**Roselle Angwin** is a Co[...] [...]d
environmentalist whose work h[...] [...]e
**Fire in the Head** banner she [...] [...]ational holistic creative
writing programme ranging from the ecobardic 'Ground of Being'
outdoor workshops, through intensive poetry, to novel-writing based
on the psychology of myth.

Roselle's first novel, *Imago*, was also published by IDP, followed by a
new poetry collection, *All the Missing Names of Love*. A prose poem
collection, *Bardo*, also appeared in 2012 from Shearsman books.
Roselle's long Dartmoor poem, *River Suite,* originally published in
1998, appeared in a limited edition in spring 2013, accompanied by
stunning water photography from Vikky Minette.

As a poet, she frequently collaborates with artists, musicians, dancers
and sculptors, often on the land. Her poetry has been displayed on
buses and cathedral websites, has appeared in numerous anthologies,
been etched into glass, hung from trees, printed on T-shirts, carved
into stone, metal and wood, painted, sung, composed to,
choreographed, danced, performed—and eaten by sheep.

Also by Roselle Angwin

**Fiction**
*Imago* (Indigo Dreams Publishing, 2011)


**Poetry**
*River Suite* (artists' edition, Mudlark, 2013)
*All the Missing Names of Love* (Indigo Dreams Publishing, 2012)
*Bardo* (Shearsman, 2011)
*Looking For Icarus* (bluechrome, 2005)
*A Hawk Into Everywhere* (with Rupert Loydell, Stride 2001)
*Hestercombe Poems and Prints* (artists' limited edition with Penny Grist, 2001 genius loci/Year of the Artist Arts Council England aided)


**Non-fiction**
*Writing the Bright Moment – inspiration and guidance for writers* (Fire in the Head/Arts Council England)
*Creative Novel Writing* (Robert Hale, 1999/2002)
*Riding the Dragon – myth & the inner journey* (Element 1994)


**Editor**
*Confluence* poetry anthology (Two Rivers/Root Creations 2010)
*Moor Poets 1* (co-editor; Wylde Publications, 2003)

# THE BURNING GROUND

## ROSELLE ANGWIN

Indigo Dreams Publishing

First Edition: The Burning Ground

First published in Great Britain in 2013 by:
Indigo Dreams Publishing Ltd
24 Forest Houses
Halwill
Beaworthy
Devon
EX21 5UU

www.indigodreams.co.uk

ISBN 978-1-909357-31-0

A CIP record for this book is available from the British Library.

Designed and typeset in Minion Pro by Indigo Dreams.
Author photo: Francis R Jones
Cover image: 'Drovers' Track', Roselle Angwin

Printed and bound in Great Britain by Imprint Academic, Exeter
*Papers used by Indigo Dreams are recyclable products made from wood grown in sustainable forests following the guidance of the Forest Stewardship Council*

I was living in the west Dartmoor area when foot and mouth struck again in 2001. The Westcountry was badly hit, and I witnessed more of it than I would have wished to. Some of my friends were affected – as of course were their animals, sometimes fatally. I shan't ever forget seeing the fields of Devon hosting white-coated figures, and gradually emptying of cattle and sheep to the accompaniment of smoke from the cull pyres on the horizons. Two farming people gave me quite a lot of time with updates and explanations: John H and Peter C, you know who you are. Thank you. Any mistakes are, of course, entirely my own, and apart from the details of the general unfolding of the crisis (for instance the injunctions on cattle and sheep movements, and the real incident of Phoenix the calf surviving, and filmed apparently walking out of the ashes) the characters and situations in this book are imaginary and fictitious.

**Roselle Angwin**

# THE BURNING GROUND

# One

## Dartmoor
## TAMAR

Someone once said to me 'Story, history – everything begins with sex, death or leaving.' I think a lot about that.

I disputed it. Starting points are so arbitrary. You don't make love and wake up thinking 'today's the day where history starts' – apart from anything else, history, after all, only exists backwards.

So I tried to avoid that neat little glibness. But it seems to be true – whichever starting point I look at involves one or the other. Sex and death both change lives, if that doesn't sound too fatuous. And leaving's a kind of loss, which is a kind of beginning, isn't it?

This beginning's nothing to do with me, though it has become my history too.

I'm telling it for the two of them because one can't tell it and the other hasn't the heart to.

\*

Picture this: an ordinary February day, for Dartmoor – horizontal sleet, blade of wind, whitey-blue smell of snow in the air. Visibility a few yards; after that, for all you know, the world has stopped existing. Even the granite tors have been flattened into nothing. Lambing season; evening; total blackness beyond the village; on the margins the faint yellowish smears that are the Prison windows, the lights barely if ever shut off.

Then for Eliot, and Guy, one in his early twenties and one not yet out of his teens, fifteen minutes that were a culmination, a conclusion and a noose around the neck of the future.

'Eliot! Call for you. It's yer old man,' bellowed Jim over the babble in the pub, and competing with the rattling of the shutters and the wild creaking of the inn sign outside.

Guy, left at the table with his half of beer, pushed down his habitual gagging resentment that whether or not their father had asked for Eliot by name, Jim would automatically have called him and not Guy to the phone. Eliot was only a few years years older, but had that authoritative presence – and the looks, too – that drew eyes to him. He towered over the other drinkers, largely farmers, in the bar, his lean frame almost foreign-looking against the stockier Devon bodies.

It was with a certain satisfaction that Guy noticed the slight lurch sideways as Eliot stretched his hand for the phone – he never knew when to stop, whereas he, Guy, 'the sensible one', never exceeded his limits, any of them. Moderacy was as much a part of his makeup as granite was of the moorland tors around here. His self-satisfaction subsided, though, as Gina, behind the bar, made a show of catching Eliot's eyes and offered a slow wink.

Guy was already shrugging on his old waterproof as Eliot loped back.

'Dad's got problems. Two ewes twinning; both first-timers, both stuck. Another one's already dropped triplets and he's lost one. C'mon,' and he fished around in the pockets of his leather jacket for the keys.

Salt in the wound. Guy couldn't find the words to say what he wanted to shout, yell, bawl: bloody hell, why Eliot the artist, not he, Guy, the one committed to farming? – so tipped down the rest of his drink as Eliot opened the door; the blast of a northwesterly, sleet-laden, whipped through and chilled Guy's face. The usual fog was blanketing the small hilltop town; even the lights on the nearby radio mast were obscured.

As they reached the car park Eliot tossed the Land Rover keys towards Guy. They grazed his hand and fell to the puddle-pocked muddy rubble that passed for a hard surface. 'You better drive, G. I've had a couple too many.'

A couple *too many!*

Eliot made no move to retrieve the keys. Guy bent.

'I can't, Eliot. You know I can't.' He swallowed and gritted his teeth. It was a source of constant anguish that Eliot had sailed through his test first time on a couple of formal lessons, while he, Guy, had failed it twice already. And he was supposed to be the practical one. 'It's Saturday night – you know what the cops are like. Even the Plymouth ones are out here Saturday nights. And I haven't got L plates on.'

'Oh for God's sake, Guy. You're such a tight-arsed old spinster. Loosen up, mate! It's only a couple of miles and you've been driving almost as long as me.' Eliot clapped his brother on the back. 'C'mon, mate. Good practice.'

'No, Eliot. No. I don't want to cock up my chances before I even start.'

Eliot made an exasperated grunt and swung round to face Guy. The corner-light fixed on the wall of the pub flickered through the trees and they regarded each other: Eliot the wolf, Guy the more domesticated canine.

Guy suddenly balled his fist round the keys and thrust it towards Eliot's face. Now or never. 'You effing drive, Eliot. You always have it your way.'

The sleet thickened and swirled between them and slicked their hair to their heads. Neither moved.

Anyone watching would have identified on Guy's normally open, pleasant face a mixture of rage, pleading and determination; Eliot's bonier, expressive features were uncompromisingly set, with a hint of challenge, and something sharper, in his eyes.

11

*Behind them the invisible bulk of Dartmoor crouched.*

*Then as if something were finished and resolved, Eliot turned and strode towards the Land Rover. Guy didn't move until Eliot, at the tailgate of the vehicle, turned to face him, then threw the keys so that they hit Eliot's boots and dropped, splashing his jeans.*

*They were to remember this moment later.*

*Guy would relive it, privately, with a kind of furious impotent agony.*

*Eliot, of course, unflinchingly took the weight, as he always had; a life-time's habit. The dual edge of responsibility of the older sibling. Eliot cut the memory off. From then on he learnt how to wipe the past from his life as surely as if it had never existed.*

*They were almost on the bridge on the unfenced moorland road before the Land Rover's headlights picked up through the blizzard two seemingly stationary objects looming on the road just feet in front of them. Too late. The double impact was blistering; a sound that neither would forget. The torn black lump of beast, bleeding so freely, so publicly, into the messy sludgy snow of the verge, congealed in their vision with the other, slighter, human form which now lay twisted and inert just off to one side of it, into a single mental image. Superimposed on that, perfectly, impossibly and coldly intact, was the just-visible motorbike, front wheel still gently swinging, in the middle of the road beyond the raw mass.*

*Whenever he heard the word 'horror' now, wherever he was, from that day on, Guy's mind would throw up this tableau. And for fifteen years, it would be all he would have of Eliot.*

# Two

Maybe one day you stop and look back: how did we all get here? But it's in the moments of a day, any day, any ordinary day, where the momentous flowers, or erupts, into your life, marking that point out forever. Before. After.

*

Friends of my parents had – still have, as far as I know – a cottage on the cliffs overlooking Cadogan Cove. We'd borrowed it for Easter.

Even with the windows shut you could hear the sea, a constant moaning and shushing as it sucked at the pebbles, rolled them over and back.

We slept with them open. Making love is so much more erotic with the sound of the waves in the background.

It was all so easy, so fast.

The pub was dark and warm; the statutory wide hearth stacked with blazing logs. I took off my jacket and sweater. Mark looked at my little jade silk chemise appreciatively. He lived life through his senses; he always noticed what I wore and how I looked and smelled. I know these things don't ultimately matter, but it all helped the chemistry.

There was good food and an abundance of it, well-cooked and unpretentious, seafood-oriented as you'd expect in a fishing village. I'm a vegetarian and there wasn't so much choice for me, but Mark – I remember because it was his favourite dish – had trout stuffed with almonds and fennel and I watched him appreciate that, too. Everything was an opportunity for enthusiasm with him, even the torrential rain we drove down in.

We had a bottle of wine between us, a deep fruity red. I

watched Mark's lips, imagined them in my hair, on my face, my neck, my nipples.

Mark lived for the moment, and lived fully. I was more cautious than he was; more intense, more serious. And he skated the edges of propriety – or sometimes didn't even approach it, outrageousness always being more his thing.

He knew I was watching him. He twinkled at me, his hair gleaming red in the firelight, raising an eyebrow. 'You know the Chilean poet Pablo Neruda? I want to do with you,' he said in a stagey whisper and a mock-Spanish accent, 'what Spring does with the cherry trees. And not once, but over and over and – '

'Mark! Shhh! You'll embarrass me!'

'OK then, I'll say it in Spanish,' he replied. 'But not now. Later. When I have you at my mercy. When I know you'll beg – '

I glared. He laughed and ran his fingers up my arm. He watched me shiver, lifted my arm and licked the goosebumps near my elbow. I felt shy, suddenly. I couldn't say I didn't like it but I was always more concerned about other people's reactions than Mark. He noticed but he wasn't deflected. 'OK. Just a taster now then,' he said, whispering a Spanish phrase or two into my ear.

'Are your knees now like two jellyfeesh? Are the 'airs on the back of your neck erect?'

'I hate the way you capitalise on my weaknesses, you BLOKE you!'

'Is that weakness as in passion for me, weakness as in inadequate grasp of the Spanish language, weakness as in being a member of the fairer –'

I thumped him, to the joy of the local fishermen leaning on the bar.

'Are you implying it's my fault that you have a strange lust for foreign tongues?'

'Far enough, Mark. Come on. Let's walk down to the cove.'
And we did, stepping in and out of the shadows thrown by the lamp outside the pub and the watery moon, picking our way over the seaweed-garlanded chains and ropes of the moorings onto the little pebbly beach, heading for the waves. Their thunder dominated everything.

Mark's fingers were at my neck; my hand in his jeans' back pocket. He turned my face towards his, kissed me gently. 'I mean it. Like the cherry trees. Now. And tonight. And tomorrow morning.' He kissed me again. 'Longer. Maybe the rest of our lives? I'll give you till tomorrow morning to think about it. Come on. Race you to the water,' and he was off, way out ahead of me, surefooted as a wild creature, the mountaineer he was, on the slippery stones and boulders.

We were young. So easy to step this way, or that. Shall we hitch to Inverness, or Paris? – The laugh in his eyes. Shall we have a pub lunch or go back to bed? Shall we get married or catch the boat to Scilly? Shall we do both?

My laughing tawny-haired man. My fiancé, so suddenly. My coiled-spring Mark, his appetite for the whole world. Now. Laughing.

He came back from the little village-store-come-newsagent's and brought coffee up to where I was sitting in a T-shirt listening to the sea by the window. I smiled and he put the tray and papers down and came over to lift my face in his hands, pushing my hair out of my eyes.

'Ah, *mia bella*, siren, how you've beguiled me. OK, OK, *guapa*, not *bella*. Just doesn't sound so good, does it? Did you know I speak Italian too? And have you thought about my question?'

15

'Question?' I teased. 'I thought it was a foregone conclusion that you'd have your way with me, as always. I didn't hear a question...'

He muttered something and suddenly swooped and lifted me. We tumbled onto the bed together.

Later, legs entwined and heads leaning together, we watched them pulling the fishing boats up the shingle slope on telegraph-pole-rollers, then spreading the nets, picking out the last silver stragglers from the meshes.

The coffee in the big white cups going cold on the bedside tables. April light bouncing off the water, shimmering and breaking and re-forming on the ceiling, gilding Mark's face. His tongue on my breasts, down my spine, in my mouth. The heat of him. The smell of sea. The salty smell of sex. The shush of the breakers.

It's all with me still.

# Three

I don't imagine I need to tell you how soulless a crematorium can be; how unfinal this final act. The neat, sanitised, hushed modernity of it all. How much worse than a church funeral, where at least there's some sense of continuity, of ancient tradition, as if there's an unbroken thread of generations being baptised, married, sent on their way from here. There's no beauty, no awe-inspiring proportions to allow your mind to transcend the shapes of human loss and longing in a crematorium, which is only, ultimately, for tidying away death, isn't it, as we might put old shoes away in a closet.

His family lived on the Somerset Levels. Only a month before the landscape would have been foaming with may blossom, fecund and extravagant in early sun. I needed storms and wind and elemental stuff to disburden myself of my grief, but that day the flatlands had the bleakness of the East Anglian fens under the still whitish-grey sky, which looked as if it couldn't summon the energy even to drizzle. Nothing, not even the water which had once been the skin of this Summer Country, seemed to move in this land scarred with dykes and ditches – perfectly level and perfectly straight – except the occasional car approaching, garish against the colourless fields and black hummocks of peat. The ditches were shrouded in duckweed or algae, and all I could think about were the bodies which surfaced from time to time, archaeological 'finds' preserved in boglands – this one with his hands tied and the garrotting wire still necklaced; that teenager with her baby by her side. Their leather-hard faces, their last meals of barley gruel still intact in their ancient stomachs.

This is the Isle of Avalon.

The Tor pointing up at the sky like an admonishing finger.

Why have you forsaken me? – Thou shalt not love.

We waited outside in a hushed cluster for the group in front of us to finish. His mother was turned slightly away from us all, one hand clutching her hat as though she hadn't noticed that there was not even a whisper of wind, motionless in a private pool of silence. I couldn't speak either, nor catch anyone's eye. His father came to talk to my parents; Mum put herself between me and him, protecting me from the need to relate to anyone. What was there left to say?

I want to do with you what Spring does with the cherry trees.

Carefully tasteful flowers, blue and white. Irises maybe – no, not irises, I'd have noticed those, something paler, less definite. Appropriate quiet music. Curtains to match both – mid-blue, a sterile shade lacking any kind of vitality. Clean.

The vicar's low voice.

His sister Hilary closed up tight like a winter lily.

The family, dignified and still, arm touching arm.

Me, a hollow mechanical toy. Rising to stand, sitting when told. Walking up to read Dylan Thomas' 'Poem In October', his favourite. Breaking as soon as I read the opening lines: *It was my thirtieth year to heaven*. He who would never see his thirtieth birthday. Carrying on, my face a streambed now.

The gasp when the vicar got his name wrong, twice – 'Martin'. Agonised silence from the family. A low angry mumble from one of his friends. The vicar flushing. But what name belonged to the body rigid and waxy in the wooden box only three or four yards away, and a million miles? If none, where had it a home now?

My cheeks hot and dry. No one sobbing or shouting or

wailing. Lips pressed, an occasional sniffle, a handkerchief proffered, a surreptitious mopping.

The curtains gliding smooth as any boat. The ancient Isle of Avalon here; this is the country of the Otherworld. Another boat sliding through the mists that separate us. Collecting the dead.

The curtains hiccuping, stalling, an incaught breath, sliding on again, swallowing the coffin.

Filing out again, all of us, keeping our eyes lowered, not speaking. We might be dead ourselves, too, almost.

Watery smiles. Hands held or shaken. Murmured exchanges. No laughter, no him to laugh.

# Four

My desk overlooks the home meadow, then the orchard, and the boulder-strewn shoulders of Wolf Tor. Some days you could imagine stepping off the craggy peak of the tor and climbing into a vast blue silence, flipping and rolling with the jackdaws and buzzards.

Today, though, is more typical – the breeze is picking up. Cloud shadows scud across the hills. Below me bantams scratch and peck in the yard; beyond them jeans and shirts start to dance on the line strung between apple trees. People coming new to the place see it as cosy, with the poultry and orchard. Idyllic, even.

I've been staring out of the window for twenty or thirty minutes, I guess: time to write. I put down the little sea-pebble I've been rolling in my palm, and put my fingers to the computer keyboard once again.

I'm nearly forty. I'm living a life that bears no resemblance, barely even a passing one, to the life I thought I was going to live fifteen years ago, except in the fact that I still write, and that I still live – or rather, live again – in the only place where I have always wanted to live, on Dartmoor: those 365 square miles of relative wilderness: granite tors, galloping amber peaty rivers, hawks, bones, ponies, bog-cotton, the ghosts of Stone Age hunters, Bronze Age agriculturalists, mediaeval farmers, rabbitmen and tinners. I can't imagine ever tiring of this place; its spaciousness, its skies, its changing faces under sun and cloud and storm and ice; the green and gold and lilac-blue of bracken, gorse, bluebell in spring; the vetches, milkworts, bilberries of summer; the amethyst tracts of heather; the bracken-rust, the black rocks and the waterfalls of winter cascading down the hillsides like tossed wild white hair...

*

Looking across all these years, I'm trying to picture what I would have been doing at the point where the boys' – the men's – lives would have been changed forever. That night. I didn't know them then, though I had glimpsed Guy and had met Bob, their father, and, briefly, Trudy their mother.

15th February 1987. That's the date on the newspaper clipping Trudy keeps tucked into the back of the old silver photo frame on the mantelpiece. Once, Guy told me, it had a photo of both boys, not yet in their teens, leaning against the tractor wheel; but by the time I got to know the family in any real sense Eliot's name was no longer mentioned, and the frame contained a picture of Bob, Guy and Trudy at Guy's graduation.

I guess that February I'd have been in my early twenties. Eliot too. If it were a weekday, I'd have been working. If a weekend probably Mark would have come down from Norwich, where he was reading for his PhD.

Where this bit of the story starts, I was working as a reporter on a provincial newspaper. Much of my work, increasingly, was features, and I was becoming aware of a consuming interest in investigative journalism.

I love mysteries and I love mosaics; and, unlike a historian, for example, my passion is not so much for fitting things together to make a logical picture but more to do with allowing disparate things (people, events, and the relationship between them) to cohere into wholeness. It's a bit like being an archaeologist, or maybe a mythologian: trying to find a way of reading meaning into patterns laid down in the past.

So think of this story as a mosaic.

21

My first meeting with the Delaney family was the previous summer. I'd completed my degree course – English and Mediaeval Studies – which I followed with a short but intensive basic course at the London School of Journalism. (I'd always wanted to write, and thought this might be a way to start.) I'd then come back down to Devon while I took a year out before travelling. I say a year out – but actually it was a really demanding year: I was working as a junior hack, as I say, on a local paper, I was doing some weekends exercising Thoroughbreds in a training yard, and one evening a week I was driving to Exeter to study for my TEFL qualification so that I could teach English abroad.

That winter was hellish, down here anyway. Interminable rain – fairly normal for the Westcountry – punctuated by the kinds of storming blizzards that left many of the moorland villages, ours amongst them, snowbound and isolated for days at a time. I remember they were feeding the ponies and cattle out on the moor by helicopter drop; a lot of animals were lost.

The roads were bad. I had come off the tarmac on ice one February night near Haytor, driving back from trying, unsuccessfully, to get home after my evening class, though why I'd gone that way and not via Moretonhampstead I don't now know; I guess I thought picking up an A road with a dual carriageway was a good idea. I know the moors well; have lived on them all my life, but I was scared, that night, in the dark and the snow. I stayed over at the pub, stumbling soaked and shivering the half mile with Bean, the old collie, and our joint night vision for company.

Same night? Can't tell you, now; spooky thought.

What else can I tell you? Perhaps I should reconstruct for you a backdrop to Guy and Eliot.

Fruit was the reason for my knowing the Delaneys in the first place.

I'd met Bob, the boys' father, that summer, as I say; the year before Guy and Eliot's accident, when I was researching a piece on old apple varieties and cider orchards for a supplement to the newspaper. Jill in the Post Office mentioned him to me, and he invited me out to Culver one afternoon. Bob was once a big tree man, an orchardist. Then when Trudy's parents died they took over the moorland farm, Culver Court; an irony for him, as virtually the only trees on the land were an avenue of beech and lime in the dip of the track leading to the farm, and a thin scattering of little stunted beech and thorn hedges topping old stone walls which offer the livestock some scant protection from the weather, with a birch copse down in the hollow. Between them, they'd planted up a new small orchard, though; too young at that stage to be fruiting in any significant way. Give it a decade, he'd said.

The middle of the moor doesn't have the gentleness of the more northerly, or northeasterly edge, where I lived then. The tors are bleak and the lanes – such as there are, because a lot of the landscape is open moorland – fenced or drystoned, where ours were all tumbling moss-covered boulders and tree-topped banks. Up near Culver the occasional tree is bent almost horizontal, arthriticky. Even in the sun of what I suppose must have been early September, maybe late August, the easterly breeze was sharp, whipping the ochre marsh grasses and skimming clouds from the sky. I drove past a little stone circle and dropped down into the lee of one of the bigger barren hills, Nattator Down, and bumped over the cattle-grid and across a small clapper bridge to the old longhouse.

Bob was in the yard, stacking a load of straw bales into one of the barns with the Massey Ferguson. (It's still in use at Culver,

23

but it must have been new, then, red and shiny as it was.) I stopped to watch, waiting for him to hear the farm dogs announcing my arrival over the rumble of the tractor. The straw gleamed amongst the puffs of dust in the gloom of the interior of the barn, and a brood of young swallows swooped in and out of the doorway.

Bob was a big-boned, gentle, quiet man, reflective and reticent. Guy was a bit like him in that way, with similar warm hazel eyes. (Eliot's are more like his mother's: Celtic throwback eyes, grey as loch water, farseeing and unreadable.) When Bob saw me he climbed down off the tractor and held out a hand. I liked his smile. I remember that he didn't wear the usual overalls or boiler suit, but cords and an old check shirt and, surprisingly, a tie.

Of course once something's history it also becomes a fiction. So I don't know if my memory and imagination have gone to work on that afternoon like yeast to grapes, but my (possibly selective) sense is of an hour or two in a place of great tranquillity, despite the unyielding landscape. And too there's the sense that all is never quite as it seems.

It's the sensory details, and the emotional atmosphere, I find, that impress themselves on memory – I don't know if that's how it is for everyone – the sound of bees in the spreading rosemary bush planted in a gap in the flagstones by the front door, for instance, where we sat on an old wooden bench.

I met Trudy. She brought the tray out and saw me looking at the rosemary bush. I can picture her still as she was at our first meeting, though from this distance I don't recognise her, as if she's a different woman altogether. A strand of soft brown hair – no grey then – had escaped from the loose coil on top of her head. She pushed it back with a copper-bangled wrist. She smiled and spoke.

Something odd happens to my synapses at this point. Do you know how it is when you're watching a film that's been dubbed: you strain to watch the characters' mouths to see what they're really saying, rather than the ascribed foreign translation? I didn't hear Trudy's words at first; perhaps a jet from Chivenor or St Mawgan went over, hillhopping; I can't remember now. But I was watching her mouth, and still had to ask her to repeat what she said. This doesn't seem at all important, but I've remembered it, so it might be. What's odd is that when she spoke the second time it was as if someone else had given her the right words to say, and I was left feeling that they were not the same as the previous ones. Strange sensation. I don't know, at the moment, what this memory means.

'My mother planted that, even though Father thought flowering bushes were a frippery; until she cured one of his beloved calves with one of her brews.'

'What do you use rosemary for?'

'Oh, everything. One of the great healers. In this case it was an infected leg wound; poor little scrap had caught its hind leg in some wire, a poacher's snare if I remember; it'd been trapped a couple of days before Father found it.'

And already I'd forgotten the momentary dislocation of a minute before.

Country people, even then, were used to treating illness in their livestock and family themselves, rather than relying on doctors and vets, and my mum had become involved in alternative therapies – despite (or maybe because of) the fact that my dad was a traditional and fairly conventional GP – in the days before they were fashionable. So talk of herbalism was nothing new, and endeared Trudy to me. She seemed a lively cheerful woman; a placid smile, and that soft, clear, unstressed complexion for which the Devon, if not Dartmoor, climate is renowned. You couldn't imagine anything fazing her. She can't have been much older then than I am now, but the woman I now know bears little resemblance to the Trudy who brought tea and scones and gooseberry jam and yellow cream out to the rickety table for us. But then we know that memory is unreliable, and after all we've all of us changed. I do know that I didn't notice then what seemed so much to epitomise Trudy later – those penetrating not-quite-accessible eyes.

Trudy excused herself; supper 'for the boys – appetites like elephants' to be prepared. Bob poured tea.

I was still appreciating being back in the Westcountry after the city. A wren whirred past us, hardly any bigger than one of the bees, and set to scuttling mouse-like up and down the cracks in the granite wall of the house. Trudy – or her mother – had conjured honeysuckle and wisteria out of the thin black soil, and the twists around the gate gusted scent towards us on the breeze. A lad of 18 or 19 came down the track and nodded to me before disappearing round the side of the house, presumably to the back door.

'Guy,' Bob said. 'My younger lad.'

'How many children do you have?'

'Just the two. Guy's at Seale Hayne. Agriculture. Following in my footsteps.' A chuckle. 'The older one's a different kettle of fish – barrel of apples, they say in Somerset – altogether. He's off in Europe somewhere; never get to hear from him. He's just finished art college.'

Did I notice then, or have I invented, the curious strained pride in his voice when speaking about the elder son – not as yet named – which, in retrospect anyway, seems significant, since it was Guy, after all, who was going to be helping on, and presumably eventually taking over, the farm?

I feel I ought to say I had some kind of premonition or

precognition, but I didn't.

We talked apples and cider and orchards. Bob listened carefully and politely to my questions and thought before he answered; and waited for me to finish scribbling each note before continuing. I remember feeling that at last I was a grownup.

Bob had been, I knew, a master cidermaker before, and was still often called upon for his knowledge of orchards to speak and advise throughout Britain and northern France. He stared over towards Wolf Tor – those unappled slopes – and I asked him if he missed the trees.

He nodded. 'Different kind of farming altogether here. Sheep and cattle. And do you know we've lost almost all our old orchards since the war? And all those old varieties gone. Have you noticed how hard it is to get anything other than French Golden Delicious or Granny Smiths in the shops? Only Coxes left, really; and I doubt they'll be long, what with scab and misshapes, and foreign competition. Russets still; and of course Bramleys. But you won't probably won't even have heard some of the old cider-apple names: Handsome Maid, Foxwhelp, Kingston Black – that'll survive blossom-drop, no bees, cold, even a summer of floods, that one, and still fruit thickly; then there's Slack-My-Girdle...'

Eventually I put my notebook back into my rucksack and stood and thanked him. A tabby cat stretched out in a flickering patch of sunlight under the mallow by the little iron garden gate yawned and blinked yellow eyes at me. As I walked back to the car a litany of long-lost apple names rolled around in my head, amber and russet and green, flavouring the late afternoon with harvest scenes: Cider With Rosie; Thomas Hardy.

27

# Five

It was summer. June, to be exact.

Mark was off climbing in North Wales with friends, in celebration of completing his doctoral thesis. He was due down at the weekend.

I was dividing my time between my parent's house and Mark's flat in Norwich, and freelancing. Mark and I were going to be looking for a house as soon as he knew which university was going to offer him a lectureship.

I'd been out riding Mum's little mare, Dancer. Her neck stretched in front of me, conker coloured, sleek and shiny; dark mane lifting with our passage. The evening sun struck auburn highlights in its ripples.

We'd come back across the edge of Cribben Tor, descending towards the hamlet in the warm scented dusk.

If you've never experienced it, it's hard to describe to you the sheer magic of riding out alone in the early evening in summer on Dartmoor. I can't think of anything that resembles it, or approaches it for utter pleasure, especially if you are aware of a synergy between you and your horse. On your own out there, you and the horse, you're in tune with something deeply primal, from which we're divorced so much of our life. Even walking on the moor lacks that quality.

I've always ridden, and feel possibly closer to the utter peace of needing nothing other and nothing more when I'm in the saddle than in any other situation. It's also my retreat and my refuge; a panacea for the soul.

Here's how it is: you come round the edge of Cribben, dropping down towards the west. You're high enough to see Bodmin Moor one way and the sea beyond Torquay the other.

Your horse's stride is a lively lope. You can hear an occasional tractor, and skylark and brambling song; otherwise only the creak of the saddle and sometimes a sheep. There may be a buzzard winding in lazy spirals.

This year's wild pony foals are already charging around in small pre-adolescent gangs, knobbly legs pounding the turf and little tails held out stiffly like loo-brushes. From time to time you encounter a small cloud of midges or a solitary bumble bee. You can smell the apricot-and-coconut gorse blossom, and the wonderful odour of sweat-damp horse.

Towards Culverstock the tors fade one on one in blue layers, and below in the valley the meadows are golden after the haycut. Perhaps there's a slender coil of smoke rising straight up from someone's bonfire. The evening starts to pool in the folds of the valley.

You're freewheeling. Perhaps you might take in, without really registering, the stooping sparrowhawk, or the scattered fleece and ribcage of a sheep dispersed among bog cotton and bramble.

Dancer and I were dawdling as we got to the bottom of the wooded track, though her ears were pricked alert as we approached home. She twirled neatly on small hooves as I leant to release the catch on the gate and draw it back towards us and she slid back and around and through in one fluid movement, automatically turning back the way we had come for me to relatch the gate. With Dancer jogging gently now we made our way down the lane with its cow parsley and dog roses. I could just catch honeysuckle spicing the dusk.

We swung in through the paddock gate. I could smell cooking from the house, and realised how hungry I was. I slid off the mare and patted her, burying my nose for a second in her mane, inhaling deeply. How I missed this smell when I was away.

As I lifted the saddle off Dancer and onto the gate I saw Mum walking slowly down the path between the grass and the peas and beans. I guessed she was picking some to add to supper, or gathering flowers for the table. I raised my arm. 'Hi Mum! I'm back!'

This is how I picture that moment now, so many years on: a freeze-frame – the tor behind me against a deepening lapis sky, the horse and I standing together and my arm raised in greeting to Mum. She was frozen, too – her arm was slower to go up and there was something odd about her face.

Then we all moved again, as if the music had restarted; Dancer snorted and lowered her head to butt my pocket gently for the carrot she knew would be in it. I unbuckled her throatlash and lifted the bridle off over her ears. Mum walked closer, close enough for me to see that her hair was sliding free of one of her combs and that she was trying to twist a smile to her mouth. My shoulderblades prickled and my fingers seemed to take forever to find, fumblingly, the catch for the chinstrap of my riding hat. It seemed imperative that I get the hat off immediately.

By the time I'd shaken my hair free of its clip Mum had arrived at the hedge between the garden and the paddock and I saw Dad coming down the path too. I couldn't move.

A last finger of sun flamed across the valley and was gone.

'Your hair's almost the same colour as Dancer's in that light,' Mum said, absently, inconsequentially.

I was very cold suddenly.

I've accepted that to live life fully means accepting that loss and pain are inevitable. Finally, now, I have. I didn't then. But what alternative do we have? Life isn't safe; and it's not possible to love safely, either. Saying yes to love, or to life, means saying yes to loss and death too. The only way we can insulate ourselves at all is to live smaller lives – restricting our risk-taking to a small circular shuffle between work and eating and shopping and sleeping.

Yes, that would be safer. Which would I have chosen back then, knowing what I know now, so many years on? If I had known what loving Mark would mean, would I have chosen not to? No choice, really, is there?

'He slipped,' Dad was saying. 'The others don't know what happened. A thick mist had come down. They were roped, but for some reason Mark's section gave way.'

A terrible unbearable silence and stillness. I couldn't breathe. Mum had me in her arms but I was rigid.

'He slipped hundreds of feet. He would have died instantly.' Dad the doctor. 'He wouldn't have known. Broke his neck. They're bringing him back.'

OF COURSE he would have known! Falling and falling and falling. Interminable. Falling forever. Why hadn't I known? I was supposed to love him, wasn't I? Why hadn't I felt that tug on empty air, that crash through space? How could I have let myself go into the hot blue afternoon?

There was a sound now on the evening air; a tearing terrible sound, a moaning, a high wail, a scream.

'Shhhh, shhhh, shhh,' Mum was saying, over and over. 'We're here. You're not alone. It's OK, it's OK.'

But of course it wasn't. How could it be, ever again?

31

## Six

Trudy told me once about Eliot's leaving. Or rather, about her foreseeing of the event in some kind of foreshadowing but subtle experience.

Trudy was fundamentally a private woman, and anyway didn't often talk about her sixth sense – it simply existed, most of the time, in the spaces between us; between her and almost everyone else, like a kind of force field, an invisible but potent distancing mechanism.

There was a time, though, when she was more forthcoming generally, like that first afternoon, and then later, for the first year or two, anyway, while I was getting to know her properly. I wonder about these things: whether there's a kind of psychic delay that buffers you after a tragedy, so that the real far-reaching effects of things take some time to manifest. Trudy's withdrawal was gradual; and not entirely the kind of introversion that comes, especially to essentially private and solitary people, with age.

The incident was minor in itself, but somehow symbolic, a threshold crossed, or at least brought into existence. She spoke of it almost casually to me in one of our rare moments of exchanged confidences that broke through our more usual side-by-side-getting-on-with-things relationship.

There was a morning, she said, when Eliot was about eighteen, when she realised he had in some important way – emotionally, psychologically – already left home. It was – again! – an ordinary morning on an ordinary day, but something unnameable changed thereafter in their relationship. And yet nothing had 'happened'…

It was the silence in the room that alerted her – then she saw Eliot.

He never got up before her, and especially on a frosty morning, still dark outside.

He was kneeling at the grate, his long back towards her, black curls caught in the neck of his sweater, very still. He had his boot-socks on; she noticed, as mothers do, the hole that needed darning.

Already he was a man – eighteen or so – and in some ways gone from her, though not in the absolute way that he seemed to go in those few moments.

As if he sensed her presence, his hands stirred; he picked up the *Western Morning News* from the floor beside him, crumpled the first sheet. She watched his shoulder blades under his sweater, saw his lean hands piling ball on crumpled ball.

Eliot never lit the fires; it had always been her job. She felt cold, suddenly. Something was wrong.

She didn't move. He picked out kindling from the basket, knobby twigs of chestnut and ash from the home meadow. The crack as he snapped them over his knee rang like gunshot in the sleeping house.

He moved methodically, unusually slowly for his mercurial nature, criss-crossing twig on twig, then reaching above him for the matches from the mantelpiece.

Still he seemed unaware of, or didn't acknowledge, her presence.

He bent sideways for larger pieces of wood. Trudy longed to throw her arms around him suddenly; clutch him to her forever, as if he were still the curly-haired grey-eyed six-year-old with the quirky sudden smile who didn't mind hugs.

Something was ebbing from her.

He struck a match, rasping twice, three times before it caught; the paper flared blue; Eliot stood up and turned towards her, tall in the low-beamed sitting room. He glanced away briefly,

33

towards the yard, its buildings already more substantial in the steel-blue half-light. In that moment she lost him; her eyes seeing only a blackish emptiness, the anchoring threads – to her, to here, to the family and farm – severed. Then:

'Hello, Mum,' – his shape cohering once again into that of her long-limbed handsome eldest son.

'Something else came into his eyes, then,' she told me. 'I knew he'd already gone.'

## Seven

There's a gap in the story after Mark. It's hard to talk about a descent, that wordless inviolable time when you can't imagine ever feeling anything again. My memory only throws up a sense of endless twilight – half-shapes, minimal motions; getting dressed, eating an occasional meal, speaking when spoken to. I suppose I must have worked; must have got through that summer and winter and the next summer somehow. Maybe it was longer. I don't know.

But even in Hades there are seeds in the fruit, and though the tasting of them seals a contract you can never again escape, so the swallowing of them yields something of nourishment, in time.

Anyone who's been bereaved will know that the returning feelings are both blessing and curse. I hadn't really expected the rage, though I know it's normal. It's just that then, as before and as now, so many years later, I expected that when I thought of Mark I would feel only love. (I had expected, of course, love to be heavily tempered with desolation.)

It took me a while to move beyond the rage. It wasn't just at him, for leaving me behind so abruptly, but also of course at life, at fate, at transience; the arbitrary unfairness, untrustworthiness of everything.

And after the rage, grief; a wild blind grief of which I could speak to no-one, not even my mother.

But now as I write this I find myself smiling at the thought of Mark. Yes, I'm over him; have been for many years, and when I think about him, as I do from time to time still, it's only with pleasure that he was in my life at all. Ah, time, knitting all these fractures, repairing the torn tissue.

*

I remember every moment, though, about the day in late September of the year after Mark's death, Michaelmas to the Christians and the equinox to others, when Mark's parents and I walked up to the top of Glastonbury Tor.

We did it the old way, taking the ancient spiral path. We hadn't really discussed this; it just seemed the right way to do it. Looking back I'm a little surprised: Mark's family is Christian, and fairly conventional. I suppose what we were doing was a pilgrimage; and when you live near the Tor the Old Ways are part of the emotional and psychic landscape just as they are of the geographical one.

It took us some time, and it was dusk when we arrived.

We'd chosen a weekday, and the end of the day, hoping there wouldn't be other people around.

It had been stormy all day, gale force winds from the west slapping our backs on the exposed side of the Tor. I was conscious of my waterproof flapping and rustling; it seemed inappropriate to be making such irrelevant noises, such modern noises. My hair was blown over my face, whipping my eyes and lips. I was grateful for the storm; I wanted more, I wanted the elements present as they weren't at the cremation; I wanted the diversion of physical discomfort. Mark's mum Lena was panting slightly, and I could hear a low moan, a tiny low moan like a sigh, escaping from her open lips.

Don had the little cardboard box containing the canister with him. He'd clutched it to his chest all the way up the hill, with both hands. When we got to the top there was a minute when we just looked at each other, not knowing what to say or do now.

Don put his hand on my shoulder. 'All right lass?'

I nodded.

Don put an arm around Lena and drew her to him. They just

stood there, head to head, very human, very mortal. You feel small on the top of the Tor, small and vulnerable. I was aware of the privacy of their grief; not sure whether I should be there at all. And I couldn't bear the silence suddenly; nor the look of anguish on Lena's face. I moved away, stumbling a little on the ruts around the old chapel.

To the west the clouds were breaking up and a lurid orange-red was bleeding around their edges. I suddenly noticed that the wind had dropped, as it often does at dusk; the silence seemed to roar until I couldn't think. The physical details of everything seemed to press themselves in on me: the smell of wet earth, the stone of the chapel under my fingers, a pebble beneath the sole of my boot, the wetness of my cuffs and at my neck. I could taste salt at the corners of my mouth – I hadn't realised until now that I was crying. I wondered whether I'd been weeping all the way up the Tor.

The gentle Somerset landscape, the quilting of fields and hedges and ditches stretched out below seemed alien, somehow, and very far away.

I felt sick.

Don was calling my name softly. I turned, and he gently lifted the box containing the pot with Mark's ashes.

I couldn't move, suddenly, for terror. Don walked towards me, his eyes steady.

'Come on, lass. It's time.' He opened the box and unscrewed the lid of the canister, sheltering it with his jacket.

'The wind's dropped,' I said, hearing my voice and despising myself for the triteness.

'We'll face east anyway,' said Don, and I had an appalling vision of the ashes blowing back and sticking to me – to my wet hair and face, to my waterproof jacket. What would I do? I suddenly felt shaken by a gust of hysterical – manic – laughter, which made me choke.

I turned and we stood in a ragged line of three.

No-one moved. I couldn't breathe properly.

Then Don passed the box reverently to Lena. I watched her; she couldn't look in it, I noticed. Don took out his handkerchief. He polished the specks of rain off his glasses, then put them back on and wiped his hand carefully, taking the box back from Lena. He put his hand into its neck, withdrawing a handful of ashes. I didn't want to look and couldn't not.

'Go on then, lad. Go on.' He opened his hand and the ashes fluttered away, some drifting down to rest on the sheep-nibbled turf and daisies. I stared at them. I didn't know what to do: turn away, go and release them? It felt unbearable.

'Be at peace then, son.' Don's voice cracked and he bent his head.

When it was my turn I slipped my hand in. I stared at the pot; didn't dare look inside. My heart was thumping. To my surprise the ashes were soft, satiny almost, but gritty, too. I flung them as far as I could. I could feel a roar like a physical pain rising up through my chest, and I turned and ran, as fast as I could, down over the rutty terraced hillside, sobbing and shouting, not caring that I couldn't see. I slipped and stumbled until I reached the hedge and stile beyond which was the lane, and then I lay on my side under the sodden hedge and cried and cried until Don and Lena caught up with me, maybe twenty minutes later.

We made our way down the lane quietly, nothing to say. Don still held the box. Lena was white, but managed a faint and reassuring smile at me.

Back in the car we attempted normality. In any case I had no tears left. Don made us laugh with a long and rambling anecdote he was telling us about an embarrassing moment when he'd put his foot in it with one of his staff. She'd asked to see him, and he had thought she was pregnant and had come to ask for maternity leave, and pre-empted her, at which point it turned out that she had just put on weight and told Don that her lover was in fact another woman – 'Every time I open my mouth some idiot starts talking,' he said. This seemed at the time unbelievably funny, and both Lena and I giggled. Release of tension, I suppose.

Don pulled up outside the fish and chip shop and we went in together, dripping and bedraggled as we were, and then drove out towards the high road. As we left Glastonbury, though, Don suddenly turned off, and backtracked, pulling up outside some public loos. He tactfully said nothing. Lena and I looked at each other and got out. Once inside, though, I couldn't wash my hands; couldn't wash the last traces of him and his life from me. I went into a cubicle instead, and numbly gazed at the graffiti until I heard Lena flush the loo and wash her hands. When it was silent again I went back out and joined the others in the car. We said nothing. Don pulled in at a field gate with the Vale stretching below us, and we all ate chips with our fingers, steaming the car windows up. I was ravenous; we were staving off death with our eating, I guess.

Don wiped his fingers and turned to me, sitting in the back of the Rover on my own.

'Well, Tamar, he was a good lad, and he's gone. We've got to let go now, haven't we, Lena? What will you do now, lass? With your life, I mean? Difficult enough the last year, I'm sure. Still, that's the worst over now. Are you going to stay down there on the moor?' His eyes behind his spectacles were sad, kindly and concerned, but I couldn't answer, couldn't think about it; just shook my head.

## Eight

Perhaps I should tell you that things are different on Dartmoor from many other places. It's one of those places where, as they say, the veil is thinner. We take certain things for granted. (Having said that, it doesn't necessarily make them easier.)

Trudy, seventh daughter of a seventh daughter, does not make the mistake of assuming that the world of the five senses is the only world of substance, or meaning.

I didn't know for a long time just how highly developed Trudy's clairvoyance was. It was useful for things like advance weather forecasts, and who might be about to visit – she had an uncanny foreknowledge, laying five places at the table before the phone call came, for instance; and Bob was in the habit of asking her where to look if an animal went missing, as if it were perfectly usual. She was accomplished with the dowsing rods, too, though that is fairly common, even now, amongst country-dwellers and moorland people.

But where most of us are aware of particular moments that have a cargo of meaning to them, or passages in our lives where synchronicity and telepathy fall thick and fast into our days, Trudy, I guess, experienced this as the norm. Occasionally I found it a little spooky: I'd come upon her completely motionless, maybe the kettle in her hand, or a carrot dripping mud into the red plastic washing-up bowl, arrested mid-action with her head cocked, as though listening; and there were times when she seemed to dwell elsewhere altogether, with a blind, bright look in her eyes and her lips moving. The first time what skimmed through my head was the absurd notion that she was playing a game of musical statues for one, and was awaiting the resumption of the music. It must have been fully ten seconds before she became aware of my presence in her line of vision and unfroze; immediately she behaved perfectly normally, smiling and pouring me tea from the huge brown pot.

I'm familiar with arcane ideas and have known various people via my mother or from my travels with well-developed psychic abilities. However I have never got used to it with Trudy, perhaps because she never talks of it, so I never know how much she sees – 'sees' – or what she knows, or what her sources are. Since that first time, though, I've been aware of a persisting slight unease when I'm near her, no matter how friendly and open she was – as she was, then. And this is despite the fact that, to a lesser extent, some of her abilities have rubbed off on me; and certainly on Eliot.

*

I don't think Trudy ever really spoke of Eliot again to me, after telling of that firelighting incident (until the events long afterwards which changed everything), except – comparatively recently – to tell me one more thing: that the same feeling, or perception, had been visited upon her the night he jumped bail some few years afterwards; and she knew where he'd headed.

His departure must have been some time in the late spring or early summer of '87 – I don't know exactly, as I'm not sure how long these things take from incident to a preliminary magistrates' hearing to the full inquest, enquiry and trial. I didn't like to ask. (Later, when I did get the chance, there was so much else that seemed more important, urgent.) But from what Trudy said, it would have been only a few weeks after the accident.

Trudy was a light sleeper where Eliot was concerned, perhaps because he was her firstborn.

When she came awake it was still two or three hours before light, though a robin had started in the lilac tree below her

41

window. There was no noise but she knew that Eliot was up; and, again, up before her.

Sometimes when it happened it was like a film unspooling, flickering behind her eyes. This was one of those times.

She heard the big latch on the front door click, and 'saw' Eliot turn briefly to look at the front of the house before bending to put on his walking boots and then shoulder his rucksack. He scratched the top of the cat's head; the animal wove in and out of his legs, nearly tripping him as he strode out, walking on the grass for silence, though anyone listening carefully would have heard the crunch of late Dartmoor frost. She didn't hear the gate go, but knew he'd headed down the track; five minutes later he'd be on the lane, heading east for the dual carriageway.

Not long after dawn broke Eliot arrived on the sliproad down to the A38. His facial hair, unshaven these last few weeks, was spiked with frost, his cheeks tight. Even with the leather jacket under the waterproof he was cold.

As luck would have it, the lorry that stopped was going all the way to Penzance.

They'd not talked of the accident at all at Culver. They'd not talked of anything of import, these last few weeks. Guy, unusually sullen and, Trudy thought, frightened, complained of nightmares, but carried on going to his courses and helping Bob with the stock, spiking the great round bales of silage onto the tractor prongs and transporting them off to the pastures, or top-dressing the peaty soil of the home pastures with slurry or lime.

Eliot had done very little, brazening it all out in silence; playing the guitar now and then, reading or seeming to read; occasionally giving Bob a hand with stock or fertiliser if asked. He didn't go out on his own; that was one of the conditions. He and Guy avoided each other, though Trudy noticed how Guy's eyes would flick to Eliot's face each time they sat down to supper together.

They'd taken to putting the radio on in the kitchen while they ate; 'news and weather', Bob declared. Trudy had protested; but the atmosphere had become so dense, so inhospitable, that she found herself being close to grateful towards the end.

A hiatus had settled over the family, holding them together and firmly apart; interminable-seeming at times.

Trudy went through a period of frantic cleaning and baking; the semblance of busy normality.

Only Bob remained equable.

She knew where he was heading. He had a schoolfriend whose brother was a share fisherman on a trawler out of Newlyn. No matter that Eliot had almost lost touch with the friend and hadn't ever spoken of fishing; Trudy watched him arrive at the quay amongst the bustle of loading and unloading, the toppling piles of herring boxes, wooden and plastic, the barrels for what few pilchards might still be there for the fishing, the crates and crab pots and scallop shells and chains and ropes and winches, the great trawls themselves, the oilskins and navy jumpers and waders, the stink of fish and diesel. She heard the mournful adult gulls and the whistling mews of the speckled adolescents; she saw Eliot stroll from boat to boat, group to group, hands in pockets, nonchalant, until he stopped by a blue and white boat, the *Mary Ellen*, whose gunwales were streaked with rust and diesel and scored by lifting gear.

Then Bob awoke and stretched out his hand to rest it on her thigh as he did every morning, and she pecked him on the cheek and rose to make a pot of tea, and didn't speak of Eliot.

*

43

Trying to catch hold of these moments in order to recreate this story is like trying to define a bird by tracking its flight. Ultimately what's left is an invisible trajectory, and the bird has gone. A reconstruction is never a true record, and there's an element of guesswork in all memory: was it like this or like this?

What you focus on – where you land and for how long – can be arbitrary.

Let's stick to a 'fact' or two.

This is what that first newspaper clipping says:

### Motorcyclist killed in head-on collision

A young Culverstock man was killed on the Moretonhampstead road late on Saturday night. The motorcyclist was travelling towards Two Bridges from Warren House when the accident happened. The man, who has not been named but was in his twenties, had apparently swerved to avoid a heifer on an unfenced stretch of the B3212 and was struck, along with the cow, by a vehicle coming in the opposite direction.

The driver and passenger of the Land Rover, Eliot and Guy Delaney, were treated in hospital for shock, and fractures of the ribs and a fractured wrist respectively. Eliot Delaney has been released from custody on bail, pending further enquiries on three possible charges: driving while under the influence of alcohol, driving without due care and attention, and causing death by dangerous driving.

I was in the office a few weeks later when the newsflash came in. I didn't think much about it at the time; I hadn't met Eliot, and anyway I was rushing to complete a feature article on the work of a local sculptor before I left for that week in Cornwall with Mark.

'Bloody hell,' said the young assistant news editor. 'Remember the guy who was arrested for that moorland accident? Eliot, he was called, Eliot Delaney. I was at school with him! Sounds like he's jumped bail. "Ports on alert", it says here. Blimey.'

I did register it, though; I remember briefly imagining how the news might have affected Bob and Trudy; pictured that tranquil bee-laden garden.

*

My life at that point changed. When I came back from Cornwall I was engaged to Mark; and you know the rest.

## Nine

I took the ferry from Plymouth to Roscoff one windy autumn day. That year? The next? England, I'd decided, held nothing for me at the moment. Once the thought had occurred to me to go abroad, find a way of starting again, I moved fast. I hoped, I suppose, that new surroundings would assuage some of my feelings, and they did help dull the edges, eventually.

I wanted to be on deck in the wind and the drizzle. I was willing the sea to manifest a minor miracle for me: a portent, a sign. I was hoping, I suppose, for a school of dolphins or porpoises, leaping and playing in the bow-wave. Instead I had to take consolation in the gulls appearing out of the mist like wraiths and gliding along with us for a few hundred yards before wheeling away, breast feathers ruffled, and vanishing once again.

Everywhere I looked was grey.

## Ten

### France
### OLIVER

The morning was worth getting up for. Light silvering the puddles. Early sun. Broken, scattered by cloud, sliding over the buildings. Smell of wet pavements. Wet foliage through the open window.

Didn't bother to shower. Pulled on jeans and T-shirt and grabbed my camera bag.

I moved amongst the traders setting up in the market. Several knew me now. I was here often enough.

'Eh Oliver,' called Yvonne from behind her poles and hangers of ethnic garments and cheap jewellery, 'you haven't had the razor yet, alors?'

I lifted my hand instinctively to my chin. A few days' stubble. Couldn't be arsed to shave every day.

'But it's sexy, quand-même,' she added, raising her eyebrows.

I laughed. 'Cheers, Yvonne,' I said as I moved on. Bit embarrassing. Yvonne, for all her hoop earrings and twinkling necklaces, must have been pushing fifty. Late forties, anyway. Christ. Old enough to be my mother.

I didn't want to be distracted. Not right now. Wanted time to think about the light. Ridge-tiles and roof slates glittering after the night's shower. Everything looked clean. I liked the way the morning light exaggerated everything. Liked the ambiguity. Corners and hidden places. Nothing yet resolved into substance or form.

Wasn't the market itself I wanted. Though its colour, its noise, its smells all filled me with a kind of buzz of purpose. What

47

I was looking for was shapes and patterns. Places where light and shadow might merge, or clash.

Started with the church spire – one of those wedding cake affairs with as many cutouts as the tin-cans we used for target practice out of school. The lower finials on the spire – don't know what you'd call them – were smothered with pigeons. Jostling fistfuls of rust and purple and grey and white.

Then M. Armandin's boulangerie doorway, low, stone-arched. Peeling marine-blue paintwork. See it everywhere in coastal Brittany. Someone had obligingly parked a pushbike with a baguette balanced across the handlebars up against the windowbox. Strictly tourist material, that shot. Even in black and white they'd love it. Couldn't bring myself to shoot it though. Walked down the cobbled street a bit. Got a couple more doorways and dark interior courtyards.

Circled back eventually towards the market. Much harder, this. Too much going on. I was hoping for one of those moments of things colliding or coinciding, so 'just right' it's almost a cliché. That's meat to a photographer. You know the kind of thing. Two Gallic faces fixed in fiery discussion, Gauloises bouncing on lips. Elderly black-clad woman gathering an armful of artichokes. Someone knocking a tray of olives so that they roll, gleaming with oil, onto the cobbles. A heap of whitebait spilling silver onto a mound of ice.

The fish stall. I set my tripod up, aimed at the pail of lobsters. Poor buggers, clawing slowly, like mechanical toys, at nothing. Takes me ages to get this kind of shot right. I'm a perfectionist. If I don't think I can get it right I don't bother. Fiddled for a while with aperture, shutter speed, angle. Changed my mind. Moved the tripod closer. Went through it all again. Copped a bollocking for blocking the front of the stall from potential customers. Moved. Did it all over for a third time.

Finally I stepped back to check the composition, and as I did so someone collided with me at speed and sent my tripod flying.

Considering I'd had a bit to drink with Jean-Yves, the gallery owner, last night, my reaction was pretty amazingly speedy – I caught it just before the camera hit the ground. Turning as I straightened I opened my mouth to bawl out the person concerned. Shut it again as I found myself looking down into a pair of green eyes in one of those faces bordered with heaps of tangled curls that look – well, never mind. I'm not a romantic. The face had a look of anxiety and embarrassment on it. She had a hand to her mouth. Glad I'd bitten the string of curses she'd been about to get.

A beat while we looked at each other. Then:

'Oh God I'm so sorry,' she said in English, removing her hand from her mouth and moving as if to touch my arm, which she then didn't. 'Oh God, did I do any damage? Parlez-vous anglais?'

Before I could speak she stepped forward, and there was a crack. 'Oh shit. That was your lens cap. Oh no. I'm a disaster these days –'

I wanted to laugh and shout simultaneously. The woman was unbelievable – two hits in as many minutes.

She looked up from the shattered lens cap to me. 'I'm just so sorry, je suis desolée; where can I get you –' Her face was flushed.

I could put her out of her misery. Didn't see why I should, though. It'd taken me twenty minutes to get as far as I had. But.

'Stop,' I said. 'For God's sake. It's OK. Really. I caught the camera, and the lens cap –' I shrugged. 'It's only a lens cap.'

'Oh, you're English, too,' she said. 'That makes it a bit easier.'

Makes what easier, I wanted to shout. It's OK to wreck my shot, make my adrenalin pump, ruin my lens cap, if I'm English?

49

– Oh yeah, I knew what she meant – easier to apologise in your own language. I said nothing.

'May I replace it though? If you tell me where to get one?'

'No problems,' I said. 'Really. Leave it. Sure I've got another somewhere. Just leave it, OK?' – Feeling pleased with myself for my restraint. Perhaps I'd still been a bit abrupt? – Just in case I added: 'What's your name, anyway?'

'Tamar. As in the river. What's yours?'

'Oliver. As in Cromwell.'

'You'd have been a King's Man, surely?' she said, green eyes watching me.

I didn't pick it up. Didn't even smile. (Royalty's not my thing, but how was she to know that?) Other things to do though. Not my type, anyway. 'I'm sorry, but –' I gestured at the fish stall. Bent pointedly to my tripod. Already the light was brightening and things were coming into sharper focus – a different kind of shot.

'Sure. Sorry.' She turned and looked at the lobsters and crabs. Some of them had their claws tied with twine. I watched her surreptitiously, under cover of fiddling with the aperture. I could see distress, or distaste, on her face as she realised they were still alive. Then she bent and picked up the lens cap and held it out to me. Christ – just LEAVE it. Her hand was little, silver-ringed, warm. 'See you around.' A quick glance up at me, wide mouth curving into a slightly nervous smile. I looked away. Started to refocus the camera. As she left though I caught myself turning to glance after her. Dark curls springing round her shoulders. Green boots, black-clad legs, swinging short skirt. Lots of swirly colours.

Shame. Could have bought her a coffee. Let her buy me one if it would have made her feel better. And wasted precious filming time? Maybe not. I'd promised myself I'd steer clear of women for a while. Not what I needed. Absolutely not. What I needed right now was dosh. Anyway women always wanted more than I wanted to give. Concentrate on the pictures, Oliver.

Found myself looking out for her the next day, though, as I rode back into Plougannis on the Honda to do an afternoon's work – 'gallery technician', which meant whatever it needed to mean, hour by hour – at Jean-Yves'. Wanted to process a handful of my own films while I was at it, see if I'd caught anything worth printing out.

Which I had. Three more for the walls, J-Y said, nodding thoughtfully. He liked the lobster – 'It has balls,' he said, in French, with the predictable exaggerated gestures. Lobsters? – Each to their own. English tourists wouldn't get it, but still.

## Eleven

Took the Honda out to Tradescat, on the coast. Left the bike chained to a stile. I had to hoof it the last kilometre or so; too rough. Suited me fine. Most people don't come out to places where you need to walk a bit. Like to be able to see the car. I needed the exercise and the head-space. Needed the wind at my back, swinging along the little white stony track with no-one around.

On the headland there's a small ruined castle. Chunky, foursquare, nothing atmospheric and gothic. It has something, though. Lonely. It's not a lookout or a fortification. Older; probably domestic. Could be strategic though too. Best homes are. The blue and white enamel signpost calls it the Manoir de Tradescat. The old maps call it Le Chateau des Fées – Arthurian stuff. Brittany's full of it.

Anyway, I wasn't here for that.

Climbed the rocks to a point above the little bay. It's a narrow shingly beach that shelves down quite a long way to the water's edge. Below the tideline the sand's a kind of soft chalky gold. There was a trail of footprints amongst the mussel shells and yellow periwinkles. Bare feet, smallish, almost child-sized. The only marks on the beach. I resisted the urge to film the prints. I could almost hear the phrases of 'poetry' that it would be captioned with. I really hate clichés, but when you're looking for prints that sell – and you need dosh – they're tempting.

I was thinking about seascapes. This shore is rocky. Lots of movement of water, undercurrents and eddies and rearing and shattering waves. Great bodies of water crashing around, all a bit primal and elemental. Chthonic I think is the word. But I was also thinking of the opposite: tiny close-focus rockpools, still and secret. Clusters of limpets. Anemones opening and closing (maybe a series of frames). Shadows on pools. Patterns made by barnacles or lacy coral weed.

The weather was good – a fast high wind so that the light was continually shifting and breaking up and changing. The water below me went through indigo, turquoise, jade and azure in moments.

I sat for a while. Bursts of sun on my shoulders. Shadows running over the water. Bit trancey, isn't it, watching the water. Like you lose your past suddenly. Sound of the waves stops you thinking.

Must have sat there for an hour, not thinking at all, before I realised that actually the sea needed a colour film. OK. Nothing doing there, then, today.

I climbed a bit higher until I reached the turf. Scrubbing-brush turf, short and bristly. How I like it. Took my shirt off. Stretched out on my back with my hands behind my head. Wind and waves filling my ears, and larks and gulls. Smell of gorse and salt wind. Yeah. No space inside my skull. No past, no future. No-one I needed to be. No-one I needed. No-one needing anything from me.

April afternoon. Bit of sunshine. Solitude.

Think I fell asleep. I sleep best when there's no-one around; these days I can't bear anyone watching me without my knowing, breathing over me, peering at me, trying to divine my thoughts. No thanks.

– What are you thinking about, darling?

– Fuck off. Though I don't actually ever say that, of course. I was brought up with some manners, even me.

When I woke the wind had slowed and there was more sun. I stood and stretched and shouldered my camera-bag, anchored to

53

my waist by its strap while I dozed.

Thought I'd go and have a look at the anemones.

Twenty minutes later and not the faintest flicker from my chosen colony of anemones. What do they do when they're not eating? Perpetual sleep? The original inerts. Are they animal or plant, anyway? All five of them dead as doorknobs. And about as stimulating.

I tickled one with a bit of twig. It sucked itself in tight as a cat's arse. Spinster's mouth. Belly button. And stayed there.

After a few minutes I stood up and prised a limpet off a rock with my knife, and winkled the flesh out. It looked a bit big for an anemone to eat whole. Besides, it would only give me two shots – opening, and closing. So I put the flesh down on the rock and sliced it. It looked like most shellfish – a greywhite gob, pretty limp and helpless-looking. It oozed a bit. I cut another one.

Lobsters, anemones, limpets. Christ. My obsession with sea-creatures was beginning to get to me.

I positioned my camera towards the anemones. I had to wedge myself into a gulley, a spit of damp sand between the shoulders of two rocks. Wriggled until I could reach both the bits of limpet and the camera. Speared a bit of shellfish with the pointy end of the twig.

Forty minutes later I had my shots of the anemones – a wonderful series of inert blobs transforming themselves slowly into surreal red-tentacled dancers, then subsiding back.

Stood up. There she was, walking away from me, boots slung over her shoulder. I'm sure it was her, Dee or Tay or whatever she was called.

Shit. How long had she been there, watching me? Why hadn't she spoken? For a minute I felt a bit spooked. But so what. Climbed up again, went to watch the sea.

## Twelve

Harriet summoned me. Not 'Haven't seen you for ages, how are you?' or 'What about a drink?' but 'You need to come visit. Staff meeting time.'

Don't normally respond to a summons like that. But Harriet offered two things I wanted: a job for the summer, and sex. A staff meeting was, if last year was anything to go by, a precursor to both.

I didn't either like Harriet or trust her. That didn't stop me going to bed with her. No, not one of those complicated intricate hidden agendas sort of situations. Supremely uncomplicated, in fact. Harriet was quite upfront. About the fact that she fancied me, anyway. Don't know if I was using her. I don't know what you feel about that. Maybe. But if so it was mutual, and our arrangement suited us both.

She was holding court when I arrived at La Bergère (La Folie, I called it). Supervising the cooking, she would describe it. They had a group in. The big group room was throbbing with wailing and chanting and frenetic monotonous drumming.

The kitchen was huge and dark. It took me a moment to spot her amidst the bustle and steam. 'Darling!' she exclaimed from her armchair by the window. She raised her glass at me. A large one, I noticed, considering it wasn't yet midday.

She caught me looking. 'When in France...'

I bent and she pecked the air near my cheek. Both sides. Her lips were immaculate, dark blood red, as always. 'No, Gisela, NOT that knife. Shift your ass, Hans, Sonia's waiting for those carrots...Sorry, Oli darling. How ARE you?' She put her hand on my arm and shoved me back a fraction, scrutinising me. She hadn't yet smiled. Noticed her eyebrows were thinner even than

55

usual. Barely there behind her excessively large red and gold specs.

'Mmmm. Like the growth. Makes you look like a bit of rough.' She widened her eyes at me.

Harriet was a large woman. Magnificent. Statuesque. Immovable. Those kinds of adjectives. Perfectly poised. She only ever wore black or maroon. Today it was both – a black flowing top with maroon pants and strappy heels. She had a huge quartz pendant dangling between her boobs. She reeked of scent, something musky dark and a bit sweet and slickly dangerous. Reminded me of something or someone, though I've never quite remembered what or whom.

She was pretty uncompromising, Harriet. Not the same thing as being honest and unmanipulative.

'Harriet?' said Gisela rather timidly.

Harriet turned her head, admirably slowly, and raised her eyebrows, waiting. I looked at Gisela, too. Where did she find them, all these willing foreign kitchen slaves? Gisela looked about seventeen, thin and blonde and frail.

'It says here only fresh artichoke hearts...'

'If you think I'm going to pay you lot an hour's worth of cooking time to peel fresh artichokes – open the tins, Gisela. No, there, in that cupboard – no, the other one.'

I heard the unvoiced exasperated sigh. Harriet raised an eyebrow at me. I suddenly realised that she too must be at least forty. These older women. She wore it well. She didn't pretend to be anything other than she was. The boss. In control. Poised, sitting there so relaxedly. That carefully cut glossy burgundy hair. It occurred to me that she dyed it.

She looked back at me. Fixed me. Knew she still had a hold over me. God knows why she did. Why I let her. But in her way she'd been good to me. That time I nearly cracked, couple of

56

summers ago. Fair's fair.

'I'm so glad you made it before lunch, Oli. Will you join us? We're going to eat in the garden, then I thought we'd have a quick tuning-in session with the group...'

Tuning-in was something I tried to avoid, even though often it was followed by a siesta for Harriet. Yes, I was usually invited. Alone, of course. But sitting in a circle holding hands with eyes closed toning the 'om' sound – well, it left me cold at best.

Before I could answer Harriet rose. 'Come and look at the programme, Oli. See if what I've sketched in for you works.'

So from the beginning of June to the end of September I would tutor a photography course again. Two weeks on, two off. Only Saturdays free for J-Y.

I quite enjoyed the Centre. It amused me. It brought me cash. And I can't pretend I didn't enjoy the attentions of all those single women who came in their droves for sun and leisure and company. All looking for something to add a frisson to their day. There were always more blokes on photography courses than on some of the others, except massage and Tai Chi, but still the women outnumbered us by a long way. Helps to be young, too. May not sound like it but I quite like people – at a bit of a distance. Or at least they interest me.

Even one week is long enough to see below the surface in holiday groups where people loosen up a bit. Once the dynamics kick in things can get very interesting. And then they go home.

Although Harriet liked to have the reins, she did trust tutors to know their stuff. She let them get on with what they were good at. Within reason. She didn't, for instance, encourage – or allow, might be more like it – intimacy between members of staff.

Her start-of-season speech. She trotted it out again now in her office: 'Our job, Oli, is to make sure these folks have a bloody good holiday. And tell their friends, and come back next year. That's what we're here for. That's the ONLY thing we're here for. That's what you're paid for. Hmmmm?' – running her nails up my spine. Fingering the quartz in her cleavage.

Harriet sat at the centre of a web. Vast. Sticky. Her threads were both subtle and not at all subtle. Can't explain that, even with the wisdom of age. Except to say that she used her charms – or her implied  promises – quite consciously. That's contrived. Hence unsubtle.

I was shocked that morning to find that her fingernails on my back provoked in me nothing. Other than a kind of mild chilly irritation. God, after a winter of almost-unrelieved celibacy too. My body at least had been looking forward to the erotic banquet that Harriet could be relied upon to provide. Particularly sophisticated and imaginative. Why then this total and unprecedented lack of interest from my groin?

Harriet's hands strayed across my shoulders as we stood and looked through the diary together. She dropped them, ostensibly to close the big year planner, brushing against the button flies of my 501s. I know I recoiled. Couldn't help it. Harriet's hands stayed where they were, gripping the edges of the diary. Her large face, three inches from mine, turned slowly towards me. I stepped back. Couldn't breathe suddenly. She was gross. Or so it seemed to me suddenly.

Shit. Confused.

'That's great, Harriet. Thanks. Must just go and say hello to Ian before I leave...' and I found myself striding away with relief coupled with anxiety. Faster than my dignity liked. My mind turning upon the new and horrifying possibility that I had suddenly become impotent. When you're in your twenties not a lot else touches that fear for sheer magnitude. In your thirties, too, come to that.

Ian was the co-director of La Bergère. Looking for him I allowed my mind to turn on what had just happened. Found myself filled with revulsion at Harriet. Her impeccably-presented front. Her neatly ordered control. The way she wielded the power of her position.

Ian was nowhere to be seen. I wanted to get out. Instead I made myself stroll down under the archway to the vegetable garden. I was walking back past the mulberry trees in the gardens towards the wall by the compost heap to collect my bike when Ian called me from the French windows of the sitting room.

'What have you said to Harriet? I saw you disappear with her. The girls in the kitchen have just had an almighty bollocking from her for nothing, and she's got her shark face on...'

Ian was the only person who took no shit from Harriet. I'd heard him call her 'Jaws dear' to her face, though usually his way was simply to disappear. I couldn't help feeling that it was as well for him that he was gay.

I laughed and kicked the bike awake, then sat astride it for a few minutes bantering with Ian. Then I heaved the bike round towards the gate and let it go.

Didn't usually let rip on the bike. Had my reasons. Today, though.

Something felt wrong. Something was missing. It had been enough before. Easy, secret, uncomplicated sex. Suddenly now it felt seriously inadequate. Worse than inadequate. False. Right now the thought of fucking Harriet was worse than the idea of no sex at all.

## Thirteen

Josselin's one of those mediaeval towns that the tourists love. Bloody history, intrigue, combat and riots. Miracles and miracle cures. Rivers. Proper pointed shiny turrets on the Huguenot – I think – castle.

Don't know what I was doing there, really. Pushing through all the summer crowds with my rucksack and camera gear. Looking for a shot that wasn't cluttered with people. Suppose I was still in search of shape and form, shadows and light. The usual unexpected angles and aspects.

The main building facing the park in what was the castle courtyard, my guidebook told me, had examples of the sculptors' art as fine as anywhere in Brittany. Pinnacles, brackets, florets, curled leaves, gables, crowns. All carved in ungiving granite. Maybe it was the granite. I'm not normally into architecture or history, that kind of stuff. Or not in those days, anyway.

I'd done the first two weeks of La Bergère with La Madame and needed to breathe. Tough going, this year. Think the course was OK. Though somehow Harriet had overlooked my need for a darkroom. I'd had to use one of the old downstairs loos, sharing it with mice and mouse-sized spiders and all the cleaning gear. H had commandeered my previous stone-floored dairy for the photocopier, excess technology and a pushbike or two. Well, at least I was out of earshot of the kitchen. Harriet's Seat of State.

Harriet hadn't been too bad, really. Considering she must have noticed that I'd snubbed her at that first meeting of the season. She hadn't exactly given me the come-on, since, though. So far not a whiff of the possibility of a lay. Was I glad or pissed off? I didn't know. But she'd been friendly in a slightly prickly way. I'd done the usual. Chauffeured to and from train or ferry. Done the boulangerie run in the morning. Split logs for the outdoor sauna and jacuzzi. Picked up guest musicians, poets, storytellers, fire-eaters and assorted troubadours etcetera for the Friday night cabaret. Fixed the lawnmower, rebuilt a wall. Oh and run a course.

Anyway here I was in Josselin on a Sunday when Jean-Yves didn't need me. I'd caught the odd frame – still on black and white – nothing that really excited me but some possibilities. Climbed the tower of the basilica to look over into the inner court, then the panorama. I wondered about collaging some shots. The fountain had promise in theory but not quite so much in practice. Wandered without a lot of enthusiasm back towards the castle, round to the walls by the river. Texture of the walls themselves in close-up and some broken reflections in the Oust below might offer something. Always this stone and water stuff. Like most photographers I enjoy playing with macro and micro.

Afterwards I paid and went into the castle itself. Found myself in the old stables, where all the antique dolls are kept. That was spooky. All those blank faces, all those dead children's hands. Horror movie stuff. Shades of Stanley Spencer, too – that strange painting of his ex-wife and daughter with the two grotesque dolls in the corner. Remembered, too, a bloke at college who took a load of photos of his girlfriend's china-faced childhood doll sprawled in the grass, legs askew and head twisted. Those remembered images combined with something about the atmosphere here did it for me. I took a couple of rolls when the custodian was back by the door, reeling them off without any attention to composition or grouping. If it worked, fine. If not, there might be images I could superimpose on other things.

I went back to the place by the basilica and found a pavement table and an espresso. Rolled a smoke, stretched my legs in the sun.

The square started to fill up, bit by bit. The late lunch rush. A couple asked me, in polite schoolbook French, if the other seats at my table were free.

'Sure,' I said in English. 'Help yourselves.'

Actually I didn't want company. I'd had plenty of that all fortnight. But you can't really say that in a cafe where all the tables are full, can you? So I carried on looking at the steps up to the doorway to the basilica. And thinking about the dolls. Newspapers and books come in handy at such times but I didn't have either.

After a while I became aware that the pair of them were looking at me. You're in a foreign place – where presumably you've come to get away from home – and you want to establish contact with fellow countrymen? Why?

The man, sweating in a turquoise shell suit, asked me whether the castle was worth a visit.

'Depends on what you like,' I said. 'It's all right. Not a lot of atmosphere. Museum bit's not bad, though.'

He indicated his camcorder. 'Wanted something for the folks back home. You're a photographer, aren't you?' – nodding at my case. 'Worth a go?'

I thought about telling him about the dolls but decided not to. 'Not a lot that moves,' I said instead, and returned to staring at the basilica.

Her turn. 'Where do you come from?'

I hate those kinds of questions. 'Oh, I live a few miles away, down near the coast.'

She persisted. 'No, I mean in England?'

I looked at her. Thin shoulder length blonde-ish hair, jeans, pale blue sweater. Nylon cagoule rolled up on the table. Neither remarkable nor unremarkable.

She was still looking at me, and suddenly she seemed vaguely familiar.

She cleared her throat. 'I just wondered if I know you?'

Now her husband and I were both looking at her. Then Shellsuit turned and peered at me.

Time to get out. Fast. I looked at my watch.

'Shit. Excuse me. The supermarket closes in a minute. Promised my wife I'd pick something up.' The lies tripped off my tongue. It was true that the supermarket would close soon though. At least until late afternoon. I gathered my camera bag and stuffed my tobacco into the rucksack with the helmet. Headed off quickly around the corner, then doubled back down another alleyway towards the river car park where I'd left the bike.

Time to head out. Call me paranoid, or cautious. What I was looking for was a quiet life.

## Fourteen

Well, bugger me if I didn't arrive for the next stint at La Folie one morning and there she was. Camera Smasher. River Woman. Another woman with questions. I nearly turned around and left again. Get a grip, Oliver.

On Sundays they did a kind of briefing session for the new arrivals before lunch. Lunch was meet-the-staff time. Then the first workshops. Up until lunch the tutors were free. I didn't mind helping out instead of hanging around. I like physical work. Need it.

I'd been clearing some rubble at the base of a wall. It was hot; stinking hot. I like it like that. Stopped to peel my T-shirt off. The air was thick with the scent of pine, and something more blossomy. There were footsteps the other side of the wall. Straightened and stretched my shoulders. The steps came nearer, though still at some distance from me. A female head and shoulders came into view. All I could see was a mass of hair caught up loosely in a flamboyant scarf. Escaped strands trailing down those elfin cheeks and curling around her neck. I leaned a little closer, very slowly. You've probably gathered I don't like drawing attention to myself. Yes, her. No question. Dressed in some kind of flame-coloured loose shirt thing with a huge belt. The perennial black-clad legs and wellies, despite the heat. Pushing a wheelbarrow with a load of greenery – weedings by the look of it, brambles and docks and stuff. On the premises, heading towards the compost heap or bonfire site near the veg garden. She didn't see me. Or at least she acted like she hadn't. After that day at Tradescat I wasn't so sure what she did or didn't see.

So what the fuck was she doing here? Gardening, clearly. But Harriet hadn't said at the last staff meeting. Not that that was much of a surprise.

Well, I bent down again and carried on with what I was doing.

When I walked through the kitchen that evening Gisela was sorting the wine for the table. *Ordinaire* from the local *cave* decanted from the plastic five-litre cask, or local cider, for the guests; a syrah or claret for 'family' – when they were in favour. (We'd replace the cask at least once an evening. Why is it that the English on holiday drink so much? The fact that it's free, I suppose.) You always knew when Harriet had a grievance with a particular member of staff. The offending member was firmly pointed to the guests' table glass decanters rather than the rough pottery staff jug (a neat and dishonest reversal of vessels) when we were about to seat ourselves to eat.

'Oliver, Harriet wants to see you,' Gisela said, timidly glancing my way. Slopping wine onto the draining board. 'She's in her office.'

I finished what I was doing – clearing up after my first session, and running off some handouts on the photocopier. Then I went to find Her Ladyship.

Not much of a surprise to see Elf in there.

'Oh, there you are,' Harriet said. I ignored the undercurrent of 'where the hell have you been?' in her tone. 'I don't think you two know each other. Tamar, this is Oliver. Oli, Tamar.'

While I was thinking about how I wanted to respond Tamar put her hand out.

'Pleased to meet you, Oli,' she said, looking up into my face. Couldn't help noticing how alive her eyes seemed. In comparison, that's all.

'Oliver,' Harriet interjected. I noted the acid tone. As far as she was concerned only she was allowed to shorten my name.

65

Actually, I hate being called Oli. By anyone.

'Hi,' I said. 'Did I see you gardening earlier?'

Before she could reply Harriet cut in. 'Tamar's brief is to clear that old vegetable patch beyond the orchard. I want to plant fruit bushes there, and a knot garden maybe. Herbs, anyway. Ian's found an old rotovator at a farm sale. You wouldn't mind giving the patch a going over one evening after Tamar's finished clearing the worst of the weeds, would you?'

Did I have any choice? But already Harriet was steaming on. 'Oli, there's something I want to talk to you about.' She started tapping a pen on the edge of her desk. 'Tamar, I'll see you in the morning. Is Janna coming to pick you up?'

'I hope so. Can I use your phone?'

'The one in the kitchen. See you tomorrow.'

Dismissal cue. After she'd closed the door Harriet gave me a long look. I didn't know what it was about so I simply looked back.

She'd find some pretext. Anything to get me alone. Put one over me.

'How was your session? How many of them came?'

'Seven or eight. Didn't count. How many are there this week? Fifteen?'

'Sixteen with Thomas. He'll only make an occasional workshop I think. The others don't know, OK?'

Thomas had AIDS, Harriet had told us at the staff meeting. When I'd met him from the train he'd looked pretty weak.

'OK. What were the rest doing today then?'

'A couple went off for a walk to the lake. One or two sat around in the garden. Thomas slept. I think the others took themselves off to Robin's Tai Chi. Now listen, Oli. Ian was stopped by the gendarmes today; dodgy tyres. But they want to see his licence and everything. Green card. Are your papers in order?'

A pretext, Oliver, a pretext.

Answer a question with a question. 'I thought the French cops were supposed to be laid back about vehicles and stuff? I've no idea where my papers are. Did they ask for staff papers?'

'I think you'd better track them down. Not like you to be disorganised. But I rely on you for driving. I hate these French roads. Be a good man –' she put her hand over mine – 'bring them in, would you? I'd be happier if I knew there was nothing they'd need to follow up.'

A caress. I just about resisted removing my hand. 'Good man' – yuck.

'And Oli –' she let her gaze travel down my body to my shorts, legs, bare feet – 'I do like brown bodies. Especially yours.' Unusually upfront for Harriet. Her style was more unspoken, more physical, normally. Maybe something had rattled her? Or perhaps my lack of advance or response was getting to her.

She left a silence. So did I. I looked out the window. I could feel her looking at me still, then she followed my gaze. Tamar happened to walk past towards the gate as we watched.

'I'm not sure about that one. Still, she cleared a lot today. I'll give her a chance. Janna says she needs the work – money, but also trouble of some sort I think. A man, I imagine. Let's hope she throws herself into the gardening.' Harriet was tapping the pen again with her free hand. I took advantage of her momentary distraction to draw my hand away from under her other one and headed towards the door.

'Must be nearly suppertime. The kitchen smelt good. I must just go and take a shower. See you later.' I swung out of the door before she could say anything else.

Her hand on mine had disturbed me. I felt restless; almost aroused, though I'm not sure it was Harriet's doing.

67

# Fifteen

She did it again the next morning – materialised beside me out of nowhere. It wasn't yet ten – workshop starting time – and I was balanced on a wall with a cup of coffee wedged into a gap while I rolled myself a smoke.

'Oliver.' Those clear assessing eyes.

'Hi.'

'Did you get a new lens cap?'

'Huh? – Oh that. Oh yeah. No problem.'

'I didn't expect to see you here. I thought you worked for that guy on the Rue Chateaubriand? The gallery?'

'I do.' How did she know that? 'Jean-Yves. Yes. I do two weeks on two off here in the summer, too. I was here last year. What about you?'

'I'm staying with some friends, and they know Harriet. I needed some work.' She leaned back against the wall, not too close. 'What's she like to work for?' Her eyes crinkled with what I suppose you'd call mischief. 'David – that's my friend's husband – calls her the Black Widow.' She turned and smiled at me questioningly.

I lit my roll-up. 'Pass. I get on OK with her. You have to give as good as you get. She's not as keen on women as she is on men.'

'She and Ian aren't partners, are they?'

'You mean lovers? God, no. Ian's not into women.'

'Oh. Right... Does she have a bloke?'

'No idea.' I paused to pick a bit if tobacco off my tongue. Changed the subject. 'Are you living here then? In France, I mean?'

'For the moment. And you?'

I nodded.

A blackbird started up in the mulberry tree and Tamar

turned to look at it. A few minutes passed. Comfortable enough.

She pushed herself off the wall. 'She's paying me by the hour. I should get going. D'you know anything about the compost heaps?'

'Not a lot. I think they put vegetable peelings in them. Maybe grass mowings.'

'Oh good. Just checking. I wasn't sure.' She twinkled at me. 'I meant do you know which one's current and which is last year's?'

'Haven't a clue. Sorry. Better ask H.'

'Guess I'd better. See you later.' She padded off – canvas sneakers today, those black Chinese slip-on things they use for Tai Chi – as silently as she'd arrived.

## Sixteen

### France
### TAMAR

I was bending over thinning out some seedlings – rocket and mustard and lettuce and cut-and-come-again and other salady things. I'd finally noticed – or rather, Janna had suggested that morning – that since it was hot, really hot, and had been for some while, wasn't it time I abandoned my leggings in favour of cooler things? I wasn't sure that I had any, but I found a vest top and a kind of narrow Indian cotton throw that I'd come back with from Morlaix market. It made a great short sarong. The warmth on my shoulders and the backs of my legs was soothing and I felt my muscles aching to unknot. I must have still been tenser than I was aware.

I stopped to stretch. The air was full of sound – swifts screaming, the stream at the end of the garden, crickets, something popping – gorse pods or pine cones – and I could hear laughter from the group room. Over by the hedge a robin was encouraging three fledglings to fly.

My thoughts drifted, not unusually, to Mark. I had been telling Janna that morning how it is that when someone dies – these all-encompassing generalisations, as if I were an authority – when you do start to feel again it's the little things that hurt most. I missed pointing out the robins; I could picture the way he'd stand, hands in pockets, watching them reflectively. The way he'd have noticed, too, the grass-snake looped on the rock by the pond, half-hidden by the ochre grasses. I imagined his uncompetitive amusement at the rivalry between the women for the attentions of Robin, the Tai Chi teacher, who was one of those classic sun-god types, all golden leg hair and inscrutably dark shades. (And, it has to be said – cruelly – a rather simpery nasal voice.)

Of course I missed the affection and the sex; of course I missed the sense of having found – I had assumed – a lifemate. These kinds of things are self-evident. And they're also almost too big, too abstract, to feel except as a deep continuous ache. There's only room for the minutiae; but my God did they hurt. I'd have given anything, anything, to see Mark clamber out of bed and don his socks before anything else – something which in 'real life' drove me crazy with unlust. If that makes sense. And the way he'd whistle the same unmelodious note over and over when he was trying to sort out a practical problem, or checking his gear before a climb. I missed the way he'd turn his head to listen to me, giving me his full attention, even when I was only mentioning something trivial.

Easy to go too far down that route. I came back to the lettuces. There were still gusts of laughter issuing from the group room. I registered that this was unusual; it was Tai Chi time and Robin took his subject seriously: it was normally conducted in complete, reverent silence.

It was laughter I missed most of all. I'm sure I must have laughed at times through those first years, but it was certainly not something I did a lot of. I've always been good at putting on a front, though; probably most of my acquaintances, if not closer friends, would have assumed I was doing fine. Which I was, in some ways; at least I didn't hoard pills any more – that had to be a good sign. And of course laughter is contagious; even when you yourself don't feel like it it serves as a reminder that grief is not the only emotion in existence. I found myself smiling as I bent back to the seedlings.

Not long afterwards I heard the group troop out for coffee-break; the animated chatter carried as far as the vegetable garden.

I moved over to the basil. Someone had piled woodchip and what looked like chopped-up thistles all around the plants. I stared. Just then there were footsteps behind me, and a shadow fell across mine, onto the bed with the basils. I looked round. It was Cromwell. He was carrying a great tower of the cut-off bottom thirds of plastic Evian bottles stacked one in the other. He put them down on the grass beside me, saying nothing, and stood a moment; then reached into his pocket for his tobacco.

'Hi,' I said, eventually.

'I've perforated the ends,' he said, as if that explained everything.

'Huh?'

'When I was down here last night I noticed the slugs had been at your basil. Have you seen the slugs here? Monsters. Rat-eaters, they are. So I brought you these.'

Unusually forthcoming. The longest speech I'd heard from him. I hadn't noticed the state of the basil, I realised guiltily.

'Was it you put the chips around them, too?' I asked probably somewhat unnecessarily.

He grunted, which I took to be an affirmative, turning his head to watch the flight of one of the swifts. His face was expressionless.

Didn't have him down as a birdwatcher or plantfancier. Full of surprises.

'Full of surprises,' I heard myself say.

He ignored this. 'Put these on at night. It'll help.'

'Thank you, Oliver. I –'

But he'd gone, loping back across the lawn and disappearing through the huge old front door. I watched his back as he crossed the red-tiled hall floor. I felt disconcerted, my initial gratitude replaced suddenly with a kind of furious irritation. How dare he interfere? And then walk away just as I start to speak. Arrogant sod. I plunged my dibber back into the warm soil with more aggression than I knew I had, and a great deal more than is necessary to make a tiny hole.

The thing about gardening is that it takes you anyway, eventually. Once you get stuck in, other things seem less important, or less overwhelming. Mum always used to say that a good therapist needs to be a good gardener too. You slow to a different pace, once you let yourself go into soil-world time. Earth's dense, after all, and it's very easy to let yourself think that you just live in air, and its faster speed, simply because most of your frame's in the vertical, especially if you're the dreamy or mystical type. Put your hands down to where your feet are and you close the circuit and come back down to the real world.

At least, that's what I was thinking when I straightened up again an hour later, having lost my irritation at Oliver and, for the moment, too, the sharper edge of my grief about Mark. I didn't know whether the calm I was feeling was an unwinding or a gentle physical tiredness, but of course it didn't matter because the effect was the same.

I picked up my sweatshirt and tied it around my waist and collected together twine and dibber and seed trays and fork and put them all in a bucket. I wandered over towards the fruit trees – we'd been picking the cherries for a week or two but I couldn't resist collecting a few handfuls more into the seed trays. I thought Harriet might be glad to put them into a fruit salad. We needed to organise the guests into a concerted hour or two with ladders – those who felt so inclined – to pick enough for the kitchen to have a serious jam-making session. The tits and blackbirds would strip the trees bare if we left it much longer, and the soft fruits alongside hadn't been netted either. I'd have to see what Harriet thought. I'd rather have asked Ian, but he left those kinds of decisions to Harriet.

My stomach suggested it might be lunch-time. I'd been joining the guests and 'family' each day; usually we ate outside, and as I rounded the corner from the orchard I could see that the two big tables under the mulberry tree were laden with food and lined with people. There was a space up at the top by Harriet, and another between Chrissie, whom I'd warmed to, and Jean-Pascal, the local farmer who provided La Bergère with some of its produce. Harriet was generous with food and hospitality; though later Oliver voiced the opinion that it was merely a method of control. In the light of what happened later I had to admit he might have been right; but at that time I gave her the benefit of the doubt.

As I took the seat by Chrissie Oliver crossed the lawn, and sat down by Harriet. I couldn't help noticing the way she placed her hand – somewhat proprietorially, perhaps? – on his arm, and left it there. It occurrred to me that she fancied him.

'Hiya,' said Chrissie. 'What have you been doing today? Are you responsible for the herbs in our salad?'

'Yes to the second bit, though the sorrel was there already, when I arrived; and I've been planting more of the same. What about you?'

'I'm going to skive off this afternoon, and go swimming. This morning was great – Tai Chi. Oliver's had us all in stitches. Bet you heard us laughing from the garden.'

'I did, actually. What was going on? Do you mean Robin?' (OLIVER? Making them all laugh?)

'No no, Oliver. He comes to the morning sessions sometimes. He doesn't ever actually say anything, but he's so funny.'

I stared at her. I couldn't quite square the Oliver I'd met with the person she seemed to be describing. 'Oliver makes you laugh?

74

What does he do?'

'It's hard to put it into words. It probably won't sound funny. But it's the way he is. He's so deadpan.' She lowered her voice. 'It took us a while to cotton on. He kind of takes Robin off; does all the movements perfectly, but just exaggerates each one a little, and a little more, and then a bit more again, until he has Robin hopping. But there's nothing Robin can do about it because Oliver's doing them right; just too much. And as soon as Robin notices he tones them down. Until the next time.'

I looked down the table at Oliver. Clearly I needed to reassess him. Yes. I could imagine that he'd have been the kind of insolent arrogant schoolboy every teacher would hate; the more so because he was clearly bright.

'I bet that really pisses Robin off.'

'Oh yes. He was mad to start with. But actually, to give him credit, he ended up laughing, too; and we even got a smile out of Oliver.'

At first I couldn't picture Oliver smiling; and then suddenly I could. I thought back. I wasn't sure I'd ever actually seen him smile as such, but I knew that his whole face would light, if he were being genuine and not just forced-polite. As I watched him, musing, I caught him looking my way. Then he turned back to Harriet, who was animatedly telling him and her other neighbour about something that involved expansive gestures. She looked over the top of her sunglasses at her other neighbour, Mike, one of the few men on the course, and then at Oliver, where her gaze rested for a few seconds. Well. So Oliver had a sense of humour; and just as surprising, I supposed, was that Robin might have, too. As for Harriet – I turned back to Chrissie.

'Where are you going to swim?'

'Jean-Pascal was saying just now that there's a deep pool in the bend of the river, so Sally and I are going to go down and investigate. Nick's going off to photography this afternoon so I'm free! How about you, love? Come too?'

'I'd love to, but I'm supposed to be working.'

'Take an hour off? Just an hour? I'm sure Harriet wouldn't mind. It'd be fun.'

'Well, maybe I could. I'll see.'

'Do try. Meet us at the front door at 3 if you can...'

Maybe I would. Time to do something just for fun.

## Seventeen

The path down to the river was secret, sandy, stony and narrow. Grasses brushed our ankles as we moved under tall sweet chestnut and oak trees.

Chrissie, in front of me, was blocking my forward view, her Neapolitan-ice-cream stripes emphasising the cheerful generosity of her figure.

Ahead of her the low-cut back of Sally's red swimsuit, disappearing into her little denim shorts, flickered in and out of my vision, punctuating the somnolent greengold darkness of the woods, urgent as a distress flare.

The path was an ancient one, frequented more by deer and badger than by humans. Here a scatter of rabbit droppings, there a magpie feather.

'Are we far enough south for there to be wild boar?' asked Chrissie, turning to restrain a bramble from whipping my face. Something about her warmth, her smile, went through me. I stared at her, feeling suddenly vulnerable, weepy, lonely. Homesick. She was looking at me, waiting for an answer. My eyes moved to the trickle of sweat moistening her temples under her straw hat.

'Um – wild boar – don't think so, no. I'd guess they don't start till the other side of the Dordogne.'

'Oh. Are you OK, love?'

I nodded.

'Wish I hadn't worn sandals,' she continued. 'Sorry I'm holding you up – I'm afraid of twisting my ankle on these loose stones.'

'No hurry, Chrissie. Free afternoon!'

'Look at Sally, striding out there up in front. She's so thin, isn't she? Too thin. Bet she swims like an otter. Ah well, at least I bounce if I trip over; and I don't need buoyancy aids either.'

I peered round Chrissie at Sally's back disappearing round the next bend in the path. Knobby vertebrae seem terribly exposed and vulnerable, don't they? Even in one who strides out so confidently.

Chrissie and I lapsed into silence. Somehow it seemed to fit the mood of the place and the afternoon.

Around us the gorse pods popped in the heat. The crickets were quiet. The dry grass whispered and crackled as we pass. Something slithered away into the bushes.

We moved in and out of sun and shade, alternately blinded by light and blinded by darkness. The effect was a little disorienting, mesmerising. After it's happened enough times you start to see differently, as if through older less physical eyes. It's as if you see from both inside and outside yourself simultaneously; or perhaps I mean from deeper inside yourself – or deeper outside.

The path now was not so much a gentle meandering descent to the river as bands of light and shade cutting the landscape up into a series of frames through which we flickered like candle flames reverberating from glass to mirror to glass.

It was a strange experience. Do you know what I mean if I say that sometimes there's confusion between movement and stillness?

It was a bit like one of those dreams where you seem to be moving forward but you don't actually get anywhere; though we did, of course, arrive at the river – I can't even add 'eventually', but probably only ten or fifteen minutes at most after entering the woods.

And by contrast the river was itself: a wide undulating ribbon separating banks. As we approached it acquired depth; the pool in the river's elbow became a chalky-green eye, all-knowing, all-seeing.

And Sally was there ahead of us, poised for a second on the bank, arms raised, her red costume blazing against the pale rocky overhang of the opposite bank. And then in one fluid movement she was in, cleaving the water.

I caught Chrissie's eyes.

She nodded. 'Told you so! Just like an otter.'

Chrissie dropped her bag and divested herself of sandals, skirt, top. She already had her swimsuit on under her clothes. As I said she was large, but had that kind of ease and unselfconsiousness about her body that people whose centre of attention is naturally others rather than themselves sometimes acquire. Fair and sweet-faced, there was something about her that made me, and I'm sure most people, feel safe.

She saw me looking at her and smiled.

'That costume makes your eyes look very blue,' I said.

'Thanks, sweetheart. God, look at Sally go. Did you bring a cozzie?'

'Don't have one. I'll just strip,' and I did, though I found myself checking the shadows in case of onlookers. The afternoon was feeling a bit spooky; a strange waiting stillness. Maybe just that kind of stillness that pools in woods on summer afternoons acquire.

Chrissie chuckled. 'Look at you. The original wild woman. Artemis? Daphne? Can't quite remember my mythology. Was Daphne the one who turned herself into a tree? Who was chasing her? Did anyone chase Artemis?'

I shook my head. 'Can't remember. Actaeon? Whoever it was who spied on Artemis bathing got torn apart by her hounds though.'

'Never mind. They're all dead now, anyway. We're perfectly

safe here. God you're so slim, too. Makes me wish I didn't find watching my weight so boring. I'm too much in love with food. Oh well.' Chrissie removed her hair clasp and redid her knot of fair hair higher off her neck. 'Race you. Look at that crawl of Sally's.' And Chrissie was in too, with a very stylish dive off the high bank.

I'm not terribly confident in the water. I love it and I love being on it – Dad sailed, and I'd learnt about jibs and booms, as well as trailing mackerel lines under oar or motor, almost as early as learning to walk. But still, I don't entirely trust water as an element. So I enjoy being in it, floating on my back, say; but I'm not a strong swimmer and I'm not good at diving. I don't like my head under water. So I slid down the bank instead, preferring a gentle entry.

The water was cool and a little murky; a clay or mud bottom, I supposed. I'd had romantic notions of clear depths and smooth river pebbles. Chrissie and Sally were out in the middle, lazing and laughing. As I watched Sally did a kind of sinuous backflip and disappeared under the surface. She seemed to be gone for an alarmingly long time, and my mind was suddenly playing panic scenarios; and just when I was sure she must be in danger she reappeared, and she and Chrissie both swam over to the bank and climbed out, to dive in again.

'Come on,' Sally said, splashing me playfully as she passed. 'No fun hovering in the shallows. It's wonderful out in the middle. It's like a great round open-roofed bath.'

Chrissie winked as she swam past. I watched her fluid breaststroke barely breaking the water, and Sally's athletic crawl sending little flurries of silver into the air amongst the dragonflies. The ripples spread and spread, dispersing until the whole surface of the pool seemed alive, shimmering and rocking gently. Easy to believe in watergods here.

I turned over onto my back and watched the different eye of sky. Against the blueness, very high up, were a couple of specks. I wondered lazily if we were far enough south for them to be kites, or if they were buzzards.

I think I must have floated off into a daydream, because what seemed like hours later I became aware of shouting. Chrissie's voice, distressed. I flipped upright, feet sinking into mud. I withdrew them quickly and trod water with my knees bent. Chrissie was racing towards the far bank at speed, screaming Sally's name. I looked around – no sign of Sally. I launched myself into a sort of overarm stroke towards the middle, my heart thumping suddenly. 'Chrissie!' I yelled. 'Chrissie! What's up? Where's Sally?'

Chrissie didn't hear me. Suddenly I saw a flash of red, below the water, moving. The afternoon contracted around me, the pool became the tight black pupil of an eye. I was panting. Everything had gone dark and still; a storm waiting to crash upon us. My chest was hurting and I could hear myself breathing, a frantic hoarse sound which I couldn't stop.

I caught up with Chrissie. Between us we'd churned the water. Even the surface was clouded. My hair was all over my face, in my eyes. I couldn't see the red flash. Then Sally's head broke the water close by; just as suddenly she disappeared under again.

Chrissie screamed again and flailed backwards, away from where Sally went down. I turned my head and saw the source of her latest fear – a snake, a water snake or grass snake, undulating away from us.

Out of the corner of my eye I caught a scrap of red again and without thinking dived towards it.

Head under water.

Then no red. Nothing except strange murky light.

I panicked and surfaced; made myself dive under again. This time I could see a shape just feet from me. Both arms and a leg were flailing.

The water was loud in my ears, pulsing. My heart.

It took me years to cross the few feet between me and the shape. Then something else took over. Something primal pushed me faster. I fumbled for the still leg. Instinct.

But my chest was bursting and I had to surface.

Chrissie grabbed my arm. With no words we both sank under again. This time my arm felt for Sally's foot and my hand freed the heel from an angle of tree root, and Sally shot up to the surface. I turned her onto her back and then Chrissie and I were swimming fast for the shore, one free arm each and an arm in each of Sally's.

I swallowed so much water I thought I would die. I could hear whimpering. My own, I realised. Sally's head kept lolling under.

We crashed and stumbled up the bank, dragging Sally's deadweight body. We let her flop onto the scratchy grass facedown. I fell onto hands and knees. I hadn't even the energy to raise my head; struggling for breath. Wheezing. Straining straining for the inbreath.

No time. No time to waste.

I crawled towards Sally's mud and slime-streaked body. God, First Aid, First Aid – what do you do first? What the hell was the acronym? ABC? Airway, breathing, cardiac? Was that it?

'Pulse, breathing – quick – '

'She is breathing. Thank GOD. Let me feel her carotid pulse – '

'But all the water she swallowed – what if she vomits? Chokes?'

'Don't panic. I'm a nurse. Yes, recovery position... OK.

Steady, Sally, steady; gently. We're here...'

And I sat back on my heels as Sally suddenly convulsed, and then retched and retched and half the river seemed to trickle into the dry grasses; and then finally she was finished and flopped again, spent, on her stomach, moaning.

An hour later we made our slow way back up the path, Sally wrapped, pale and shivering, but alive. None of us talked much until we arrived at the lane, where Sally seemed to cheer up; and as we walked back into the garden, Chrissie and I either side of Sally, arms around her, we were all laughing, Sally too, albeit weakly. These brushes with danger or death release laughter sometimes, don't they? – And there was Oliver, in the hammock under the oak.

As we came through the arch he closed his book and got up and left.

'Something we said, obviously,' said Chrissie; and we all laughed again, hysterically, until – the after-effects of shock, I suppose – all we could do was subside weakly onto the grass.

## Eighteen

It wasn't much of a surprise that Oliver didn't give me the benefit of his company for a few days. Not, of course, that he had before. But God, these arrogant aloof men. He slouched round the place as enigmatic and unreadable as ever, but I couldn't help noticing that he seemed to leave a room – any room – each time I entered. What's a woman supposed to make of that? Nothing, maybe. Coincidence, maybe.

What I also noticed was how much time he and Harriet seemed to spend together. He even drove her to the supermarket outside Pontivy, and helped her carry the shopping in. I was surprised. I knew he did a lot of the stuff around the place but I didn't have him down as the domestic type.

\*

I was getting on well in the herb and vegetable gardens. The crops were good – fat courgettes and yellow patty pan squashes and little green and purple and cream dwarf beans; plump tomatoes, and peppers and aubergines ripening nicely. My basil plants were superb, huge-leafed, juicy.

On this hot morning there were fritillaries doing their thing – dancing prettily – under the willow, and bees drowsed around the lemon balm's little white flowers.

I'd put the sprinkler on the herbs, and was pinching out the elbow shoots in the tomato plot one morning, swimming in the pungent bruised smell mixed with the fragrances of the damp herbs, when I heard the murmur of voices just over the wall. One sounded like Harriet's, which was a surprise. She didn't like the heat, and almost never left the cool of her office, except to sit under the trees to eat, with her huge floppy hat on. In fact I could only hear Harriet's voice, but I didn't think she'd be talking to herself. The voice got nearer and two heads approached. Yes, Harriet. And Oliver. Oliver was tall, but Harriet's head was almost level with his. I carried on pinching out, moving along the row. Some of the plants had come loose from their ties, and as I bent to re-stake them the scent was almost overpowering.

Next time I looked up Harriet was sitting down; or from the position of her head I assumed she was. She must have been leaning back against the wall – and unless she'd brought a rug with her, on the bare ground. Another surprise. Oliver was still standing, a foot or two away from her, back to me and the wall. As I looked Harriet put an arm up and pulled him down beside her, then leant towards him. I could only see the tops of their heads, but from the angle of hers I would guess she was nibbling his neck. I felt embarrassed, uncomfortable. They must have known I was there; Harriet had checked what I was going to be doing only an hour or two before.

I made myself look back down at the tomatoes; but after a minute or two I found I couldn't stand it. My heart was thumping. It was too hot. I brushed off my knees and picked up my trug and walked over to one of the herbaceous borders to do a little weeding, well out of sight of anyone, guest or resident. One of the great things about the gardens at La Bergère was their size.

I thought about other things. Anything. About my day off tomorrow. About going to the market to pick up some stuff to cook Janna and David some supper. About how long I might stay – in France, at La Bergère. About whether I could find a horse to ride. I wanted to go to Carnac, and I also wanted to look at the forest around Huelgoat. That would be good to explore on horseback. About what I might do if I was still here in the winter, when the Centre would have wound down to be open only to people wanting to rent it in family groups or parties over

Christmas and New Year. I wondered what Harriet and Ian did then? Harriet, I knew, had a flat in London still, but Ian I knew nothing about really.

Then I thought about Mark, just a little.

Just before lunch I was walking past Harriet's office to go and wash my hands, and became aware of raised voices. I couldn't help stopping.

'I'm not your fucking slave, Harriet. When did I last have a morning off?' – Oliver.

'Not tomorrow, Oli. Thursdays are no good. I need you here.'

'But it's the only bloody day when I don't have an afternoon session!'

'Tough. Ian's off then and I need another member of staff. Most of the others do morning sessions.'

'You're being a shit, H. I don't know how the fuck you manage to keep your staff. If that's your attitude you'll bloody well lose me, that's for sure –'

At which point I carried on walking towards the bathroom. A second later the office door slammed open and Oliver stormed down the passageway out towards the garden. I heard his bike roar, and then there was silence.

Harriet, at lunch, was as poised and implacable as ever, as if nothing had happened.

\*

The following Wednesday I was just clearing up to go home when Oliver materialised in the garden beside the fig tree. He stood under it for a minute. It was laden with fruit; some greeny-purple, some already ripe and softening. I glanced at him framed in fruit and to my horror the image of a scrotum arose in my mind. I know I flushed. I bent down again rapidly, hoping that at least some strands of my tied-back hair would cover my face. Oliver strolled down and leaned against the wall across the salad plot from me, one long leg crossed over the other, and took out his tobacco packet.

'Hi,' I said. I was aware of him watching me as I pushed up my sleeves and tucked the loose strands of hair back behind my ears. I was suddenly conscious that I probably had mud streaked on my face from watering-in the new plantlets.

As usual he didn't say anything, so I carried on gathering up twine and marker sticks and pens and plastic labels. His silent presence, coupled with my discomposure – shock, even – at the obtrusion of such a blatantly sexual, albeit unbidden and unexpected, image in my mind made me a bit uncomfortable, and I dropped the twine, which unravelled. Of course.

A few minutes later he still hadn't said anything. I straightened up, all the garden bits piled in my arms, and glanced at him. My ability to make small talk had vaporised. ''Bye then,' I said, feeling stupid, and turned.

He pushed himself off the wall – I was beginning to recognise his movements – and moved – the word I want to use is 'uncoiled' – towards me. I didn't know whether to keep going, or stop. I kept going, slowly. He reached his arm out towards my head and I kind of flinched, or quivered.

'Whoa,' he said. 'Did you know you have goosegrass in your hair?' – dropping it to the ground. I was mesmerised by his forearms, suddenly. Strange what you notice, isn't it? I hardly dared look at his eyes.

'What you doing tomorrow?'

'It's my day off.'

'I know. That's why I asked.'

'Oh! – Ummm; I hadn't really thought...'

'Fancy a trip to Carnac? If you can stand bikes, that is...'

I was stunned. I opened my mouth to say that I thought he couldn't take Thursdays off, then thought better of it. I didn't know what to say.

'It'll have to be dawn. I'll pick you up. At your place. OK?' – And again he was gone, into the late afternoon sun; and shock was still banging through me in waves. And I couldn't breathe. I felt transparent, as if he could see my mental pictures. And once again I felt anger at the sheer bloody arrogance of the man.

## Nineteen

Did I sleep? Did I hell.

I thought I was through with all that. I hadn't thought that any man could get to me now; not after Mark.

So I lay there all night, my thoughts chasing each other. I kept thinking of the fig tree; feeling my face heat up in the dark. And I felt twinges of irritation, too. Considering how cross this man made me, I couldn't quite imagine either why I'd agreed to go with him, or why it was that the thought of him caught my breath.

I lay and watched the first fingers of light outlining the leaves of the lime tree outside my window in Janna and David's garden. It can't have been past five o'clock, and already it was hot. I wondered what 'dawn' meant. Any minute now, possibly.

I got up and crept into the shower; then had a moment's panic about what I should wear. It would be hot; we'd be on a bike; and Carnac was some distance. It would be good to wear something other than my usual work clothes. I brought myself up short. What did it matter? In the end I put on jeans with a white T-shirt and my green boots, and tucked a jumper and my sarong and canvas sneakers into a rucksack.

I was just combing my hair when I heard the bike pull up. Should I tie my hair up? Would he have brought another helmet? Should I have thought about food?

I picked up my rucksack and took my boots back off to tiptoe down the stairs. In the kitchen I scrawled a note for David and Janna – for some reason I hadn't mentioned it last night – and opened the door. There was an owl hooting somewhere in the distance, and already a noisy clacking of jackdaws in the beech trees.

Oliver was straddling the bike, looking the part in leathers.

89

Black and lean. I glanced at my clothes. Oh well. And yes, he had a helmet over his arm. Of course he'd have thought of that if he'd invited me.

He lifted his visor and we looked at each other. His eyes nearly creased in what might have been an almost-smile. Fleetingly, he lost a fraction of the tension I suddenly realised was habitually in his face. I didn't have time to register my nerves.

'Put your bag in the other pannier. I brought a flask of coffee. You been on a bike before?'

I shook my head. I couldn't believe that I hadn't, but I hadn't. I expected him to say something sarcastic, like 'sheltered life', but he didn't.

'You'll like it. You're an adventurer. Just lean into the corners. Not away. Hang on to me if you get nervous.'

Did he think that would make me less nervous?

'You'll need a sweater.'

\*

At first it was frightening, then it was exhilarating. I got the impression that Oliver was being careful, not taking risks that he might take on his own. He was steady, careful on bends and when overtaking. I hadn't expected that. I was very conscious of my thighs either side of his; I tried not to lean against him, and I couldn't put my arms around his waist. I hung onto the chrome bar behind me.

I wondered why he'd asked me; and what I was doing saying yes.

I suddenly remembered thinking to myself the week before that I wanted to visit Carnac.

The wind made my eyes stream until I remembered to pull the visor down; although with my hair still whipping my face even from under the helmet visibility was still virtually nil.

The sun rose. There was a scrappy veil of mist low over some of the fields. The countryside flattened out a bit, and soon we started to pass fragments of stone avenues, like rows of petrified trees left behind from a great felled forest. There was gorse, tall red seed pods – irises, perhaps? – and an occasional cottage whose back wall was conveniently created by menhirs.

My bum was numb.

Oliver slowed and turned onto a rutted track. Everywhere I looked great stones loomed or leaned, like large animals, singly or in interrupted avenues. For a moment I lost a sense of time – I mean era – until the bumping of the bike grounded me firmly in the late twentieth century.

Oliver switched the engine off and the sudden silence roared in my ears. He steadied the bike with his feet and turned his head back to me, gestured that we should dismount. My legs were stiff. I had to put my hand onto his shoulder to lever myself off. We took off our helmets. I couldn't get my fingers through my hair. The air was thick with the scent of gorse.

'There's an unbroken row down there –' he tilted his head – 'worth seeing. Coffee first?'

He propped the bike and I went and leaned my weight against one of the nearby stones. It was hot. The far distances shimmered, making the stones look strangely fluid and insubstantial.

Oliver came over and squatted against the neighbouring stone and took his jacket off. I expected him to reach for his tobacco, but he unscrewed the Thermos lid and poured coffee, and then handed it to me. 'Sugar?'

I shook my head.

'Good. Haven't any.' He stood up again and stretched. 'God. You OK?'

'Thank you. Yes. That was great.' I felt shy suddenly, and

91

touched that he'd thought of coffee – real coffee – and a bit strained after my sleepless night.

He turned his head and looked at me. It was the first time, certainly up close, that he'd done more than glance. He opened his mouth as if to say something, then stopped and looked away into the trees.

I sipped the coffee and offered the cup to him but he shook his head. 'In a minute. Need a pee first.' He strode off into the trees at the edge. I listened to bees and swifts, let my thoughts drift, sipped.

He came back rolling a smoke and held his hand out for my now-empty cup. He drank his in a moment, flinging the last few drops onto the hardened earth. 'Right. Just want to walk the alignment before we head on down towards the coast.'

'Am I invited?'

'If you want to be.'

'Which alignment is this?'

'One of the "kers"; Kerzhero, perhaps. There'll be a sign. They're pretty amazing. About a thousand of them, some of them nearly three times your height.'

'You've been here before...'

He moved his head in what I supposed was a nod, and strode off ahead of me, helmet over his arm, shielding his eyes from the sun.

I didn't mind. I strolled, touched the stones, forgot about time, and work, and Mark.

*

Looking back over these years the 'feel' of the area and the sites we visited remains with me, inarticulable but substantial as the little perfectly spherical grey-white sea-pebble I still carry in my pocket that Oliver picked up and tossed to me at Locmariaquer, though the individual places have blurred in my head into a series of unlocated shining images which I can call back like a litany.

There's the little homely dolmen, brambles encroaching, in a field full of bullocks where Oliver stepped aside at the entrance for me to go in front of him, fending off inquisitive drooling muzzles (I didn't mind the cattle but I was pleased that he thought of it).

The climb up a small hill between pine trees and past gardens, and then the many steps down into a wide round chamber, Oliver ahead of me with his cigarette lighter flickering.

The ancientness of it all; some of the megaliths 6,000 year old mysteries.

The fabulous swirly carvings on the supports and interior of the *pierres-plates*, by the sea, where an intense local youth insisted on escorting us, and made a lot of the idea of lungs, breath and spirit in the engravings. Turning around and swallowing the whole expanse of summer sea and sky.

Walking back past oyster beds and mimosas. The smell of pine resin.

The spill of crimson and saffron petals from a great stone trough of day lilies where Oliver and I sat on the steps of a small chapel, side by side. Me slipping inside the chapel to swap my jeans and T-shirt for vest top and sarong as the heat bled us. Feeling strange disrobing in a church.

And, strongest of all, a moment where we stopped alongside a kind of little lagoon, walking on the seawall. By a trick of the light the sun, behind us, made in the water haloes around our heads, striations radiating away, streaming outwards like the irises of a pair of eyes. As we watched a waterbird broke the surface and our haloes swam towards each other and merged, then broke up and rippled away. We were both standing very still, neither of us speaking. I knew – know – that Oliver had seen what I had seen.

'Mandorla,' he said. I found I was holding my breath and trying very hard not to look at Oliver. Before I could follow up on the word mandorla he stretched out his hand. It seemed, his hand, to hover for an instant in the air between us, like a falcon. Then he brushed my cheek briefly, and dropped it; and I turned to him then, held his gaze. We didn't say anything, and we didn't kiss.

## Twenty

I didn't know how I'd meet Oliver the next morning. How I would be. Had everything changed? Or nothing?

As it happened, he wasn't there when I arrived, and his bike wasn't in its usual place.

It was still only August, but there'd been a dew in the night and the leaves in the garden were outlined with moisture. The air was still. I could smell heat beginning; the stone walls were already throwing it back. I suddenly had an intense irrational longing for thunder, for lightning chopping the sky up.

I kicked my boots off at the back door, propped open as usual with a huge white quartz boulder. I dropped my bag in the utility room and went through into the kitchen to put the kettle on. Ian walked through the kitchen and smiled vaguely in my direction. Harriet was nowhere to be seen, but even when she was absent her presence managed to make itself felt in the staff dynamics. Hans and Gisela and Sonia were all in there, but somehow the kitchen seemed to contain enough energy for a dozen people. The air jangled. Sonia grimaced at me and carried on with what she was doing, grating coconut blocks. I stood beside her and lifted a mug off a hook. I felt jumpy. I wasn't sure whether it was the lack of Oliver or the atmosphere.

'Hi,' I said to Sonia.

She gave me a tight smile.

'What's going on?'

'What do you mean?'

'You all seem wired.'

'You try spending twenty minutes with Harriet this morning. We've just had to. She's in a right strop.'

'What about?'

Sonia glanced at me and widened her eyes, shrugging her

shoulders exaggeratedly. 'You tell me!'

There were footsteps in the hall and my heart accelerated. My hand shook as I lifted the teabag out of my cup.

Sonia noticed. 'I could ask you the same question?'

The footsteps went on by. Was there a pause outside Harriet's office? To my intense aggravation my mind was leaping around like a mayfly, listening to every noise, every distant voice.

Sonia scraped the pile of coconut shavings into a bowl and put it beside a smaller bowl full of kaffir lime leaves, then lifted a handful of lemongrass. She looked across at me again.

I inhaled the fragrances in the kitchen: clear, citrus; so much in contrast to the turbulence I was feeling. I had an intense need to talk about Oliver, and to ask Sonia what she knew about him and Harriet. I looked at her smooth skin and neat blonde hair, pulled back into a high ponytail for cooking, and opened my mouth. From the other side of the room Hans suddenly snapped at Gisela, who dropped a knife with a clatter.

'Oh for God's sake, you two. Just leave it,' Sonia sighed.

A beat. I pulled back and closed my mouth. Somehow my relationship with the house team wouldn't allow this intimate gesture towards friendship. I was a bit on the outside; and I knew I kept myself a little apart, private. I found myself saying instead: 'What are you cooking?'

'Some kind of Malaysian korma thing. Or maybe I mean Thai. Or Madras. Thai. Making it up as I go, actually. Friday feast night.' She stripped the outer leaves from the lemongrass and glanced back at me. 'What's going on with you?'

'Nothing,' I said. 'It's too hot in here. Must go and water the basil before the sun reaches the beds,' and took my cup with me, grabbing a biscuit as I went. I had an urgent longing to be on Dartmoor, high up, on my own; not in this place where tensions seemed to brew today under everyone's polite smiles and where

Harriet held all the strings, tugging them as she saw fit.

I literally bumped into Harriet as I walked out the door, spilling tea down my bare legs below my shorts. Harriet didn't move. 'Shit,' I said. 'Sorry. Did I get you?'

'You'd know it if you did,' she said curtly. Her eyes behind her glasses were hostile. 'I need a word with you.' She turned and sailed towards her office, clearly assuming I would follow.

She knows, I thought to myself in panic. Then – of course she doesn't. How could she? And anyway, what's it to do with her? I drew a breath. I hoped she hadn't heard it.

Harriet stepped aside to let me in in front, then closed the door and leaned against it, folding her arms. I felt at a distinct disadvantage in my shorts and bare feet. I remembered a Tai Chi power-stance that Sally had shown me from one of Robin's sessions ('Drop your attention to your belly, to the hara, below the solar plexus,') and surreptitiously adopted it, feet a little apart and parallel, knees just very slightly bent.

Harriet looked at me. 'Do you know where Oliver is this morning?' she asked, enunciating clearly. Her voice was steely.

'Of course not,' I answered, quite truthfully. I was about to tack on 'why should I?', but thought better of it just in time. I braced myself for the next question. She was watching me. Would she dare ask where I'd been, what I'd been doing yesterday? Surely not. My legitimate day off was absolutely none of her business.

'We're into truth and honesty here, Tamar.'

She took my breath away. I couldn't believe what I'd just heard. I was too stunned even to respond, except to stare at her.

She watched me.

I found enough presence of mind – just – to summon some words. 'What exactly are you implying, Harriet?'

'He didn't come in yesterday. I didn't give him permission

not to.'

I was close enough to see a pulse at her temple. I could also see the slightest discoloration of her skin at the hairline, as if she hadn't taken as much care as usual with her dyeing. I was breathing fast. I made myself take a moment before responding.

'That's not my business, Harriet.' I astonished myself. I didn't know I could be so cool.

She raised her eyebrows. Her face, otherwise, hadn't changed since I'd bumped into her. I had an intense feeling of mistrust of this woman.

Then, suddenly, and to my now redoubled relief, there was the noise of a motorbike outside. I glanced at the window, unable to stop myself, and then back at Harriet. She too was looking at the window. To my consternation her face for a moment was unguarded, and something very like pain flashed across it; gone just as quickly, replaced with that hard look. My heart thumped. I knew instantly that my instincts were right. There clearly was, or had been, something going on between the two of them. Under my immediate fury, jealousy and confusion something almost sympathetic twanged, then was gone as suddenly.

Harriet turned back to me. She gestured to the door with her head. 'You can go.'

I marched out without a word, enraged at her gall, the injustice of her implied accusations, my being summoned, my summary dismissal, my confusion. I could feel hot tears stinging my eyes. I went out through the front door, just as I heard Oliver's footsteps heading round to the back, and fled to the herb garden, gathering my boots en route.

By lunchtime there had been no sign of Oliver. I guess I had half-expected him to come and seek me out. As the morning drew on it became harder and harder to think of going to find him, more and more difficult to imagine what he might be feeling, what I might say.

Today gardening didn't soothe me.

It got hot. I could feel sweat dripping between my breasts. I took off my vest top and tied the scarf from my hair round my boobs and twisted a twig through my hair to hold it high on my head, away from my face and neck. The backs of my legs were burning but I didn't want to go to the house to get sunscreen out of my bag. Harriet's words were banging round and round in my head, like the blackbird I'd found trapped in the new strawberry netting yesterday.

I took my boots off and squatted down in the soil and started to lift all the weeds I'd hoed from amongst the vegetables, and forced Harriet out of my head. Instead I went through yesterday again in my mind, examining every movement or word of Oliver's to see if I could translate them into a language I might understand. Every so often I caught myself glancing up, expecting Oliver to appear under the trees, but he didn't.

The crickets went quiet. Too hot to be out in the sun. I stood up slightly dizzily and went to stand in the shade of a tree. I wasn't sure I could face anyone for lunch. But I was starving. There was a well over near the wall, still in shade, and I moved to sit on its cool stone rim. I needed water; running water preferably, but any water would help. I leaned to look down into the dark eye of its water way down below. The shaft was lined with little ferns growing out of the stony cracks.

I needed some water to drink, too. I needed calm; and then I needed to bring some sandwiches out to eat here. Perhaps I could lose myself in a book. I'd brought a Margaret Atwood novel with me, as I had daily, but had still not got beyond the first chapter. And that too was in my bag, in the house. So I'd have to either face it, or stay here, hungry and thirsty, and with no distraction.

Almost as if she'd heard my thoughts Chrissie appeared. I knew she and her husband had booked for a fortnight but I'd hardly seen her this week.

'Chrissie! You're an angel! Or at least an answer to a prayer. Where've you been all week? And is it lunchtime?'

'Nick and I've been sightseeing. We did the courses pretty intensively last week and thought we'd just be tourists for a bit. Gorges, chapels, châteaux, enchanted forests, calvaries – we've done the lot. Art exhibitions. Harbours. Lakes. Tay, have you burnt your shoulders? You silly woman. Why didn't you come and ask for some sunscreen?'

'I'm OK. I've got some. I just wanted to clear this bed. Is everyone at the table?'

'Pretty much. Are you going to join us?'

I shook my head. 'Sorry. Can't face people today. Bit tired. Chrissie – sorry not to explain, I just can't – please would you be a darling and bring me some bread and cheese? And some water? Would you mind?'

'What, out here?' She studied my face. 'Are you sure? And are you sure you don't want to tell me?'

'Sorry. I just can't. Would you?'

Chrissie's pretty face creased in worry for me.

'I'm OK. Honest. Just not feeling sociable.' I couldn't catch her eye.

'OK pet. Just give me five minutes.'


By early afternoon my head was spinning with the heat and I realised I'd have to go home. I'd borrowed a pushbike to save Janna having to drive me; it was only about four miles, but if I didn't go now I suspected I wouldn't make it.

I'd have to tell Harriet.

I was dragging myself across the lawn towards the house

when to my relief Ian appeared. Through the open window I could hear chanting, Harriet's voice dominating. The scent of over-sweet incense drifted out. I could picture Queen Harriet sitting on her low chair – everyone else would be on the floor or on cushions – on the kilims at the top of the room, under the portrait of Sai Baba, hands together and eyes not-quite-closed. Where did Oliver sit? He hadn't been there the one time I'd ventured to join in.

I suddenly felt sick. I'd had enough of this place. They could stuff their rituals, their New Age facades, their gurus, bells, Hopi ear candles, reiki. Under the sweetness and forgiving light, the unconditional love to which their many pastel posters and hand-lettered notices enjoined us there was enough suppressed rage, as somebody once observed, to fuel several rockets.

And I was sick, sick, sick to the guts of all these emotions, all this messy human complexity.

Ian put his hands on my shoulders. I winced. 'You're burnt. Sorry. Are they sore? Are you OK, Tamar? You look pale.'

'No, not really. Too much sun. Headache. I'm going to have to go home. Will you tell Harriet?'

'Of course. Are you going to be all right on your bike?'

'I think so.'

'Hmm. Hang on, I'll drop you back. It's only a mile or two. Come on. You wait here and I'll get the keys. Cover your shoulders up, for goodness' sake.'

Ian strode off.

I called after him. 'Ian, can you grab my bag? It's in the kitchen or utility room. Forget which. Green rucksack.'

He turned and raised his thumb in the air. I tried to remember if I had a sweatshirt in my bag. Possibly. I sat down on the grass and closed my eyes. I could smell the wisteria.

There was a roll of thunder from somewhere.

'You're going to get your storm,' said Oliver's voice.

My eyes flicked open. He was looking down at me, hands in pockets, his grey eyes focused intently on mine. As soon as I looked at him, though, a remoteness displaced the depth in them that I had just seen.

I felt shocked and confused. I couldn't think what to say. His words circled in my head, not making any sense. I hadn't mentioned storm to anyone. I was sure I hadn't.

I now felt faint as well as sick. I closed my eyes again, and then Ian was there, jangling the keys. 'Come on, Buttercup, let's get you back. Now.'

I got to my feet. Oliver was strolling away.

As we left, fat drops of rain were starting to rattle and roll off the mulberry leaves.

## Twenty-one

I had the weekend to recover. On Saturday I'd felt pretty weak, and had spent most of the day in bed, alternately sleeping and watching the curtains blow in the wind. Through the window in waves came the sounds of Saturday in a French village, albeit a French village subdued by the annual August exodus – cars and car horns, vélos, the rising and falling of voices; unidentified clatterings and bangings; chinks of coffee cups or glasses on metal street tables; the occasional thonk of the ubiquitous boules.

'You don't have to go back, you know,' Janna said, looking at me the next morning. She had some troubadour music on the player; it seemed strangely plaintive and otherworldly in the heat and light of August. Janna tore off a piece of croissant and dipped it in her coffee. I still hadn't acquired that taste. 'Harriet's not easy. There are always comings and goings at La Bergère. People are always leaving. I'd hate you to feel you had to stay for my sake, because I mentioned it in the first place. You don't have to protect me, either. Harriet's not a close friend.'

'Thanks.' I smiled at her gratefully. 'I know.' I picked out a plum from the great green glass fruit bowl. 'But I need the money. And I really enjoy the gardening. And I might just as well be here as anywhere.' I heard what that sounded like. 'I didn't mean that like that. I really appreciate what you and David have done for me, and I've really appreciated your friendship and hospitality. I mean the inside of my head's the same whether I'm here or in England. At least here there aren't any reminders.'

'Of Mark, you mean?' Janna's eyes were kind. 'Does it still hurt so much?'

I nodded. I looked down at my cup. 'Sometimes. It's easier when I'm occupied. What would I do if I stopped gardening?'

'What about your writing, love? Journalism?'

'I haven't kept the contacts up. And you have to stay on top of it all the time. I don't even read the newspapers here.' And what a relief that had been. Not having to cope with other people's tragedies, global disasters, everyone's pain on top of my own.

'I suppose. What will you do in the winter?'

'God knows. I don't like thinking about it.'

'Will you go back eventually?'

'To England, you mean?' I thought about it. I supposed I would, ultimately. It was all very well to live from day to day – in fact it was proving crucial right now – but I guessed that there might be a time when casual labour wouldn't be enough. What would I do then?

'I guess you'd always be welcome at your parents?'

'Mmm. Yes. When I say "home" that's still where I picture. But Mum mentioned that Dad was thinking of doing a locum in Scotland somewhere, maybe the Western Isles, so I don't know how much of an option that would be.'

'Does that mean they'd sell up?'

'I don't know. That scares me. I feel so – rootless.' I could feel hot tears pressing again. I turned my head. 'Can I have some more coffee?'

'Help yourself, love, of course. Would you pour me one, too? Anyway, see how you feel tomorrow. Don't think about it all today. Do you want to wander down towards the market with me in a mo? Sometimes they do that Sunday fair thing this time of year. Shan't stay long. And after that there's always a book and the hammock, if the girls haven't got there first.'

## Twenty-two

When Monday morning came I knew I was going to go back. On Janna's insistence I took a large sunhat with me. I felt stronger, but thought I'd give myself a gentle day, and maybe just do the morning if it was still as hot.

It was hot; but with a faint haze and a breeze that smelled of the sea.

I followed the shade around as much as I could, weeding the flowerbeds and beans, and then pinching out elbow shoots in the tomatoes that were still fruiting. This last proved too hot, so after lunch I removed myself to the orchard to gather the unblemished windfalls and then to strip the ivy from the walls. Since I still felt lethargic and weary, I made myself stop to sit down periodically.

Oliver hadn't been at lunch. I wanted to ask someone whether they'd seen him, but couldn't think who. I couldn't ask Harriet, and I didn't want to ask the house team. I'd not really made contact with the other tutors, who weren't necessarily the same week by week anyway. I could probably have asked Ian but he was at the other end of the table and was engrossed in conversation with a handsome if rather petulant-looking young guy who looked like a poet. And Chrissie had left on the previous Saturday, and the group was entirely new.

Some of them looked interesting and approachable. We all, I knew, watched a new group to see who would be easy, who would help hold it together, who would present a challenge. Not being either tutoring staff or house team exactly, I always felt slightly on the periphery, but Harriet made a point of inviting everyone involved with La Bergère to the Sunday morning meeting. Perhaps it would be more truthful to say she expected everyone to be at the Sunday morning meeting, but Janna had rung in on my behalf on Saturday night to say I wouldn't make it.

There was a daily debriefing for tutors, I knew, at six, by which time I'd usually have gone. I wondered if Oliver would turn up for that, at least.

I caught myself thinking about him over and over, still puzzling everything out – our trip to Carnac, the nature of his relationship with Harriet, what he'd said about storms. Or had I imagined that, in my heat-stroked state? Had I imagined his arrival on the lawn altogether? I could ask Ian that, too, but I felt a bit shy about it.

I needed to be back amongst my non-verbal plants. Plants on the whole didn't provoke questions that didn't have answers. How wonderful if the simple answers to plant needs could be adapted to humans'. I saw an easy bullet-point checklist in my mind:

- Learn about your specimen. Watch it. It will tell you what it needs by its behaviour.
- Find the right place for each plant. Find the company it needs, and move the company that is not beneficial.
- If poor-looking, compost, water or feed. (Check which is needed.)
- If overshadowed, give more light.
- If withered, offer shade and moisture.
- Remove stones and choking factors.
- Protect from frost.
- If sickly, cut back.
- Remove dead wood.
- Remember cycles, seasons, the effect of weather and climate.
- Remember to allow fallow time, dormancy.
- Remember to feed the soil.
- Remember how much goes on out of sight. The visible part above ground when it's ready for emergence is only

one aspect of a long process, manifesting its growth in its own time.

- Don't keep digging it up to look at its roots.

I remembered the vegetable garden at home. Mum's wisdom about it.

I pushed my chair back abruptly, and stood up. Harriet turned her head and looked at me over her sunglasses, then turned back to her neighbour.

As I walked away from the table I found myself thinking about my bullet points. I'd forgotten, lately, that I'd ever been a writer, but Janna's question about journalism had stirred a hint of restlessness.

I mulled it over as I went to the potting shed to rummage around for some heavy canvas gloves to start to strip the ivy after I'd picked up the windfalls. I found some and carried them over to my rucksack in which – force of habit – I still always carried a notebook and pen. I took the whole lot and went to sit beside the well.

'Number 1,' I wrote, 'learn about your specimen. Watch it. Read up on its habits, if you can.'


When later a voice beside me where I bent over straining and yanking at the lower tenacious ivy stems said 'Fancy a swim?' I was so engrossed in thinking over angles and directions for a piece of writing I forgot to be surprised.

I straightened up. 'I don't really swim,' I said. 'But I like being near or in water. Where did you have in mind?'

'There's a pool down in the river. I'm going down now.'

I looked at him, shading my eyes from the sun. 'OK. Give me five minutes.'

## Twenty-three

We didn't talk much on the path going down. That was OK. When we got to the riverbank I said: 'Do you remember that day the other week when Chrissie and Sally and I all came back giggling?'

'No.'

'You got up and left the garden as we came in.'

He didn't respond.

'Sally nearly drowned here. We thought she was going to die.'

'Christ. And you were laughing?'

'That was afterwards. Shock and then relief, I suppose.'

'Why the – why didn't you say something?'

'You'd gone,' I said.

He stripped off. I hesitated a moment then decided I'd go in too, if only to float on my back and look at the sky and exorcise Sally's near-ghost. I kept my vest top on but took my shorts off, trying to remember what knickers I'd put on that morning.

Oliver was off the bank and gone, swimming underwater. I lowered myself in and launched off gently, on my back. The cool water poured over my shoulders. In the middle of the pool the water was so slow it hardly moved at all. I let myself drift, just gently moving my hands to stay afloat. Occasionally the wash from Oliver's passing rocked me slightly.

I closed my eyes.

When he surfaced beside me I jumped.

'Thought you didn't?'

'This isn't swimming,' I said. I turned my face a little. His face was beside and towards me, dark hair flattened and streaming. His eyes in the forest light, this close, were almost indigo more than grey, and for once not completely guarded. He kind of sat in the water, keeping himself afloat with his hands, and looked at me. He was about two feet away. I could hear his breathing, see the droplets on his face glistening. I felt naked, and turned my face back, looking up at the sky once more. I'd like to say that I maintained silence out of being cool, but it was just terror.

There was a tiny movement and he'd gone again, under the water.

The next time he spoke he was a few yards away. 'Got to go. Meeting at six.'

'Yes.' I roused myself and put an arm over my head, followed by the other one, in my version of a backstroke. I didn't want to leave the pool, the stillness, the privacy, the sense of a tryst.

I was wringing out my hair with my back to him; and suddenly he was behind me. He lifted my hair out of my hands and held it high; then put his lips to the back of my neck. I froze. I could feel his body, cold and wet, touching my spine and buttocks.

I have this awful propensity for taking myself out of myself at meaningful moments. I suddenly saw us as if in a film, and couldn't suppress a laugh. He dropped my hair immediately and stepped back.

'What?' he said in a cool voice.

I put out a hand. He let me touch his arm for a moment, then withdrew it. What do you do with plants that are sensitive to everything, that can't bear much human contact? Leave them alone, I suppose. 'Oliver. I'm so sorry. It was just suddenly so romantic I could hardly bear it.'

He just kept looking at me. He didn't respond. My heart rate quickened. I wasn't sure whether I felt fearful of him suddenly, or just nervous.

'I wasn't laughing at you. I promise. I just suddenly saw us as a film clip.'

He was pulling his jeans on, buttoning them, picking up his shirt. Moving too fast.

'Oliver. Please...'

He was lacing boots.

I crossed the distance between us and squatted beside him so our heads were level. 'Oliver. I loved our day together the other day. I loved coming down here with you. It's just that I don't know what's going on.'

'Snap,' he said, and stood up, pushing past me to take the path back out and up.

'And another thing. I need to know what's going on between you and Harriet.' I was amazed at my bravado; but now I was feeling angry.

He didn't stop walking; not fast, but determinedly. He also didn't reply. I picked up the rest of my things and followed. I hadn't thought of myself as an angry person until recently, and now I could barely contain my fury. I also felt ridiculous challenging him in just a vest top and wet knickers. I put my shorts and espadrilles back on and caught up with him.

'It's almost as if she has a hold – '

'No-one has a hold over me, no-one. Get that?' His voice was hard. 'She makes rules, I break them. She doesn't like that.'

'That's not what I mean...'

He swung round. 'Then what the – what do you mean?' His eyes held mine.

'The other day. In the garden.'

'I don't know what you're talking about.'

I felt as if I was talking to a complete stranger. I couldn't be bothered, suddenly. I felt completely wiped out.

I stopped for a moment and leant against a tree and took a few breaths. Oliver was waiting for me round the next corner.

'She was good to me,' he said without looking at me. 'She was good to me when I was in trouble a year or two back. OK?'

I couldn't help myself. 'Are you lovers?'

'No,' he said shortly. And that was that.

At the gate to La Bergère he reached out and touched my shoulder, very briefly, and then loped off towards the house.

# Twenty-four

## France
## OLIVER

I know when things are getting dodgy. Survival instinct, it's called.

She was getting under my skin. Dangerous.

But luckily it was my fortnight with J-Y. I still went to the occasional end-of-day debriefing at La Folie, just to show willing, really. Wasn't ready to give it up yet, though too much more of H la Control Freak and she'd not see me for skidmarks.

After the river though it seemed like a good idea to cool it for a bit. Get on with photos. Not sure what was going on with Riverwoman. This kind of teasing keep-your-distance stuff. Knickers and vest top in the river, letting me see her with the wet cloth almost transparent. I could picture her perfectly: small breasts with their nipples visible under the green cotton, laughing eyes, water from her hair running down her body. Her just standing there, unself-conscious, natural. Hadn't thought she was playing with me. But then. You wonder. Doing an Ophelia in the river then good as smacking me in the face when I touched her. Felt like. And then her going on. Sorry. Sorry. Like when she trod on the lens cap. If she'd just left it.

Truth is I felt a bit bad about it. Guilty. Over-reacting? Maybe. But there was my past. And as for my future. For her sake. And mine too.

Couldn't afford to get soft.

Maybe time to split. Things getting heavy.

Getting it in the neck from J-Y, too, the next morning.

'You English, your humours. You come here like a great

112

raincloud. Qu'est-ce que se passe avec toi alors? Huh?'

'Just not into talking this morning, OK?'

'Les femmes?'

'Or not.'

'Well, I want talking. I want your – what do you say – *avis* –'

'Opinion.'

'– on this filming. What you think? She works, or not?'

I looked at the contacts. One of his 'filmings', all black and white French moodiness. L'atmosphere, or whatever the word is in French. L'ambience. Cliffs and rocks and shrubby trees.

'Where is it?'

'Crozon. She works, or not?'

'It's OK.' Didn't feel forthcoming.

'Mais merde, Oliver! Fucking hell. You leave early yesterday, you don't talk now, you don't look at my pictures. I'm boss, yes? I need you to put your finger out.'

'Pull.'

'PULL!' He was shouting now, slapping the desk, glaring.

The bell rang and a couple of punters entered the gallery. Germans or Dutch from their clothes and blondness. For some incomprehensible reason the northern Europeans seemed to like my lobster print. I cheered up fractionally. J-Y did the usual 'Bonjour monsieur 'dame' stuff and then turned and glared at me again.

'OK. Keep your hair on. Show me again.' I wasn't ready to leave here, either. And he was a good bloke. Not his fault. I took another look at his pictures, pointed to one, then another. Yes, there was a handful that could bear blowing up. I told him. Gave him what he asked for. He punched me in the back. At least with another bloke you could cut the crap.

I went out and got us beers – if you can call that pissy blond

French stuff beer – and some filled baguettes for lunch. J-Y turned the notice to *fermé*. We went out into the square that passed for a courtyard behind the gallery. Pulled the heavy metal and wood chairs up to the table.

The old woman upstairs and to the side had strung her washing out from the top of her steps across to a strut on the shed wall. Great pink bloomers. Capacious white brassières – far too voluminous to be called 'bras', hoists, more like – not at all chic. She looked after the pots, and the stone steps up to her door were filled with geraniums and great leafy things and jasmine. She had a canary in a cage by the door. Some little quail crept around in their aviary thing at the bottom of the steps. I felt sorry for the rabbits hutched into their hardboard rectangles, piled one on the other. Tamar would hate it. Tamar? Get out of my head, woman.

J-Y looked at me looking at the rabbits and nodded. He lifted the beer bottle to his mouth and then wiped his mouth with the back of his hand.

'Les femmes, eh, Oliver?'

'What d'you mean?'

'Trouble with les femmes, you?' He was grinning.

I shook my head. Then said 'Yeah. Don't know why I bother.' The easy answer.

'Uhuh?'

J-Y was married. He had a couple of small dark-haired children. Nice enough kids. He seemed content enough, in an irascible French way. I guessed he was in his late thirties or early forties. Suddenly seemed inconceivable to me that someone could meet a woman, love her, be sure, declare his love for her, get married, have kids and stay married.

Have kids. Almost a pang I had there. Must've been the beer. I didn't want kids. I worked out very early on that I didn't want to bring more children into this godforsaken world of ours. Too many without what they need already. A paternity suit at college helped that along – failed, as it turned out; I was far too careful for that kind of thing to stick. Nonetheless, I'd checked in and had a vasectomy. Just to be sure.

In the courtyard I brooded on it all. It's all about consequences. That's the law of karma. Our thoughts manifest as actions; our actions bring effects in their wake. Sometimes they're predictable; mostly they're subtle. We have to live with those consequences. Yep. Potted history for you. And believe me when I say I know about consequences.

Less easy to put a condom on your mental and emotional bodies. Though some schools of thought in Tibetan Buddhism invite you to consider the beloved as she will be when a decaying body.

'Eh bien?'

'Eh bien what?' Suddenly I had a strong urge to tell J-Y everything. Impulse. Be free of it. Couldn't ever talk to anyone about it all.

I looked at him. Appraised him. What did we have in common? Photography and gender. I could try him. We did understand each other.

'Une problème?'

What was the problem? My past, or my present? Didn't like to think about it.

Perhaps it was about how to get away. I couldn't always breathe.

'I can't breathe,' I said. Didn't really mean to.

J-Y nodded slowly, looking at the table.

'You don't want her, then?' he said eventually. 'She is not interesting?'

God. How simple he made it sound.

115

I considered his response. Something came clear. I didn't know whether I wanted her or not. That's what.

No. Actually I did. Question was whether I could afford to want her.

He was right and wrong.

And the moment had gone for the rest.

'Cheers, J-Y,' I said, and lifted my bottle to him. Just then the phone went in the office behind us and he got up to answer it.

I leaned back and stretched my legs out. Good to feel sun. This was my present. Right now.

Thought about the afternoon and whether J-Y would want to print his own frames or whether I could practise my toning on them. That gave me an idea for some of my own prints of rock strata. Pushed my own chair back and went to look through the negatives.

## Twenty-four

J-Y's gallery was on two floors, joined by an old open wooden staircase. Not sure what it was originally. Granary or something. It overlooked the river. Très chic.

It was L-shaped. Downstairs the till and then the office (phone, fax, photocopier, desk, espresso machine and – most important – fridge for beer and wines 'pour les clients'). All tucked into the foot of the L.

Upstairs the gallery space – pitched roof and original timbers. Interrupted by the mouth of the staircase and by a deep alcove which opened onto the old wooden loading bay – or if you were an arty type you'd call it a minstrels' gallery – flying out on cantilevered timber buttresses over the street. J-Y had had some terribly tasteful wooden turned railings made up. Stop the art groupies from stepping backwards in drama, price-shock or drunkenness. Finding themselves flailing around in empty air over the street. Leave it open, I'd say.

The darkroom was through a pair of doors opposite the staircase.

The whole thing was well lit. Several tall windows, tiny spots on tracks between the joists.

J-Y had decided I should be trusted to hang the late summer show. Alongside the artist, that is. Item: Artist – one of those dark glamorous Frenchwomen. You see them even in the villages. Too young to be so sexy and cool. All arched eyebrows and determined lips. Smooth hair. Gold earrings. Neat legs. Looked like an executive for Dior rather than an abstract painter. I guessed she was around my age, roughly. Twenty-five, six maybe.

From the deliberate way J-Y had introduced us he was up to something. As usual. Couldn't say I liked her stuff but it was kind of firm. Like her mouth. Opinionated. That was OK. At least she wasn't apologising.

We disagreed on the first picture. It was a huge dark strong canvas with a clever ratio of light areas that invited you to walk through it. It needed the full space of the wall to the left of the darkroom, facing you coming in.

Initial impact is all when you're hanging abstracts. (Besides, it was the only one that was strong enough to occupy the prime position.) I tried to explain that individual location was as important as sequencing, neighbours, in a show.

She – Lorraine – wasn't having any of it. She wanted it on the wall to the left of the top of the stairs. Its effect would be completely lost. In my opinion. Of course.

So we fell out immediately. She took her arse in its tight little pink silk number over to the loading bay for a sulky cigarette. Stood there, hip jutting, staring moodily (she'd positioned herself sideways on) down at the river.

I ran my hands through my hair. Fuck. Fallen at the first fence.

Turned my back on her. Perched on the top step of the flight of stairs while I worked out my next move.

That's how I saw her come in. Ophelia. As she came into view she looked up at the sign swinging from the balcony: 'Galerie Châteaubriand'. Or maybe she was looking up at Lorraine looking down at her. Je ne sais pas. Anyway there she was, hand poised on the brass door handle. Not quite coming in. Fuck and double fuck. Just my luck, two femmes difficiles at once.

She looked like she took a breath, then opened the door. Hesitated again. Didn't see me. I drew my feet up and swung my back against the wall so I could see her in the security mirror but hopefully not be seen myself.

J-Y came forward, all charm and French sincerity. I looked at him through her eyes. Yep. She'd probably fancy him. Black hair, black T-shirt, lean black jeans. No belly considering how much alcohol he put away. Shame about the shoes though – shiny black slip-on jobs. The French have no shoe sense. I looked down at my own leather walking boots. Done me proud – hundreds of miles over Europe and still looking good. But shoes apart J-Y scored. Those French bastards – even the ugly ones have something. He wasn't really good-looking. Features too big. But even I could see she'd think he was sexy as hell.

She smiled at him. I wondered if she'd caught the garlic-laden breath yet, or the suave underarm. Had he hit the Armagnac this early in the day?

My God, he was going to give her the tour. Smarmy bugger. She wasn't looking around her. Had she come in for me, or what? But was listening to J-Y, smiling and nodding. Her hair caught the light, red bits glinting.

They both of them stopped in front of the horse that dominated the downstairs. An armature of copper wire infilled with driftwood and bits of sea-glass. The anatomy and the grace of the pose exact – you practically expected it to neigh. J-Y moved on, but she made a little gesture and just stood there. For minutes.

Then I realised that my lobster print was also in her line of vision. I thought. I craned forward. Yeah. She walked towards it, stopped. Looked. Kept looking. Moved forward again.

J-Y came back. She gestured at the print.

'Un anglais,' I heard J-Y say. 'Oui, that's right, Oliver. You know him?'

I couldn't hear what she said because Lorraine was tapping on her shiny black heels impatiently my way. 'Alors. We begin, yes?' The lacquered fingernails drummed against her big canvas.

119

I got up. Stood there too. Facing her. Didn't say a word. She stared at me, her lips pushed forward a little. I was getting the fullblown petulance. It amused me.

'OK,' I said. 'You stand them where you want them, and I'll hang them.'

Her face flickered. I realised she'd wanted a fight.

You might have noticed that 'obliging' is not my middle name. Put my hands in my pockets and went to look out over the balcony. I expect I whistled. I do at times like that.

Aware that the voices downstairs had stopped.

Behind me, all on her own Lorraine was generating enough tension to blow all the circuits. The sharp snip-snip-snip of her heels seemed to me wrong in that space. Or perhaps I was getting over-used to women who walked silently. Lorraine made me think of carrion crows – they way they stab at their prey's eyes. Lorraine's black spikes.

I ignored it all. Leaned over and looked at the river. Watched a boat. Thought about J-Y's prints of Crozon. Let my thoughts turn around my own laborious building and fading of the anemone images. Trying to figure out a way of collaging them. The images needed to overlap – tentacles unfolding and flaring and closing almost simultaneously. I liked my original idea of dancers. Juxtapose them with picture of human limbs, or animals' legs or something?

Must have been absorbed. Suddenly realised I was alone in the gallery. None of the other three was anywhere to be seen. Though I heard the murmur of voices from the courtyard. Tried to picture the trio: Lorraine tall, lithe, scented, hot pink, glossy black hair pulled back, neat gold clip. Tamar bird-like in rusts and greens, gypsy hair. J-Y in rock star blacks. What would they talk about?

Went down the stairs. Turned the sign to Closed then locked

myself in the darkroom. Plenty to do.

Ages later J-Y came and banged on the darkroom door. A torrent of French abuse accompanied the thuds.

Waited till he stopped to draw breath and then opened up.

He was alone. He turned the only chair around and straddled it. 'Fuckin' 'ell Oliver,' he said, with exactly the intonation I use.

'Have they gone or did you eat them?'

'Oh merde.' He threw his shoulders up and flicked his hand at the wrist. 'Les femmes. Oi-oi-oi. The big one she was en colère.' He mimicked Lorraine, leg crossed, lighting up, pouting. He remembered his own cigarettes, pulled them out, tapped the base, offered me one. I moved my head to indicate we should move out to the balcony. He talked around his cigarette as he bent his head to light it. 'She says you have not helping her.'

'Didn't help her.'

'Alors. I say I will help. She moves her head "no". She wants you.' He grinned. 'The little one, l'Anglaise, she's something different. Or else. How are you saying it?

'Something else?'

'She's chouette, mignonne. She just keeps watching Lorraine. Then she suddenly gets up, shakes my hand and – she goes!' He spread his hands and lifted his shoulders again.

He remembered something. 'She says she knows you.'

'And?'

'And rien. C'est tout.'

We both leaned on the balcony, watched the river, watched the boats, smoked in silence. That's what I like about blokes.

## Twenty-five

Couldn't hack what was going down around me.

September now. Season of mists and fucking melancholy etc.

Things quieter in the gallery. H needed me till mid-October this year. If I wanted time out now it would have to be courtesy of J-Y.

There was a world out there. I seemed to have spent the summer shuffling back and forth between two small spaces. Out there and in my head.

Wasn't going to wait. It wasn't, I wasn't.

Friday evening then I kicked the bike awake, tent strapped to the back. Time to clear my head out.

Tempted to cruise southwest towards the coast but thought I quite fancied woodland. So motored towards the Fôret de Paimpoint.

Could feel things dropping away behind me. Stress, I mean. Like shedding layers. Who needed all this shit. Who needed more than wind, road.

Silence except the sweet engine. Which stops you thinking and takes you where you need to be.

Light thrown at you. Moving at speed beneath trees it flickers so fast it can do your head in. Breaks your thoughts up and chucks them out. Like epileptics. In fact it can trigger epilepsy. If speeds and wavelengths coincide right. I'm not epileptic and I like the oscillations. Strobes.

Christ. No thinking. The road was striped. I was striped. The day was a tiger. Light flickering.

So when I landed up in serious woodland my head was already

cleared out. Thank Christ.

Coming off the road and bumping down tracks.

Late afternoon. Very still. Sun. No one about, anywhere. Virgin fruiting woodland. If that's not a contradiction. Everywhere chestnuts and berries and mushrooms. Red, gold, green.

I like that about France. Hide yourself away and live off the land.

Did that the previous autumn down further southwest, in Les Landes. Unpopulated, parts of the southwest still. The living's easy in autumn. Hide away. Take odd jobs – prune a few vines after the harvest. Tractor driving – ploughing, hedge-flailing if you can find a farm with hedges. Miss England for that. Chainsawing for all those neat French woodstacks. Lift oysters towards Christmas. Right through September October and November I stashed my bike and tent in woods back of the ocean and gathered what I needed. Shellfish when you're sick of chestnuts and mushrooms. Snare the odd rabbit or pheasant. Lift maize. Bit of casual labour.

Quiet. Suits me fine.


There was a stream. I could hear it. Through the trees the glint of a lake. Lots of châteaux and lakes in this bit. Legends – this is Broceliande of the old stories. Merlin the Enchanter. Excalibur. Knights doing their chivalrous bit and all that. Funny thing though but the present stops mattering here.

I parked the bike up. At the edges of the wood the ground was quite hilly; big boulders and little gorges.

No noise. Except squirrels churning up the leaves. A jay. A woodpecker. And the water.

I sat a bit. There was a trunk over the river I could stretch out on, so I did that and watched the water. Mosquitoes and damselflies. Sometimes a fish bracing the current. Like a small dagger, light glinting.

Daydreaming. Then her face, below me in the water. I even glanced over my shoulder. Spooky. Fucking hell. Where the fuck did that come from? Even here. Under my skin. Couldn't settle after that, couldn't sit still.


Found a place for the tent near a single pine tree away from the damp boggy bits. Wheeled the bike out of sight of the track and unloaded my gear.

Plenty of bracken. I took my knife and cut a couple of armfuls to put under the groundsheet, then spread the base of the tent out. Could feel my spirits rising. Yeah, home. This nylon rectangle.

Had to find a log to knock the pegs in. Hadn't expected the ground to be hard. Thunk thunk thunk in the still afternoon.

They were shooting somewhere in the distance. You know that really pisses me off about the French. Sure I'll take a rabbit if I need one. But it's about respect, you know? I take what I need and I take it with care. They just blast what they fancy, if they see it moving. English aren't much better, I know. But you see the results in the French woodland. No songbirds worth talking about. Poor buggers.

Anyway. Got a good stash of dead wood; good dry wood. A fire without smoke would just do it. All I needed. Clear water. Camp fire. Book – *The Magus* that summer it was. Read so little anyway it saw me right through. Stars, later. Clean air.

I could feel myself unfolding. You know how it is. Like I'd been put away damp and had got stuck in my own creases.

Could breathe again.


Lay on my back later in the dark among the debris of the forest floor. Looked up through the pine branches at the constellations. No light pollution. Couple of glow-worms over on a rock. You know how so much being turns into non-being?

One last fag and then I smothered the fire and turned in.

Woke some time before dawn. I sleep better outdoors. Don't need to recover from all those people you aren't seeing. Pulled my boots on and went down to wash my face. Thick ribbon of mist over the stream. Thought I'd follow the length of it to the lake. Walking into thick cloud suddenly. Couldn't see the other shore; and as I walked towards it I too was swallowed in mist and lost my bearings. No sounds except plops of water from branches. A couple of waterfowl took off over my head.

Bogland; huge submerged branches like crocs; crack willow and sallow and alder. I stumbled around the margins in the black mud. Wanted to walk right round the lake; had no idea how big it was. Had all day though.

And arrived at a château. Completely fucked, of course. Probably magnificent in its time. Was alerted by a sluice gate, and the huge sluggish grey carp at the pool's edge – it must have been stocked once.

Stone pillars and an iron gate, chained but not padlocked. The chain links fell apart, rusted right through, but the gates were corroded nearly solid. I forced them.

A carriageway. Completely overgrown – self-seeded beech and lime saplings all over the track from the avenue of trees. Fungi. Gardens sprawling and derelict. Round turreted dovecote – with doves. Choked stewpond – waterlily leaves the size of tennis racquets.

Wooden front door rotting at the hinges. Sad, somehow.

Lifted the door open. The jagged base scraped the stones and left a slimy green trail. Inside in the hallway a canopy of cobwebs and thin light through a tall grimy window. A huge freckled mirror. Fucking enormous. My reflection suddenly. What a shock. Coathooks. One blackened ragged straw hat, ribbon greened with age and mould. Spooked me, that – human detail. Wall sconces; no bulbs. A broken empty basket colonised by snails. Dead leaves. Mouse shit everywhere.

The house was utterly still. Of course. Half-expected to see a huge clock, hands stopped at some significant hour. Expected to hear music. Spinet or harpsichord or something. Christ.

Ahead of me a wide stone staircase. I resisted it. Maybe some other time.

The house felt – somehow – dunno – as if it were only resting; moored, not permanently planted. Vast silence. I wanted to creep; instead I shouted out as loud as I could.

Then I couldn't move forwards suddenly. Stepped backwards, quietly, and pulled the door closed.


Mist was thinning now. Still no sounds outside except for the lap, suck and drip of water.


Had this strange sense that if I turned round the château wouldn't be there.

Didn't test it out.

Seemed important to heave the great gates back into position. Closing it in on itself.

126

## Twenty-six

### France
### TAMAR

'God Oliver you made me jump!' – arriving like that into the early morning, barefoot in the grass of the lawn.

He'd been away for a bit. I'd missed him; then as September unfolded I'd been grateful for the chance to concentrate on work, and think about my future.

I'd been looking up into the foliage of the mulberry tree, noticing how day-by-day its little fruits were swelling and softening.

He came round and stood in front of me, slow, deliberate. He had to duck under the branches to do so. The first time I'd seen him do that – approach me directly for the purpose of gaining and holding my attention.

He put his fingers into the front pockets of his jeans and leaned back against the tree, one leg crossed over the other.

'How are you?' I asked inanely, feeling a rush of pleasure and confusion reddening my neck and rising towards my face. 'Where've you...' I stopped myself. Don't ask him personal questions. Remember the plants.

He ignored my words but carried on watching me. I could see he was reading the colour in my face.

That now-familiar gesture, pushing himself away from the tree with his shoulders, extricating his hands, reaching into a back pocket for tobacco, papers, lighter.

He took his time rolling up. I could feel in me the usual fascination mixed with something approaching irritation. And fear. Well, nervousness.

He lifted his eyes from his hands to my face, then bent to

lick the edge of the Rizla. Did I imagine it, or were his hands shaking? I suddenly caught a glimpse of something vulnerable under his cool deliberation.

'Something I want to show you. Got a couple of days? You OK with tents?' His eyes for a second were pleading; the expression gone as soon as I registered, subsumed into his usual guardedness.

My heart started thumping hard again. What about Lorraine, I wanted to ask. I knew he was up there, that day in the gallery, and Lorraine was so furious when the three of us were out in the courtyard later that I had imagined something going on between them. I caught myself, my absurd jealousy. Where had that come from?

And Oliver and I had barely spoken since the river afternoon.

I didn't know how to answer.

He lifted the rollie to his lips without taking his eyes from my face. Something rustled in the leaves above us and he looked up. The blackbird flew off and we both watched; a momentary safe diversion.

Everything I wanted to say seemed either far too personal or trivial and clichéd. I put my hand up to push my hair off my face and he stretched his hand out and caught mine.

A long moment. I stopped breathing. He dropped my hand.

'I'd really like you to come,' he said, catching my eyes for an instant before pushing his free hand back into his pocket.

I could imagine what that declaration had cost him, and felt a wave of tenderness in my solar plexus.

'When? Where? Do I need to bring a tent?' – And then felt embarrassed. Of course I'd need a tent.

For a moment I saw something mischievous chase the customary wary look out of his eyes.

'Depends whether you'd prefer to share mine,' he said, dropping the butt of the rollie onto the ground and crushing it. He bent and retrieved it and put it in his pocket. 'Got to go and see Harriet. Are you coming up to the house? Coffee?'

It was a bit easier to talk to him side-by-side strolling. 'Where were you thinking about? Somewhere in particular?'

'Yeah. Somewhere I think you'll really like. You're into atmospheres and stuff. Found this ruined château. Thought it might give you inspiration. You're a writer, aren't you?'

I felt absurdly touched. 'How do you know that?'

He shrugged. 'Everyone knows. What do you write? Poetry and stuff?'

'A little. Mostly journalism though. That's what I was doing in England. I'm not sure what I want to do with my future though – I mean my writing future. That's one of the reasons I'm here.'

'Taking a breather?'

'Yes, I suppose. What about you?'

The guarded look came back. 'Oh, I just like it here. For the moment. Suits me fine to be doing what I'm doing. No plans.'

'What were you doing in England?'

'Oh, this and that. Building up a portfolio.'

'Photography?'

'Yeah. Lots of commercial stuff – magazines, news items. Ads. And I did some commissions for National Geographic, and some other travel mags.'

He turned to me suddenly. 'Is there someone back home for you?'

'How do you mean?'

'Thought you might have a bloke or something.'

I wanted to tell him about Mark, but couldn't. 'Not any more,' I said.

129

We'd arrived at the kitchen door. Already the sun was releasing fragrance from the herbs I'd watered earlier – basil, tarragon, peppermint.

He pushed the door and stood aside to let me go first. 'Speak later,' he said.

Despite the sun I was stiff and cold when we arrived at the marshy edges of the lake, having left the bike with its laden rack and panniers in the wood. Everything was still. The water was dark and unreflective. It was almost as if the landscape was suspended in a vacuum. I had the strange sense that if I opened my mouth to speak my words would drop into the silence and vanish, unshaped and unvoiced.

I could hear Oliver squelching up behind me. He rested a hand lightly on my shoulder. Neither of us moved for a few moments, then I turned my face towards him. He brought his cheek towards mine. I could feel his breath.

A heron flew over, languorous heavy wingbeats. Both our heads, a slow almost imperceptible synchronised movement, followed its flight.

Still his breath.

The afternoon stretched.

'See the frog?' – His words the first either of us had uttered since arriving. We moved apart a little. He turned to head up towards the top of the lake and held out a hand behind him for me. I could feel him trembling. I was, too. We picked our way via the green and ochre tussocks over the black mud.

There was a lot of water backed up in the deep channel behind the sluice, and extraordinarily black mud the other side, maybe three yards below. The sluice gate was topped by a deep blackened timber, fissured and slimy-looking. Oliver loosed my hand and leapt from the bank onto it, landing with bent knees and outstretched arms. We both looked down to the outlet. A slender trickle of water, dirty-green algal weed, and uninviting stinking mud to a depth, judging by the channel behind, of at least several feet.

'Wouldn't want to fall in there,' I commented. 'Bit like Conan Doyle's Grimpen Mire back home on Dartmoor.'

I'd barely finished the sentence when suddenly Oliver's legs seemed to give way, and he swayed, tipped forward, arms flailing for a long moment, right on the threshold. There was a splintering groan from the timber beneath his boots. Then he fell. Mercurial, he managed to twist himself upright before he hit the mud. He sank almost immediately to his thighs. I gasped. 'Oliver! Are you OK? Did you hurt yourself?'

The look of surprise on his face was replaced swiftly by his habitual guarded look. 'Do I look OK? I am, after all, sinking.'


You know how it is when you witness something happening and you have the sense that it is going to impact on your future? – The next hour was the time when, like Persephone eating those pomegranate seeds of Hades, I allowed myself to be bound to this man irrevocably. Yes, of course if someone is sinking you don't leave him to drown. And yes, of course you risk being pulled under yourself.

That's not the issue, though, so much as the fact that we were already in that liminal space – people who know they are to be lovers, but haven't yet quite pulled off the garments of separateness.

And of course what they don't tell you in the myths is that you never quite inhabit the same springtime garden in the aftermath; that your corn-poppy meadow will now always also sport those mauve and purple blooms amongst the red.

And that's OK, too. To be fully human means drinking the bitter draughts, too; I don't mind that. To go into the darkness with a light is to know the light. To know the darkness you have to walk in the dark. Who said that?

The day was still. I've said that already, too. After Oliver's words he too was still, silent, not struggling. At first he seemed to be simply immobilised where he had landed; after a long minute or two where I was also unmoving, too shocked to know what to do, I realised with a rush of terror that the mud was indeed beginning to engulf him, centimetre by centimetre. He really was sinking.

I remembered with another shock *Pincher Martin*, one of my O-level texts. For an unreal and probably brief period we simply stared at each other. His face was ungiving, if white. God knows what he was thinking. I couldn't tell. Or imagine. What do you think if you might be about to drown, in those moments before – as surely he must – you start to fight both the realisation and the soon-to-be-realised reality?

What I was doing was fighting a powerful urge simply to run away. My mind had thrown up a picture of that day when, innocent, I had ridden Dancer back across the golden evening moors prior to hearing the news that rearranged my future, and without which I guess I wouldn't have been where I now found myself.

I felt my imagination, my memory, close down before I could picture Mark's falling. I thought I might fall. I felt my mouth open on a scream.

Oliver's voice, low, fierce, forced through his teeth, cut across. 'Tamar. Tamar! For fuck's sake FIND A PLANK! NOW! For Christ, NOW! PLEASE!'

132

I opened my eyes. Stared. Couldn't think. I heard his words but something wasn't connecting.

The splitting timber had taken part of the sluice gate with it. As I watched, the water backed-up behind started to spill over in a slender trickling braid; then a little more.

Oliver's eyes were frightened. 'Tamar! For Christ's sake! I'm sinking! I'm going to drown!'

And I moved. I tried to run but could only wade, impossibly slowly. Ankle-deep in globulous black mud. Couldn't see anything. Couldn't think. A plank. A branch. Anything. I grabbed a willow branch. Too slender; snapped in my hands. Tried to yank a log out of the marsh but couldn't lift it.

Out of sight of the sluice now. All I could hear was my breathing and the bog sucking at my feet. Suddenly I was terrified again; I felt my cheeks and neck tight with it.

I couldn't hear any sound from Oliver. I fantasised that it was a dream; that with enough willpower I could wake up.

But no. My nape prickled with a terror that he might already have sunk; suffocated in this black bog.

I tripped, and the mud plastered my legs and trunk, slapped into my mouth and eyes. Things crawling. I gagged. I hated this place, its slimy brooding. I think I was sobbing. Please God, please God I promise, I promise...

As I hauled myself up I made myself think. Breathe slowly, girl, just breathe. My heart was still clattering and my ears hummed with fear. I wanted to vomit. Breathe. Plank. Branch. Plank. Think. I watched a dry yellow willow leaf spin in a non-existent breeze.

Think. The drop from the top of the sluice gate couldn't be much more than ten feet. Surely. If the banks were anything to go by. The channel must have a bed. It was possibly stone-lined. The depth of mud would be measurable, finite. And it only started

133

around what must be the halfway mark. He would be OK. Surely he would be OK. He couldn't sink more than three or four feet, surely. Five at the most. He wouldn't – couldn't – suffocate.

For an instant I relaxed.

But he was sinking and there was now a thin but steady flow of water coming over the lip. And he still couldn't get out. I waded again. A branch was my only hope. I took hold of another, thicker, one and pulled. It came away in my hand. Rotten.

Oliver's voice, higher now. 'Tamar! Where are you, for Christ's sake?'

'Coming!' I yelled. 'I'm coming!' My heart was thumping my ribcage so hard my body was shaking.

Then there, just in front of me. The hull of a rowing boat, exposed ribs protruding.

I'll spare you the details and the agony, the minutiae of trying to break and haul struts designed to withstand battering.

But I did it. Just.


Oliver had sunk another few inches when I staggered back with my muddy booty clamped to each side of my ribcage, dragging leaves and twigs and marsh plants with me. The mud was swarming around his waist. I needed a rest and didn't dare. I could barely see with the exhaustion of exerting myself.

He was shivering. 'Just lay – just lay –'

I forced a calm voice. 'I know. I'm going to. I've rescued sheep like this. Here, look – crawling boards for you. I'm going to fetch another one to straddle the channel for you to hang onto. And there's still a painter attached to the boat. If it's not rotten I'll bring it too.'

'My knife – where's – can't reach my pocket. Hands too cold...'

'No need. Slates. Sharp edges for cutting. Here, look. Hold

on. Just hold on...'

'Tamar, whatever – whatever I was standing on – sinking too. Don't know how long I've got...'

'I'm coming. We'll do it –' though I wasn't sure. My voice was shaking.

The planks held. They were too short to lay across the channel from bank to bank but I managed to bend an alder bough to Oliver's reach; and slowly, so slowly it was agony to watch, he finally dragged himself by inches out of the mire; flopping, at last, his length onto the planks.

I leaned as far as I dared and tossed the rope to him, both it and myself tied to the tree behind me. Twice I missed. The third time his reactions were too slow and it uncoiled into mud. The fourth time, though, he caught it. The rope had nearly had it, but sufficed. It held.


And so it was that we found ourselves, at last, in each other's arms; wearing mud and leaves like participants in some strange vegetation rite, stretched on the firm margins of the marsh, surrounded by bog cotton and water mint and mosquitoes.

It seemed like hours before he stopped shaking and his teeth stopped chattering. I clasped him tight against me, his head pressed against my cheek, our sodden garments between us. His hair was wet against my face, and I could feel his heart pounding. The afternoon rolled over us.

The layer of mud and sweat between us started to warm up, and finally he turned his head and opened his eyes, looking into mine. His expression was, for once, completely unguarded; he met me. This was, I sensed, the closest I might get to the real Oliver.

He closed his eyes again and moved slightly in my arms. 'Tamar...'

135

Then his parted lips were moving across my breasts. 'No bra. Did wonder...' His hand gently lifted the hem of my shirt and slid across my stomach. I could feel his breath through the fabric of my T-shirt.

My nipples hardened. My own breath seemed so loud on the still air.

Oliver groaned. Against my thigh I could feel him stirring. 'Christ, Tamar, I want you. I really want you... do you mind?'

'What do you think? – I want you too... I wasn't sure...'

'You're shaking. Think I am, too.'

His face was streaked. He moved to look me in the eyes, then slowly lowered his lips to mine. Our bodies were pressed together, pelvis to pelvis. His tongue was on my lips, between my teeth. I could taste mud, and salt.

At length he lifted his head again. His eyes were smiling. 'We're steaming,' he said, and laughed. 'I'm sorry about all the mud. Do you think we could take our shirts off?'

I wriggled free and lifted my T-shirt over my head. So much for its earlier whiteness.

Oliver, too, had removed his shirt. I could see a pulse beating in the hollow between his collarbones. I touched my finger to it. He exhaled and ran his own finger down over my breastbone. 'You're beautiful. Really beautiful –'

I reached up and pulled his head towards me. His eyes held mine. Something in me loosened, went out towards this man. So long. So long...

'Didn't shave this morning. Sorry...'

'I didn't notice. Can't see for mud, anyway...'

'You do know, don't you, that if we make love now, two people like us, it'll change our future? – We won't be able to just walk away, forget each other.'

'Why should I want to do that?'

'Just checking.'

'Oliver – I'm not on the ...'

'The Pill? No. Didn't expect you to be. Don't strike me as someone who'd want to mess with her body like that. It's OK.'

'But – umm – my – period's due... you don't – ?'

'Mind? No. Wouldn't notice anyway, the way we – it – all is. Are. Do you?'

'Mind? Not if you don't. Not at all...'

'I promise not to hurt... And with your period due we're – ah – OK without condoms. Yes? OK. Shhh...' His lips closed on mine again, gently.

His hand was between my thighs; then at the button of my jeans. I lifted my pelvis and he eased the wet denim down my legs. I could feel myself moisten. He unbuttoned his own jeans, wiped the worst of the mud off his hands on them, grinned wryly at me. 'Not quite the romantic scene I'd hoped for – '

'You mean you'd planned this?'

'Not as such. Not like this. Come here – '


There is something exquisite and unrepeatable about the moment of entry – the first time – with someone with whom you are in love; the more so, of course, when that moment had previously seemed so unlikely. Even the mud couldn't wipe the sheen off the moment; and maybe the recent danger heightened it all. Whatever, I have never forgotten that first time: the greengold light cast through the willow leaves flickering on his face as he lowered himself towards me, lighting those grey eyes. Nor have I forgotten the physical feel of him, the tip of him. Even these years later with so much else between.

In those moments I knew for certain that this was the man with whom I wanted to be. That sense of your destiny, your future, coming towards you.

After, we lay, bodies touching and almost dry, mud-emblazoned.

I looked at him, touched his face. 'I think we've known for a while, haven't we?'

'What?'

'Well, this.'

'You mean that I might be falling in love with you?'

'Are you?'

'Maybe. And maybe we recognised something. In each other. At the market.'

'All that time ago?'

'Maybe. Even though you wrecked my shot, and my lens cap...' He turned his head and kissed my fingers. 'Hadn't planned on you having to save my fucking life before I could make love with you...'

'I hadn't planned on dragging you out of the mud, either... And by the way I know I didn't wreck your shot. I've seen it.'

The edges of his mouth almost smiled.

We were quiet.

Then: 'I've been trying to avoid you. Don't need to fall in love. Shit, it's the last thing I need... Hey, I was going to show you the castle. You still up for it?'

'Are you? You nearly drowned...'

'Suffocated, anyway. Forgotten that. Come on –'

He took my hand, pulled me to my feet. Put his arms around me. 'Fucking hell, Tamar. I think I love you. Now what?'

## Twenty-seven

### France
### OLIVER

Thought I was fucking drowning. Well, suffocating. Which is worse. Black ooze creeping up my trunk. Treacling. Hugged by mud. Terminally. Fuck.

They say that your life flashes in front of you, don't they. You want to know what I was thinking about? – Whether I'd left the panniers in sunlight – didn't want to wreck the film in my camera. All I could think about as I watched the black line swallow my thighs, then my cock. Well, hadn't used that in a while anyway. But Christ I needed a piss though.

No sign of Tamar. No sound, either. Would've given anything to see that flaming bush of hair approach. Preferably with rescue – couple of burly French hunters and a ladder or two. My God.

Murder for a cup of coffee. Roll-up. Couldn't get at the papers and tobacco, of course, and they'd be wrecked now anyway.

Jesus, the cold. If the mud doesn't get you the cold surely will. One thing is certain.

Found myself yelling for her. Nearly in tears, like a bloody woman, for God's sake. The relief when she answered my call. I wanted to laugh. And the sweetheart! – Laden like a donkey with great slimy wooden spars. Could barely walk. Plastered. Mud, I mean. Her T-shirt – the way its wetness clung. Perhaps I'd never get the chance to tell her what lovely tits she had.

But. Maybe we'd do it – get me out of there. Maybe, after all.

Then the ground beneath my feet started to give way. More

rotten planks or something. Lurched a bit lower. My arse had never been so cold. Couldn't stop my teeth chattering. Wanted to yell at her to move it. But I could see she was coming as fast as she could.

Gave up at that point.

Then she was there. Come in, she said, I'll give you shelter from the storm. And she knew what to do. As if she did this all the time – dragged wankers like me from bogs. Madonna of the Mud. Christ. Not a lot of dignity left. Having to be rescued from the mud.

We were lying there. Couldn't do a lot else. Hard to breathe.

Under the smell of slime another smell. Her. Close. She was wiping mud from my face. My eyes and mouth. With her T-shirt.

Wanted to sob.

Wanted to fuck her, hard. Long. Could feel her breasts against my cheek. Wanted her so hard my head swam. Thought I might love her. Christ. Be in love with her.

And so we did it. Strange feeling. As if I knew her all the time; knew the feel of her. Wanted to be with her. Wanted more. Wanted to sleep in her arms. Didn't want to sleep. Wanted a quiet place, just her and me, a long way from all this. Everything.

Wanted to be with her.

## Twenty-eight

### France
### TAMAR

Well, we never did get to the château. If it ever existed. When Oliver spoke of it it seemed unreal, but as if it would be also visible to those who search for it, in the right way, at the right time. Almost a cross between the Grail castle and that château in *Le Grand Meaulnes* – I remember that too from school, from A level French – icon, symbol of all that might be, if only...

But what did I care – such a beautiful evening. Such a magical night.

I went off to wash in the stream. Oliver had said he was off water for a while, though I noticed he had cleaned himself up anyway.

He got the tent up, and then we lit a fire. We used – ceremoniously, as if in gratitude and propitiation – the planks and spars of Oliver's rescue.

Oliver had thought to bring things that a vegetarian might barbecue – whole peppers, courgettes, aubergines; goat's cheese. A baguette of course. Olives. A bottle of wine, rich, mulberry-red. And fresh figs, from the tree at La Bergère.

We found cêpes, chestnuts, wild oregano.

We used our fingers, drank out of the shared plastic lid of the Thermos. The vegetables, of course, were charred on one side and almost uncooked on the other; there were a few casualties, sliding off sticks or dropped abruptly by burnt and severed ones into the flames – no matter. We laughed. I'd brought bananas – soft now after the day's warmth – and almonds and chocolate, and tinfoil to wrap them in. I tucked them into the embers, and we remembered them in the early hours, long after the fire had died down. We talked, laughed more, listened to each other hungrily, kissed. Kissed again.

The smoke drifted off into the night, the blue September night hoary with stars and, later, a nearly-full hunter's moon. Somewhere an animal rustled, an owl called, was answered.

You know how it is when, for a few moments, or hours, you feel completely in step with the universe? The harmony of the spheres? That feeling by which you navigate later, by which all relationships are measured; by which you realise that so much of your life until that point has been wanting, though you never knew it... I'm not sure if I've ever felt quite so relaxed, before or since, with another person. Surprising, given our history up until that point. And maybe 'relaxed' is not exactly the word; I think I mean 'at ease'; 'fitted with'. Connected; to myself, really, my real self, as much as to Oliver and, beyond us both, to everything else.

We made love again.

It must have been dawn when we drifted off; a light sleep, as it is with a new lover. From time-to-time we surfaced, caressed, touched lips, adjusted a hip or a shoulder, sank again into intimate separateness.

I guess it was around six when I came awake finally. A green-ish dawn light was seeping into the tent, and there was a faint crack of a twig somewhere off towards the stream. Through the tent flap the woods smelt olive-green, smelt of humus, early leaf-fall, mushrooms. I could just see a thin glow of autumn sun sliding between the branches in the east. Oliver was propped on one elbow, leaning towards me. He smiled and set a light kiss on my lips.

'Just nipping out for a pee and a rollie...'

Who knows what happened in those few minutes? Or whether I

had simply tuned out what my instincts might have told me earlier?

Oh, he came back in. He kissed me. We talked, stirred the fire, brewed strong black coffee. Strolled in the woods. He took my hand, drew me to him, sat with me on a log straddling the river. 'Wanted to bring you here,' he said.

Later the same day we packed, headed back towards La Bergère. I had thought we'd be staying longer, but Oliver only had the clothes he'd fallen in with; dry now, but hard and muddy. 'I'm cold, still,' he said. 'Don't quite know why. Can't shake it off. Chilled to the marrow. That fucking mud. Thought it'd got me.'

I guess a different woman might have been alerted? – I still believe, too often, what I hear. My grandmother used to shake her head. 'You wear your heart on your sleeve, girl. Toughen up. Don't believe anything you hear, and only half of what you see...'

Anyway.

Oliver propped the bike but left the engine running. He took his helmet off and put my rucksack down and put his arms around me. 'Tamar, that was a wonderful time. I loved being with you.' He looked at me, at my eyes, then bent his head and brushed my lips. He straddled the bike again. 'Maybe we'll do it again. I'm away for a few days now. Speak soon?'

'We never did get to the château,' I said, not sure what else to say.

'I know. We will.'

He rocked the bike off the stand and lifted one foot onto the bar. His mouth smiled, but his eyes looked sober. Frightened, even. He fastened the helmet, turned his face towards me again, and was gone. My heart was jumping.

It wasn't for ages that I realised that while he knew a lot about

143

me, I knew almost nothing of him; nothing beyond his day-to-day life at La Bergère. Should that have told me?

## Twenty-nine

### France
### OLIVER

Someone once told me they used to torture people by tying them to two horses, then sending the horses off in different directions.

Couldn't stay, couldn't go. Bloody mess.

Then knew I couldn't do it. Couldn't stay. Couldn't take her down with me. And I couldn't see how I wouldn't, the way things were.

And she was a journalist, too. Too risky.

Felt like some guy in one of the Greek myths. Can't think who. Damned if you do; damned if you don't. Couldn't lie to her but couldn't tell her the truth, either. Some things you can't say, especially if the others concerned are alive. Better to split now, before we got in any deeper. I didn't have a future. That simple. I've thought about it over and over. No way out.

Who wants to be a fugitive forever? Or a fugitive's wife?

Knew it when I woke the next morning and there she was. Sleeping. Breathing by my side in the green light from the tent. Flap open. One bird singing. Her hair flung over my chest.

Had to get the hell out.

Too much at stake.

Chest hurt. Couldn't breathe. She was beautiful.

Christ.

Ashamed.

Just couldn't risk it. Thought it might not matter. At first. Not that she'd judge me. She wouldn't. She was too – good. But I'd judge myself.

My woman. If anyone. Sure about that. Made her mine. Couldn't be with anyone else.

No doubt about that.

I knew I was being a shit.

Didn't bargain on missing her so badly though.

## Thirty

### France
### TAMAR

I guess you get to an age where you start to realise that the events in your life have about them a circular, or cyclical, quality. At least, I did. How is it that I've arrived here again? Different players, different time, same theme. A kind of death, though of a different order. Some might say that that suggests a higher sweep on the spiral journey.

And same setting for this overwhelming sense of grief, as it happened.

The bow-wave peeled away, a tight clean tinny curl of water. Dawn, this time; and heading the other way. Back. (Home, I could say, though I had no idea what 'home' might now mean.)

I went on deck.

Egrets lifted and landed in the distant shallows.

No dolphins. A mournful, whistling young herring gull, flecked salt and pepper, sitting on the railing, breast feathers flattened by the oncoming breeze.

The ferry steamed out of the harbour. We passed the Ile de Batz and then there was nothing ahead but ocean.

## Thirty-one

### Dartmoor
### TAMAR

'You remember the Delaneys, Tay? Out at Culver? Didn't you meet them at some stage?' One of Louise's early morning phone calls, concurrent with rushing the kids through the routine of breakfast, teeth, football boots, sheet music, have-you-done-your-homework and don't do that and then the walk to the school bus.

Her voice came and went; I could hear water gurgling, children shouting, a cat mewing for breakfast. I pictured Louise rushing from room to room, cordless phone tucked between her ear and chin, thick not-quite-blonde bob swinging over the mouthpiece. The Delaneys? Oh yes, Mr Delaney – Bob, was it? – and the orchards.

'God, that's a long time ago.'

'What? Can't hear –'

'Long time ago,' I shouted.

'Battery's low. Listen, Tay, I've got to go. Wanted to tell you though that they're advertising accommodation. If you're still wanting to get out of town.'

'Of course,' I said. 'Thanks! Got a number?'

I scrabbled for pen and paper and jotted down the number she gave me.

'Bye,' she said, and the line went dead.

I haven't mentioned Louise. She's been wonderful. I don't quite know at what point she turned into my closest friend, but she pulled me through the time after Oliver, and we've remained close ever since.

We didn't really know each other before, though we met through working on the same paper before I went to France. Now she was freelance, fitting her work from home as an editor around three children and her husband, Mac. She still lived on the edge of the moor, where she always had.

But I bumped into her on my first day back, when I returned to Dartmoor from the Roscoff / Plymouth ferry, not knowing where else to go. My parents had rented the house out while they were in Scotland, so I'd booked into the Court House Inn overnight, and there she was, Louise, in Culverstock market the next day when I wandered in; and she had a spare room which she immediately offered me. So I stayed with them for a few weeks; then I found a job – undemanding, temporary – in an antiquarian bookshop up in Bath. I wanted somewhere new, with no associations. I needed time to recover and think; decide where I wanted to be and pick up the threads of freelancing again. I signed up for a copyediting course, and rented a small cheap flat – nothing special, but it had a little private courtyard garden, which sold it to me.

I knew no-one.

Bath is a pleasant city, as cities go. During the two years I spent there I shifted a lot of stuff, as the therapeutic jargon goes. I didn't mind my solitude, I found. Some days, of course, it was hard – lonely; and there was what sometimes seemed like an unending well of grief: Mark's death compounded by Oliver's betrayal. And I missed the moor.

I spent a lot of time on my own; but I also went out – concerts in the Pump Rooms, poetry readings, exhibitions. I made some friends; went out with a couple of men; told them I wasn't ready for a 'serious relationship'. Visited my parents near Oban a couple of times; toyed with moving up to the islands. Too far north, too much dark, too far away from Dartmoor, I decided in the end.

Increasingly, though, I lived for the weekends when I managed to get away and stay with Louise and walk, walk, walk.

It was 1994. I was thirty. I needed, I thought, to stop freewheeling; to find what I wanted to do with my life; where and how I wanted to live.

Sometimes the universe listens. Sometimes it moves with you. Often you just need to pay attention.

On the way into work that morning, after Louise's call, I picked up a copy of *Vision*, the environmental and arts magazine. In the little office at the back of the bookstore I flipped it open while I had my coffee break – and they wanted an in-house copy editor, three days a week. At their base. In Devon.

I rang the editor immediately – David who ran the bookshop was good like that, and knew I was 'only temporary' – as I had been for two years.

Twenty minutes later I looked like I might have three days' work a week plus some commissioned features – pending interview and clippings' file.

That evening I rang the number Louise had given me. A woman answered – Trudy. I wasn't sure if she remembered me; unlikely, though she was polite when I mentioned my visit all those years ago. But she was friendly in a quiet way; and yes, the room was still available. It was actually more like a small annexe, she told me – a small sitting room or study, a middle-sized bedroom, with a bathroom and tiny kitchen and porch below. It had once been a dairy and store. Yes, there was a view of the moor.

I sorted everything in just over a month. And so I came back to Dartmoor, and went to live with the Delaneys.

## Thirty-two

The Delaneys were in conversion to organic. *Vision* favoured life story features over theoretical articles. Within days of moving in, I had my first article, without even leaving the farm. I talked to Bob, tailed him and Guy around the farm, asked them about their approach to organic farming, as well as their reasons for changing; and then had each of them speak into a tape recorder about the whole process of conversion: its limitations as well as its benefits. The magazine sent out a photographer, and the piece came out a couple of months later. It felt like a validation; confirmation that I'd done the right thing.

I remembered the feel of Culver. I took the rooms unseen, on trust; the Delaneys too agreed to let me rent them without our meeting, though they did take up references. My sitting room was very small, but lovely – on a corner of the house, it looked out over the tors towards Culverstock one way, and in the direction of Cornwall and my namesake river the other. I put my desk under one of the windows and installed my computer. As I wrote my first piece I could smell the honeysuckle against the wall below me, and the clean green air of the moor-soaked river at the bottom of the valley. They had been mowing the meadows, too – it could hardly have been more idyllic.

Within weeks, I was settled to the extent that I could scarcely remember life before Culver.

Guy, of course, was no longer the boy I'd met in passing all those years ago. In his mid-twenties now, he had that look about him of a man who fit his own skin, and his life, perfectly.

Transcribing the notes I'd made from our conversation, and gazing out at the moors in moments between, my eye was caught by his figure passing from time to time – tinkering with the engine on the quad bike, moving sheep from one of the home meadows up to the newly-mown Newtake field with the tractor and trailer, lifting a gate off its hinges to get the baler through the narrow gap between granite posts.

Always the dogs were at his heels. That touched me somehow; I found it endearing, even though of course dogs do shadow their owners. Though quite a solid man, Guy moved around the farm and about his tasks with that particular grace and agility that strongly physical men embody. I had seen it in Mark, too: that earthy comfortable-in-their-shoes quality.

I enjoyed watching Guy, as I had Mark when he climbed, or ran – it's always a delight watching someone who fits so neatly his chosen environment and lifestyle.

It was obvious from the beginning – I mean from our first conversation as adults – that Guy's dreams – no, aspirations, Guy wasn't a dreamer – Guy's aspirations and ambitions centred on the farm, stopped at the farm. I don't mean that negatively. Farming was what he did. He loved it; it was what he'd been born to do. End of story.

When I first arrived at the farm this second time, Guy was on hand – briefed, I imagined, by Trudy – to help me move my stuff. I'd acquired very little – books, of course; a few CDs; but other than that really only my clothes, a couple of rugs and cushions; a moody painting of the moor by a friend; a dozen or so plants in pots, my desk and computer. I'd hired a Transit, and Guy opened the gates for me, then came around to the driver's door and opened that too. His handshake was firm, his hazel eyes warm and interested and steady. Brownish thick hair, pleasant face – not astonishingly handsome but easy, mobile, ready to smile.

'I'm Guy. Bob and Trudy's son. You must be Tamar. Find it OK?'

152

I took off my sunglasses. 'After a fashion. I used to live on the moor. Got a bit lost though coming the long way round – I was a bit nervous about the width of the van. I did visit here once, years ago. I didn't meet you properly, though. God, I'm exhausted.'

'Long journey then. Here, give me that. And that. I'll just ask Mum to make you a cuppa, then I'll give you a hand.'

Later, Trudy insisted I had dinner with the family. I remember being absurdly emotional at the warmth of their welcome.

Guy seemed unshakeable; dependable, older than his years. In those days, I never saw him lose his cool. He was one of those people who were there when you needed them – quietly, without a fuss. I had to take the van back to Bristol the day after my arrival, and I'd intended to catch the train back as far as Newton Abbot and then get a taxi.

'No matter,' Guy said. 'I've got to go and get some fence posts and udder cream and stock feed, stuff like that, anyway. The merchants are over that way. I'll pick you up from Newton station. Tell me when?'

I needed a car. I was due to start at the Vision office two weeks after I'd moved in. If I was careful with what little money I had, I could just about manage to run something not too costly. I mentioned it to Bob, casually, intending simply to ring around various local garages; the next day Guy brought round the local CarMart, knocking at my door and then waiting diffidently. 'Thought it might be helpful. The local man's got a couple in – have a look: Hills' Garage in Cross Street.'

'That's really kind, Guy. You didn't need to do that. Thanks though.' I was pleased; but also a little surprised. Taken aback, I suppose I mean. I was used to sorting myself out alone. I didn't quite know how to relate to this helpfulness. They were treating me almost like family. I liked it; but I also wanted to be careful to remain independent.

He was gone before I could say more. 'Got to go and check the lambs for fly-strike. See you later.'

'Any luck with Hills'?' Guy had his back to me, hands deep in the bowels of the tractor's engine. He didn't look round.

'How on earth did you know it was me?' The big male collie, Fly, came over and pushed his nose into my hand. I pulled his ears gently.

'Your footsteps didn't sound like either Mum or Dad. Complex process of deduction, you see.' He grinned up at me over his shoulder. 'Where are you off to, anyway?'

'Thought I'd go up the footpath for a walk. I need a break from the computer.'

'Getting to you, is it? Couldn't stand it, myself. Chained to that thing day after day.'

'Well, I've got to a tricky bit in that article I'm writing. I seem to think best when I'm walking.'

'Well, now, that I understand. I do all my thinking when I'm active, myself; in the milking parlour or out up in those hills with the sheep. Grand. Fresh air, big view, no damn electronic thing beeping at you.'

I noticed for the first time a slight Devon burr to his accent; the long vowels. Something about his old-fashioned use of the word 'grand' endeared him to me, somehow. His lack of pretension. 'You do long days, don't you? Weren't you out baling till late last night?'

'Hear the tractor, did you? Hope it didn't disturb you. Yep. Best time of day, that and the early morning.'

154

I smiled. 'Of course you didn't disturb me. I'm a country person myself.' Why did I need to tell him that? 'Must get on. Got another 2000 words to write before I stop today.'

'Blimey. How long's that?'

'Three or four pages, I suppose. A4.'

Guy stood up and wiped his hands on a rag. 'Hmmm. That's the piece on conversion to organics, still?'

'Yes. I'll let you see it when it's done. Actually you ought to, anyway, in case I've misquoted you or got my facts horribly wrong. Is that OK?'

''Course. Any luck with that car of yours, by the way?'

'Well, the garage you mentioned has a little Peugeot for sale. 205. Not too old.'

'They're not bad. How much is it?'

'Eight hundred.'

'Tax and MOT?'

'I think so.'

'Well, I'd go for it. Not diesel, is it? Not expensive enough. How old is it?'

'Can't remember. He said it was in good condition.'

'Well, worth a look, certainly. Want me to come too?'

I looked at him. 'I was going to get the AA to look. I forgot my membership had lapsed, though. I haven't needed a car in a while. Do you have time?'

'I can make time. Be glad to have an hour or two off.'

'Well, if you're sure. I really appreciate that, Guy.'

'Well, I've been around machines long enough to know a dud when I see it. When d'you need to go?'

'Tomorrow? Could you do the morning?'

'Yep.'

'You're a star. I'll ring the garage.'

'And by the way, you don't have to stick to the footpaths,

you know. You live here. Take the dogs, if you like.'

I bought the car. Or should I say 'we bought the car'? I handed over the money and took the keys; Guy did the negotiation – not easy for someone as independent as I am, or was. I concede that Guy knew much more about cars than I did, but I still felt odd about it; especially when the garage owner referred to me as Guy's girlfriend. 'I'm not, actually,' I said calmly. 'Guy's my neighbour.'

Guy grinned. 'And friend,' he said. Mr Hills winked at him. I pretended not to notice.

'Can I buy you a pint? It's the least I can do,' I said as I got into my new car and Guy strode over towards the Land Rover.

'You bet,' he called over his shoulder. 'The Three Feathers? Do you want to follow me?'

'I know where it is; but OK, you lead.'

'I didn't offend you, did I?' His eyes looked slightly concerned, genuinely interested in my answer. It struck me, not for the first time, how mature he seemed for someone who must only have been twenty-six or -seven.

I'd thought at first that Guy reminded me of Bob, but actually close to he didn't really resemble him, except maybe in similarly coloured eyes. I realise now that farming men often have that slow-moving, deliberate quietness: a kind of bone-deep calm. Comes from being around animals so much, of course. It's generic rather than genetic, perhaps.

We were ensconced on a bench under the oak tree in the pub garden. He held my eyes.

'When?'

'When I said we were friends.'

156

'Of course not! We are.' I looked away.

'I hope so,' he said, and took a draught of beer. He wiped the foam off his lips. 'Mmm. Needed that. Thirsty work, spending someone else's money.' He laughed up at me. I noticed how his eyes were lit when he grinned. 'They brew their own here, you know. Taste?'

'I'll stick to my spritzer. Can't tell one beer from another, I'm afraid.'

'We'll soon change that... What brings you back to Dartmoor, then?'

How do you answer that in one sentence? 'Many things, I suppose. I was tired of being away, really. I was brought up here.'

'Your mum and dad still here?'

'Yes and no. They're in Scotland at the moment for a while – my dad's work.'

There was a silence between us for a few minutes. We didn't know each other well enough for it to be comfortable, and I was searching around for something to say when he beat me to it.

'How long did you live in Bath, then?'

'Oh, a couple of years.'

'Before that?'

'France.'

He looked surprised. 'What were you doing there? – Not that it's any of my business – '

'Gardening. I've friends there.' I changed the subject. 'Tell me about your life, Guy. Have you always been at Culver?'

'Since I was young, yes.' He looked down at his beer. 'Bit weird, isn't it, still living with your mum and dad at my age.' He looked back up at me and grinned self-deprecatingly. I smiled back. I'm a sucker for self-disclosure in people, openness. 'Just that farming's my life, and the farm's here. Dad's OK at the moment, but there'll be a time I suppose when he can't manage

157

any more. Besides, there hasn't been any reason not to. Hard to beat the area. Have thought about Canada or New Zealand from time to time, but why? I'm not really a grass-is-greener type.'

I wanted – out of sheer nosiness – to ask him whether he ever got out, had a social life, met women, but didn't like to. I was afraid he might misinterpret my intentions, too.

Once again he filled the gap. 'It's OK at home. We all fit around each other. The house is big enough; I've got my own sitting room if I need to bugger off on my own to read or watch the box or something. We all eat together, though. I think Mum likes it. I've got a little sailing boat, too; so I get out on the river from time to time. Not often, mind; especially this time of year. Shame.'

'Oh? Where do you go?'

'Down into the Sound, usually. Plymouth. Or down onto the Tamar. It's a single-hander, so I trailer it. Sometimes down onto the Yealm or somewhere. You should come out some time – there's room for two, at a push. Done any sailing?'

I shook my head. 'Not for ages. Dad sails, but I've never been a strong swimmer. Listen, I've got to complete that piece I was writing this afternoon, and of course I'm starting my new job – the other bit of it – tomorrow. D'you want a sandwich before we go?'

'Are you going to have one?'

'Could do. I'm hungry.'

Eating together breaks the ice, doesn't it? By the time we arrived at our respective vehicles we were laughing and chattering like old friends.

## Thirty-three

When I got home after my first day at *Vision*, there was a basket on my doorstep: broad beans, eggs, a fat bunch of parsley and a jar of Bob's honey.

I went and knocked on the back door immediately. Bob opened the door.

'Mr Delaney, there was a lovely surprise on my doorstep. Was that Trudy?'

'Call me Bob, lass, for goodness' sake. Well, we want you to be happy in there.' He pushed his reading glasses up onto his head. His eyes smiled kindly at me. Who else had called me 'lass'? Mark's father, of course. Suddenly there was a lump in my throat.

'You've all been so good to me. Thank you so much.'

'Oh, it's nothing. Forget it. Nice to have someone back in those rooms. Shouldn't stay empty when there are so many people needing homes. Ah, there you are Trudy – '

'Hello, dear.' Trudy was pinning her hair up. It was mostly white, now. 'How was it today?'

'Oh, it was good. I really enjoyed it. Listen, thank you so much for the things on the doorstep. You're all so kind to me.'

'Do you want to join us for supper, dear?'

'That's really kind; but I think I need to go and have a bath and be quiet. Besides, you've already given me supper!'

'Guy picked the beans. His idea, actually.' She smiled at me. I couldn't help noticing that sadness seemed permanently to linger at the corners of her mouth, though. 'Well, if you're sure...'

\*

I suddenly seemed to have a lot of energy. Work was good. Robert, my boss, the editor, was both fun and funny, and a man whose integrity and commitment to what his magazine stood for was inspiring. He seemed to genuinely appreciate my first piece, both in conception and execution. 'This is exactly what we want, Tamar,' he told me at the staff meeting on the following Monday, after I'd completed my first two days as copy editor and handed over my article on the Delaneys. 'Your style fits ours, and I need my staff to be self-motivated. Let me know what you'd like to work on next.'

The drive back home across the moor was stupendous.

One evening I borrowed the dogs and took a long hike up over the top. Guy had told me of a circular walk that I'd not explored before; one that took in several of the megalithic remains, including the Bronze Age village of Grimspound.

As I clambered through the hut circles and on up to the top dusk was pooling in the cleaves, and the sky to the west was apricot and rose and lilac; there was that stillness peculiar to dusk, broken only by an occasional rustle of a small animal in the bracken by the path. I climbed up through the clitter on the tor; the sky darkened to indigo, and I realised that we were almost at the solstice. A turning point.

I stopped on the rocks, and sat with the dogs at my feet until the first stars appeared, and a moon, then we slipped back down the other side of the hill.

My mind was as unruffled as a still pool. It took me a while to recognise the feeling, to name it: yes, happiness.

Guy must have heard the orchard gate latch, because he came out of the big barn into the yard. 'Good walk? – I'll show you the longer version of that some time. What about this weekend?'

'Love to some time, Guy, but I've got some things I need to do; some more writing.'

'You the kind of writer who can't talk to anyone when she's

in the middle of a piece?

"Fraid so...'

'Oh well. When you've time.'

'Thanks, Guy. Goodnight.'

I was sitting at my desk in my window a week or two later. It had been a busy time; I'd only just had a chance to properly unpack. A dedicated phone line had been installed, now, too. It looked like I'd committed myself for the long haul, I realised with a shock. The day before I'd been to the local auction house with Louise to see if I could pick up some bookcases and a chest of drawers and cupboard. Her husband, Mac, had dropped my purchases off on his way to work that morning, and I had finally sorted my little house out, more or less.

I'd hardly seen the Delaneys except to wave at from a distance for days.

Suddenly there seemed to be a lot of work. Robert wanted me to do a piece on GM crops, and then another on farmers' markets. 'They're going to be the next big thing,' he said. 'Give it a couple of years; more maybe for us down here. But they've got some up and running in the Cotswolds. Fancy a drive?'

So that took care of next week; and just now he had emailed me for my opinion on a press release that had come in, with a view to running a piece in Vision. The flyer detailed a major new woodland sculpture trail with an emphasis on environmentalism on the edge of Exmoor. The feature editor was keen; she was possibly going to interview the individual artists involved herself, but I would write up the background and cover the installation. I thought it looked great.

I was checking out the sculpture trail website when I was aware of someone making a lot of noise in the yard. Curiosity took hold of me, and I craned past the computer to see what was going on. Guy, welding a batch of galvanised hurdles, as far as I could see; though why the need for such a commotion was less clear. I was about to sit down again when he glanced up at my window, then pointedly turned his back to me and bent back to his welding. Quietly, this time. Strange. Then I saw the notice tied to his back with baler twine. 'WHEN' it said, in bold red capitals, handwritten on card. I puzzled over that for a minute, as I sat back to my screen.

Perhaps fifteen minutes later the noise started up again. Intrigued, I glanced out. Guy didn't look up. 'WILL', the notice said this time. It occurred to me that this might be for my benefit. Well, maybe. But I was working. I dropped back down in my seat.

Then a third time. 'YOU'.

The next time I looked he'd gone. 'When will you.' I puzzled over that. I carried on with what I was doing, but my mind circled over the aborted phrase. I could make no sense of it at all.

I wondered about calling in as I went past their door that evening, on my way in to see Louise, but thought better of it.

I didn't think about it again till Friday; then there he was, back to me, going through the yard gate. 'COMEFOR', the red letters all cramped together. I opened my mouth to call him, but he'd disappeared round the corner. I hesitated a moment, smiling to myself, but carried on towards my car. Ah! There was the completion, taped to my driver's window: 'ADRINK?' This time I laughed out loud.

His head appeared over the wall. He was grinning. 'Well?'

'Ten out of ten for ingenuity!'

'Good to hear you laugh. You normally look like you're carrying the weight of the whole solar system –'

'Do I?' I was genuinely surprised. But yes, I supposed the last couple or three years hadn't been the most fun years of my life.

'You haven't answered my question.'

'Which was?'

'When are you going to come for a drink?'

'Umm. Not sure. Busy time... maybe next week?'

'I'll keep you to that. 'Bye.' And he was gone.

## Thirty-four

It was my second full summer at Culver. The Delaneys had been considerate neighbours, as well as landlords, to me; a second family, in effect. It had been an easy peaceful time; my life turned on rhythms that I liked. Guy had become a good friend: I gave him a hand with the farm from time to time; he fixed my car; we often walked together on the moor, sometimes incorporating a pub into our journey; and occasionally we took the dogs to the coast for an evening stroll or swim; now and then I went sailing with him. We were easy together – we talked about lots of things; Guy turned out to be well-read and interested in current affairs. Sometimes we simply walked together in silence. Other times we laughed together. Always I enjoyed his company. I didn't think beyond that.

Of course, it changed. Sometimes these things just manifest themselves: apparently out of the blue, although in retrospect you can usually see that actually it was slow but inexorable progress towards that moment of no return – which is so often, in itself, an inconsequential point which arrives untrumpeted and seemingly arbitrarily at that moment when – well, when the moment is ripe, I guess.

I picture it now as a tableau: musical statues. In my memory, nothing moved for an unimaginable length of time, though in actuality it was probably only a minute or two. I say 'nothing', but in fact, closing my eyes now to picture the scene, there is a skylark, rising and rising, dropping its song back down through the thick hay-scented air towards the dusty late-summer earth.

Sometimes at Culver, on an easterly breeze, you can smell salt in the air from Dawlish or Torbay. Or at least I like to think I can. That day, though, it was too hot, too still. The air seemed to have soaked up all the fragrances of the summer hedgerows: a muscat-yellow cocktail of bedstraw and woodruff, dry grass, dog rose. On the track early hips, sloes and bullaces ('mazzards', Guy called them) sat fatly amongst the bright berries of bryony and honeysuckle. Already Trudy had made the annual batch of rowan jelly; the jars crowded the shelves of their larder, conducting light. On the floor below them, as well as in my little porch, were baskets of early windfalls.

In the yard now everything was still except for the dogs, panting in the shade of the house close by. And Guy and I, too, still: about three feet apart. I could feel sweat trickling in my armpits and between my breasts; self-conscious suddenly in the silence I was fighting the urge to glance down at my top.

I was also very conscious of Guy. I noticed as if for the first time how big his hands were – strong capable farmer's hands, equally at ease with pistons and combine harvesters, shearing sheep and delivering calves. My senses seemed to be on high alert. I was very aware of the smell of him – warm, earthy, male; comforting, sweat-tinged. I intuited, rather than smelt, an edge of nervousness in his odour; simultaneously smelt my own fear.

He held my eyes steadily with his own.

There was, I think, an uncompleted sentence hanging between his mouth and my ears – or was it my mouth and his ears?

Then one of us must have crossed the yard of earth between us, because our arms were round each other and my face was pressed to the top of his chest, where his hair curled over his T-shirt and tickled my cheeks and my nostrils were full of him, and all I could hear was the rapid thump of his heart and my own blood singing, and all I could feel was the heat of him and his breath stirring my hair.

Then from somewhere there was a clang of metal – a gate or

a pail or a dropped spanner; my mind skittered sideways and we gently drew apart, and as if by agreement carried on with what we had been doing before that moment, separately; though for the rest of that day, no matter where I was, I felt his eyes holding mine.

*

It had seemed simple. A man who made me laugh, with whom I felt at ease, who loved me deeply, and whom I too had started to love; maybe not with passion, but with a great deal of warmth and affection. Mature love, I imagined, at last. Where had passion got me? And my home here on Dartmoor, with people whose rural lifestyle I respected and related to. A security I hadn't known as an adult. A woman would be a fool to turn away from it. Wouldn't she? Eventually, after he'd asked me three times, I married him.

## Thirty-five

Flashforward to 2001. I woke from a dream of pomegranates. You remember the story of Persephone? I mentioned it earlier. She sealed her own fate by eating half a dozen pomegranate seeds on the invitation of Hades, Lord of the Underworld. – Such a simple action, which confirmed that she now belonged at least in part to the Underworld.

Looking back over a life you can perhaps pick out those moments of consequence, those moments of choice where a step this way instead of that can set in motion the effects of which the step is a cause, start the reverberations which can fracture or heal the future.

Oh yes, I'd eaten the seeds. By the handful, with Oliver. And now, years later, by marrying the man I had.

And so, I now see, had Trudy; for these gifts come at a cost, and donate, too, their own gift of vision, of forescribing the future. What her seeds were it's not my place to say here. But her gift is hers; and although I cannot say I have the Sight I have a certain sensitivity to it.

So I knew by looking at Trudy. Years of practice.

Trudy didn't talk much these days; but then, I guess she was never especially voluble. Small and quiet though she was, she carried that aura that powerful women have – matriarchs even – and it was she who created the atmosphere at Culver. I'd got in the habit of watching her; she was a kind of weather forecast, as I've said already; an early storm warning.

So I'd noticed. Minutes before Bob came in her shoulders had gone rigid, and her knuckles around the bottle she was warming for the orphan lamb were white with tension. When the back door opened she didn't lift her head, though I spotted what

167

might have been a slight quiver in the newly-cut tips of her silvery hair.

Bob took forever to take his boots off, toe to heel. They fell against the open door. Chill February rain streamed over the lip of the gutters above him and cascaded over his sodden jacket. He stepped into the scullery and shed his waterproofs before plodding to the kitchen table to sit down.

I glanced at him. His face these days looked tired. Sad.

'OK, Bob?'

'All right.' He didn't look up.

Trudy deftly tested the milk with her free hand on the other wrist, and then hoicked the lamb from under her arm onto her lap.

I stood up and moved the kettle back onto the hotplate and turned round.

Bob raised his head. He and Trudy stared at each other. She tipped her head at him questioningly. The lamb sucked at the bottle.

The kettle started to boil.

The whistle rose to an unbearable pitch, drowning the downpour outside. I'd made the tea and sat down again with the book I'd been making notes from before Bob said more.

'Possible foot and mouth at Collapound.'

'What?'

'Waiting for confirmation. Got the MAFF vets in.'

'Foot and mouth? Oh, no!'

'What'll happen if they find it?'

'Probably shoot the lot. How far is it, eight miles? Six?'

Bob was hunched, large veiny hands dangling between his knees. The cuffs of his shirt were damp. He stared down at the floor between his feet. He answered himself. 'Aye. Six miles too close.'

168

'How can it be foot and mouth? The last time was thirty years ago!'

'That's what they're saying.'

In the ensuing silence the rain was loud. In a box by the Aga the cat stretched and yawned. The lamb finished slurping and started to wriggle. Trudy put it down and stood up and shooed it towards the door.

'I'll do that. I've got to go out to the barn anyway.'

'D'you want your tea first?'

'In a minute.' Bob stood again and followed the lamb out towards the scullery. His boots as he donned them squelched.

Trudy and I looked at each other. Bob's words still hung, thickening the silence. Simultaneously we glanced at the window. The rain still tumbled through and over the gutters, poured off the porch overhang, crazed the windows. I'd moved beyond my misery at the unending rain; we were all simply resigned to it.

'We'll need to unblock the drains,' said Trudy. 'I don't know where all the leaves come from this time of the year.'

As she said this I suddenly realised how rarely Bob attended to those things any more, and how Trudy had extended her realm of responsibility – normally the house and, before I took it over, the garden – to include the yard and outbuildings.

'I'll get some more wood in,' I said, bending to lift the great willow basket.

I noticed we didn't mention Bob's bombshell. There seemed to be a lot of things we didn't mention these days.

As I pulled on oilskins and boots to trudge across the yard to the woodshed – the old stone goosepen by the main gate – the full impact and implications of Bob's news hit me.

A lot was at stake. Guy was off at market today, his weekly escape from the farm, chance to chat to other farmers and keep an eye on the competition as well as share – if only in non-specific comradely side-by-side small talk – the trials and despairs of farming.

Guy's increasing involvement with the farm had manifested itself in two strong pedigree flocks of sheep – the black-faced Dartmoors with their resilience and their ancient lineage, and a new flock of Wiltshires. He had been thinking of winding down the Friesian dairy herd, and the handful of little belted Galloways, and was wanting to bring in a new bull – 'new blood' – for the growing Culver herd of South Devons, already well-established and respected as one of the strongest herds in the West, and fast becoming a sought-after bloodline. Just suppose Collapound were confirmed as foot and mouth positive. If anything were to happen to Guy's herds and flocks the result would be devastation; worse than devastation, financial ruin as well.

I sloshed through the slurry in the yard. Despite the rain the sweet smell of the silage that Bob had opened for the cattle from the baled stack in the home meadow caught my nostrils and for a moment lifted my spirits. I'd become a true farmer's wife: as long as the hay was in and there were logs in the woodshed I could feel secure.

By the gate the last of the snowdrops nodded under the weight of raindrops, and the little wild daffodils in the banks of the track were just showing ruffs above the calyces.

My fingers felt for the little pebble I always carried in my jeans pocket from Brittany. The last legacy of those days. I hardly thought of Oliver any more, but the pebble was my comfort. Any trace of roughness had gone, in all these years of its life as a touchstone for me.

As I bent to the door of the goosepen the rain trickled down my neck and just as abruptly I reverted to a now-familiar state almost approaching panic; or at least a sense of cabin fever, mild claustrophobia weighted with irritation and resentment. How had we ended up here, all of us, in this silent *folie à quatre* where what was voiced was kind but distant, and what was unvoiced was consuming us – well, me, anyway – with a dull but insistent banked-down fire? And this daily round, daily battle with rain and mud, merely to survive? And by means which I, a vegetarian, could hardly condone?

One of the outdoor cats had wriggled under the ill-fitting door and was curled on top of the logs on a scrap of old hessian sacking. She squeaked and rolled to expose her belly, and as I bent to oblige with the requested tickle I felt myself soften.

It hadn't been an easy time for Guy, either. He didn't deserve more trouble. As Bob aged so Guy increasingly assumed responsibility for the farm, for steering it through the varying requirements for subsidies, for ensuring its survival through cashflow crises, BSE, TB panics, and the challenge of sustaining and marketing the organic meat that he was committed to producing. There were the inevitable and frequent losses of stock – to disease; to flukes – both 'acts of God' and parasitic; to weather, and increasingly to the large number of vehicles driving too fast in poor conditions on the unfenced moorland roads alongside which much of the Culver stock grazed.

On top of all this he had a wife who was at best disinclined to be directly involved in the agricultural processes that all led to one end – slaughter; and at worst was downright hostile to both the means and the end. I loved the farm and the animals, but increasingly found it hard to swallow the fact that our continued survival was dependent on their death.

And then there was the matter, before my time, of a large sum of Bob's capital ransomed to Eliot's flouted bail.

And of course these stresses were all reflected in our relationship, I mused, as I brought the axe down with rising vigour on the sawn-up boles of the ash we had felled last winter. I'd got into a swing now, a ring-thud-split. Guy was a good, decent, kind man and deserved somebody who cared for him, backed him totally, understood his passion for his animals without judging him a hypocrite for their function as exploitees in our lives. And who wasn't herself a hypocrite. In other words, someone who loved him wholeheartedly.

He didn't need this news. Did he know by now? He must surely have heard at market.

God, I needed to get out. I needed to see Louise, to share a pot of coffee with someone who wasn't either silent or talking quotas, the fluctuations in value of live and dead stock, or the price of calcified seaweed this year. I felt a twinge of guilt even thinking this, but by God I needed to laugh.

## Thirty-six

Louise rushed in to the riverside café, late as usual, scattering raindrops. 'Sorry, darling, so sorry. Fog on the Nattadown road. Look, got you some flowers.'

'Mimosa! Just what I need – so sunny. But this time of year?'

'Garden. We're more sheltered than you, remember.'

'You don't know how much I need cheering. Thanks – just perfect.'

Louise looked at me with concern. 'You do look a bit down, Tay. And you're going grey!'

'Thanks, L. Tactful as ever!'

'Actually I envy your silver streaks. Can't wait to lose my nondescript locks to something more showy.'

She settled, shedding coat, scarf and bags and showering the table with rain.

'Go on, then, Tay, tell me all. How's that lovely man of yours?' Louise, having finally, the last year, struggled free of Mac, the charismatic but congenitally unfaithful and fiscally and emotionally unreliable father of her three boys, regarded the stable and loving Guy as a minor god.

'Guy? Oh, he's fine. A bit of a blow about the foot and mouth though – you must have heard?'

'What, down here? Shit. No, I hadn't. Where?'

'Possibly at Collapound, so Bob said. Certainly at Hatherleigh.'

'Collapound. That's just round the corner, isn't it?'

'From us? Yes. Five or six miles.'

'My God. Guy must be worried out of his mind.'

'I haven't seen him. He's out at market, and Bob only heard this morning. You know Guy though – he simply won't take it seriously until he sees the evidence. But yes, couldn't be much

173

worse, it seems to me, after all this rain and flooding, and the price of beef only just stabilised after BSE. And the price of organic feed.'

'Still trumpeting the organic corner?'

'Of course. You remember that documentary I contributed to all those years ago, the Country programme, when they were still in the process of conversion? – Bob was convinced that there was a connection between BSE and CJD and organophosphates, and the piece drew quite a lot of media attention. He's not the only one, but he has become a hot name on the subject. More committed than ever. Won't buy in unless the stock have all been born and reared organic. He's become a bit of an expert; gets to speak around the country on it. Guy's just as convinced, though he's more laid back than Bob about the politics of it all. Less of a crusader.'

The waitress arrived. Louise looked at me, her head on one side, smiling wickedly. 'I think this woman needs a cream tea,' she said.

I opened my mouth and shut it again. Yes. I seemed to have become so abstemious these days. A cream tea was exactly what I needed. The waitress looked questioningly at me. 'Lovely. Please,' I said. 'And you too, Lou?'

Louise looked at me searchingly. 'You nearly said no, didn't you? You've become so ascetic, Tay. You're a puritan at heart, aren't you?'

'I was listening to a programme about anchorites yesterday. Yes, I do yearn for a simpler way of living. I'd have made a good anchoress.'

'Surely your life's simple enough? You hardly go out, Tay. You spend a lot of time closeted away, reading and writing and thinking. Not talking to anyone. Scarcely a life of glamour and hedonism...'

'Anyway. A cream tea's just what I need today.'

'We should have gone to Hamelbridge, had a cream tea by their fire and walked to the Wisht Wood. Or walked first and come back to steam and dry out by their fire... Where were we? What were we talking about?'

'Men. Or organics, I think...'

'Oh yes. You and your future. Didn't you have plans to be involved in growing for the organic veg box scheme?'

'Well, yes, obviously that would be my preference. But Guy and Bob don't think it would be viable and they don't have time to help me with it. I can't do it alone. Had to let that dream go, for the moment.'

'Aren't there any subsidies for organic veg growing?'

'I think so. But it's not just that – it's also convincing Guy.'

The waitress came with our teas. We were silent while we split our scones, piled clotted cream and strawberry jam. 'I feel like a tourist,' I said, with my mouth full.

The café was busy – market day – and hummed with voices, fragments of conversation. The windows were steamed up; it felt comforting to be so cocooned.

'Are you two getting on OK?'

'Me and Guy? Oh, we don't really ever get on badly. Never have. We don't really row, or anything. He's great. I'm lucky. We just don't always see eye-to eye.'

'Does any couple?'

'I don't know.' I was fiddling with the knife; feeling anxious suddenly. 'Why d'you ask, Lou?'

Louise watched me over her coffee cup, her grey eyes serious. 'I'm not sure. Something about your tone of voice when you talk about him. Do you love him, Tay?'

'He's a lovely man. Kind, caring, affectionate.'

'I know that. That's not what I'm asking. Look at me, Tay.'

I didn't know how to respond. I didn't ask myself that question. Life was as it was, and I had committed myself to it.

'Tay?'

I glanced at Louise and then away.

'You're not happy, are you?'

'Guy would have liked us to have children. He didn't really get over all that fuss last year.'

'You mean the fact that he might be infertile?'

'Well, the fact that I didn't conceive. We're only guessing that it's him because I seem to be OK. He's refused to go for tests, though. He can't quite accept that it might be him, and he won't quite believe that we can't. Or don't seem to be able to.'

'Are you happy? – You didn't answer my question.'

'Well, given everything. It's not a bad life. Great place to live. I have my own study to hide in, and my writing work. Guy's generous. He's a hard worker and he loves me. He's a steady man, too. I know he won't ever play around. The family's good to me. And I have the horse when I need to escape. And you.'

Louise didn't respond, just watched me.

I carried on. 'Well, of course it's different from the life I thought I'd have. When I was younger. Isn't it for all of us? But I love the moor, as you know.'

'How long now since you came back from France?'

'God knows. Years. Eight years? Nine? Something like that.'

'So you two must have been married for – what? Six years?'

'About that. Five, anyway. But I've lived there for longer, of course – remember I rented the room there to start with, before Guy and I got together. That's – I don't know – seven years maybe? And I was with you for a while, too.'

'Mmm. I remember the first time I met Guy – those steady warm hazel eyes fixed adoringly on you. I noticed because Mac's eyes were always everywhere – noticing everyone but me. Guy's only ever gazed at you, hasn't he?'

'Yes. I'm lucky. He gives me a lot of security.'

Outside it was still pouring. Schoolchildren were streaming past, hoods up and satchels banging. Cars with their lights on. The sky closing in.

# Thirty-seven

Guy had heard at market. When I came back the two men were leaning propped on their hands over the kitchen table reading a copy of the Westcountry Gazette, exchanging a word or two now and then.

Guy looked up at me. I noticed how he slouched these days, more than a 34-year-old ought to. He smiled at me, but only with his mouth. 'Guess you've heard, love. Bob tell you?'

'Yes. Appalling. What's the paper say?'

'Well, there's still a ringfence around the Essex abattoir and farms in the area. Collapound's the first suspect here on the moor, though looks like there's another confirmed near Hatherleigh. But they say they've contained it, don't they, Dad?'

'Hatherleigh? But how? How did it get here?'

'Likely infected sheep or cows taken to the slaughterhouse in Essex from up north. Cumbria, Northumberland or somewhere. Guess a cattle lorry might have brought it back down here.' Bob passed his hand over his eyes. 'Yes, they're saying they've contained it... We'll see.'

'Or stock bought up at one of the markets upcountry somewhere. That's what they were saying this morning in Culverstock, Dad – bought-in stock. Enough people do it, though. Never had any trouble before. Probably won't come to anything.'

'Is it airborne or carried on clothes or cars or hooves or what?'

'They don't know, Tay, quite. There may not be any obvious connection or contaminate. Or it might be both. That's why it's not been eradicated. Always the chance of infected meat from abroad, too.'

'And animals from the north taken all the way to Essex?

God. Why?'

'No small slaughterhouses left. It's normal, love. The abattoir at Hatherleigh has deliveries from all over too. Hundreds of miles.'

I swallowed.

'Look.' Bob's finger jabbed the paper. 'They're talking of closing off the moor. And from this morning no movement of animals anywhere for a week. Not so bad for us, but some poor bastards'll suffer. No fodder left this time of year; grass-keep a quagmire and no cashflow to buy more feed.'

There was a look of despair in his eyes as he glanced at Guy. I couldn't bear it.

'But it's only a week, Bob.'

'Maybe, Tamar. Maybe.'

'Come off it, Dad. You're such an old bellyacher. Save your whingeing. It hasn't happened yet. Might just be scare-mongering. Keep us all quiet.'

Bob moved stiffly towards the radio for the six o'clock news. Big Ben, normally so comforting, seemed menacing tonight; the pause between the peal and the first stroke poignant. There are times when you feel that the darkness really is squatting just outside the door, maw agape, waiting to swallow you whole for the slightest transgression. Get a grip, Tamar. It's February, nadir of the year, and you're sick of rain and mud. That's all. And anyway March is only a couple of days away. Nothing's happened to us. Yet, said the little voice.

'...Foot and mouth has struck again. In the newest outbreak, at Hillsworthy in Devon, two thousand sheep have been slaughtered following confirmation, with a further two thousand one hundred belonging to the same farmer due for slaughter...'

We all stared at each other.

'Christ,' said Guy. 'Christ. Four thousand at one stroke. That

179

poor sod'll be getting legless tonight.'

'Not if he can't move off the farm. They've confined the Hatherleigh farmers and their families, haven't they?'

'Let's hope he's got some homebrew in then. Talking of beer: Dad? Mum? What would you like, love?'

'Cider for me, son. Cheers.' Trudy and I shook our heads. Trudy collected the enamel bowls to feed the cats and the dogs. I put the others' casserole and my jacket potato with a slice of last night's cheese and spinach pie in the top oven. Bob continued: 'We'd better go and stock up on disinfectant to do a footbath and a straw barrier at the end of the lane by the cattlegrid. That's what they're suggesting up in North Devon.'

'Yep. Everyone'll be in panic mode, stockpiling. Load of bloody old women, farmers when they're worrying.' Guy winked at me. 'You're as bad as the rest of them, Dad. It'll all blow over in time, you'll see. But if it keeps you happy I'll go in and get some disinfectant first thing.'

I found myself, as so often in this meat-eating family, torn between my loyalty to this kindly adoptive family of mine and my principles. I knew they cared for their animals, but it was the human costs they would count. And not unreasonably. But I wanted to scream. What about the animals? It had got to Devon now. Four thousand dead sheep already; how many more to go? What right did we have? What right, to put cash above welfare? And about that, as usual, I held my tongue. I loved these people.

But while the campaigner in me was rattling the gates, the journalist in me, I noticed, wanted the facts. At supper I couldn't hold my tongue.

'How serious is it?'

'You mean the disease, or the current situation?'

'Well, both, I suppose. How likely is another major

outbreak?'

Bob shrugged. 'Who can tell? They say they're confident they've caught it in time.'

'How many animals were killed in the last outbreak, Bob? It was the late '60s, wasn't it?'

''67. About four hundred thousand. Maybe more. And a few hundred in that minor outbreak on the Isle of Wight in '81. '67 was bad, lass.'

'Four hundred thousand? And there's no antidote?

Bob shook his head. 'Time, maybe. What farmer's got any to spare? Or cash resources? Hard enough as it is without having useless animals eating their heads off and you with no income. And there's always the spectre of another epidemic after the '81 crisis.'

'That won't happen again, Dad. They've learnt from it.'

'And anyway there's a vaccine, isn't there? Can't they vaccinate?'

'Won't. Can't sell the meat to Europe then. They say.'

'Didn't you say that the French and the Dutch vaccinate anyway?'

'So I've heard.'

'So isn't that a spurious argument?'

'Big Brother, Tamar. It's money that talks. And there are farmers who would rather have the compensation than useless live meat, it has to be said. If compensation's on the agenda, that is. They're not really talking much about that.'

'And us? Organic farmers?'

'We're not exempt from legislation, love.' Guy grimaced cynically. 'Depends on which way the wind blows.'

'What are the Soil Association saying?'

'Guy's right. The law may be an ass, but once it's spoken the law is the law. Hard to see what they'll say. It's early days. The

SA'll be pushing for preservation, and the preservation of rare breeds, for sure. My bet is that after a few more cases they'd start pushing the vaccine option.' Bob stared off out through the window at the black night. The rain was still sluicing. 'Need to move those lambing ewes back closer to the house again. Trouble is there's almost no grass in that home meadow, and the stream's burst.'

Trudy spoke. 'You're looking tired, dear. Shall we get an early night?'

He nodded briefly and looked back at me.

'Let's hope it doesn't come to that. But vaccination? Don't know what their line will be. Ultimately it's down to Nick Brown at the Min of Ag and his cronies though. And the NFU and Scudamore, the chief vet. Any one of those says shoot, they'll shoot. Shoot first, ask questions after.' Bob sighed heavily and turned his attention back to his plate, mopping up the juice with a piece of bread.

'Pudding, anyone?' said Trudy.

## Thirty-eight

Guy and I arrived in the yard at the same time; me from digging sodden vegetables for that night's supper, Guy in the Land Rover from town. He jumped down and let out the sheepdogs, who wove and danced around his feet, spattering mud on his jeans. 'Go on with you, Fly. Get out of it Jess. Hi darling; how are you? Seen Dad?'

'I think he's in the milk parlour. Or out with the young heifers.'

Guy kicked his boots off and dropped the bale of wire he had under his arm in the porch. 'No disinfectant. Whole bloody lot gone. I don't believe it – a couple of cases of blistered noses and people really are panicking. No more deliveries till next week.'

'How can you say that? You heard the news last night. Four thousand sheep slaughtered at Hillsworthy. That's not just a few blistered noses.'

He took my wet jacket and hung it beside his to drip onto the flagstones. 'Well, OK. Yes, that was bad.'

'More than bad. Terrible. Shocking.'

'But what's the point in panicking? It's probably only orf anyway. Plenty of that around. Doesn't hurt them. Mind you, nor does foot and mouth, usually.'

'How lethal is it?'

'Very few fatalities. They recover. – Hi, Mum. Want some tea?' Then over his shoulder to me: 'This bloody siege mentality. Melodrama. How the English love to panic.' He picked up the kettle. 'By the way I got you the mag you wanted. Is that your cover story? "Back to the Garden – one man's dream" – is that the piece on the Eden Project? – Like the title.'

'Oh, I think it's been used before. Thanks for remembering to get the mag.' I piled the vegetables in the sink and dried my hands to go and pick it up. 'So you don't think it's much of a problem?'

Guy put the kettle on and came over to drop an arm round my shoulders. 'What? Eden? Well, I wish I'd thought of it first... Oh, getting the magazine, you mean? We-ell, you can see me all right later... OK OK. You can put the breadknife away. Foot and mouth, you mean? Nah. Should be containable. Any writing done today? What about a piece on f and m?'

I swallowed my irritation at his blasé tone. It was a pattern between us – the more seriously I took things the more frivolous his response. I hated it. 'A bit. Any news from Culverstock?'

'Depends what you mean by news. The Farmers' Co-op's run out of sheepnuts. That Rebecca girl of Simon Mason's been running him around again. What does he expect, girl that age with an old fart like him. Someone's giving away a young cattle dog because he bit the head off a chicken. Sled Wilson pranged his car...'

'Guy! Stop messing. Take something seriously for once, for God's sake! I mean about FMD. As you well know.'

'Seriously? Everyone's taking it all far too seriously all ready! But since you ask. Not really. The National Park have banned walkers and riders. DCC closed all the footpaths last week, as you know. There's talk of culling the deer. And even the ponies.'

'Horses can't get it!'

'Of course not. They're not cloven-hooved! But they can carry it.'

'God. Of course. So they really are taking it seriously?'

'Well, they've got to look like they're taking precautions, haven't they?'

He took a mug out to find Bob. Ten minutes later they were both back. Guy's good humour had evaporated. Neither of them was

184

talking.

Trudy pushed the biscuit tin towards them. Bob shook his head.

'What's the matter, dear?'

'Collapound's confirmed.'

Nobody said anything for several minutes. I looked at Guy. You could hear a log spitting in the Aga.

'My God,' murmured Trudy. 'Poor Johnny, poor Rosie. They've only just had another baby, too, haven't they?'

'What will happen, Bob?'

Bob just shook his head. I could see Guy gearing up to make a crack of some sort. I narrowed my eyes at him. From the way he subsided I guessed the news had shaken him too.

For a few minutes Bob didn't seem able to speak. His cheeks were working. I could see him fighting himself and realised he was close to tears. I allowed in the knowledge that I loved this quiet gentle man, my father-in-law, enormously, and that I relied on him. And that I couldn't bear his dignified sadness. He had never treated me with anything other than kindness and respect, and he regarded my and Guy's privacy as of paramount importance; but we had, I knew, some unspoken understanding of each other.

He looked up at last, in control of himself. 'John May's been taken to hospital with heart trouble. The old boy.'

John was Johnny's father, and Bob's chess mate. He looked away again. 'And they're in there slaughtering now. You must have heard the shots.'

'They've lit the pyres up at Hillsworthy and Hatherleigh. You can see them in the distance from Culverstock.'

'Oh God. How awful. Many?'

'Yep. Thousands of animals blazing away. More to go.'

'On local radio they were saying they might have to cull the moorland ponies, just like you said.'

'Did you see Spotlight? The cameras had got Johnny and his brother making a straw and timber pyre. All those cow carcases piled up in the yard, where the kids can see them, streaming muck and blood. All bloated and stinking. Makes that Hirst fellow's sculpture look like a bloody tea-party.' Guy sniffed and rubbed his hand across his nose. 'Johnny there – big beefy Johnny – snivelling like a girl. He must have lost nearly a thousand head of stock, with all the sheep too. Guess they killed those out in the meadows.'

That sharp sick feeling again. We stood in the rain in the yard, Guy and I. Bob was between us sitting on the quad bike. No-one spoke for a bit. In a matter of days foot and mouth seemed to have become a permanent foreground spectre.

The rain poured down our necks. Fly was digging a hole in the yard, and we all watched him. Too much to say, and too little.

The rain had flattened my hair against my face.

'No point in standing out here getting soaked,' I said. 'Have you just come back from the top pastures, Bob?'

Bob nodded. 'Checking the ewes. Need to move them down but the pasture's still saturated. Going to give the Mays a ring to see how old John is. If we can do anything.' He hauled himself off the quad bike and stomped towards the house. We both looked after his departing back.

'Old misery-face. Anybody'd think he was the Ancient

Mariner, the way he goes round like a thundercloud.'

'He's sad, Guy. And distressed. He's not usually this miserable.'

'Face like a wet Welsh Sunday.'

'Well, he's getting on a bit. And John is his mate. Aren't you worried, too, with Collapound so close? – I had nightmares about it last night.'

He came round the bike and hugged me. 'You great softie.' He held me back from him and looked me in the eyes. He must have seen my anxiety because he was quiet for a moment before responding. 'OK, Tamar. You're really bothered, aren't you?'

'Of course I am!'

'OK, yes, of course I'm concerned. For us, but especially for the Mays.' He stared off across the fields towards Collapound. 'But what's the point in worrying? May never happen. Leave it alone till it does. Come on, I need some tea and some of that cake of Mum's.'

'Have you spoken to Johnny or Rosie since they heard?'

'Nope. But Dad said last night they were all confined to barracks. No school for the kids and no going out anywhere.'

'Hardly a holiday for them. I wonder whether we should offer to do some shopping?'

'What, and take it to them? Bring back f & m to our animals?'

'God, of course. Well, maybe we could leave some shopping at the foot of the lane.'

'Yep. Good idea. Come on, then. Let's go and catch Dad before he rings off.'

## Forty

I could smell the alcohol still on Guy's breath when we woke. He propped himself on an elbow and tickled my lips with his tongue. 'Well, Bo-Peep, no more nightmares about burning sheep, I hope?'

I snapped. 'How can you joke about it, Guy?'

'Better laugh than cry, sweetheart. But I'm sorry you're upset. Would you like me to help you forget it?'

Which of us needed oblivion? I'd noticed how much he'd drunk last night, sitting by the fire after supper in front of the TV. We'd disappeared off to our little sitting room beneath my study, the one whose window framed the great Cedar of Lebanon at the back of the house, beyond which rose the slopes of Wolf Tor. We rarely got the chance to spend time alone, and I'd hoped we might forget about it all and talk about something else, maybe listen to music, watch a film or read a book or play backgammon or something. Something normal. But he'd put the TV on and watched the news bulletins ad nauseam.

He was still watching me. His mouth twitched at the corners.

I reminded myself that sometimes he teased when he was too upset himself to voice it. Nonetheless it made him distant from me. I felt obscurely guilty at the thought. 'What did you have in mind?' I responded, as I knew he wanted me to.

'We-ell,' he drawled. 'What about starting with – this? And this? And this?'

Afterwards we lay for longer than usual and watched the grey light start to creep through the uncurtained windows. The rain had died to a low murmur.

'Seven-ish, I guess. Soon be time to put the clocks forward. That'll feel better. The equinox.'

'Mmm. What are you doing today, love?'

'I've got that piece to finish on the watermill and gardens at Trescarrow for Rural Life. I was going to spend the next couple of days tailing the vet – do you remember? – for that other feature. But he's probably been called up for MAFF testing. Must ring him and find out. Anyway this afternoon I'll go into the library maybe – I said I'd drop Trudy into town for her dental appointment. What about you?'

'Got to check some equipment. Gear up for lambing. Ought to trim some feet, too.'

'What, in this weather?'

'Well, we're not likely to suddenly hit a heatwave, are we? The farming life, Tay. You should know by now.'

'Shall I pick up that stuff for Rosie and Johnny? She needed nappies and sterilising fluid pretty desperately. And the usual shopping.'

'Assuming it's OK to drop them at the lane end. – Hey, don't do that, or I might have to seduce you all over again... Do that again!' He launched himself across the bed at me. I evaded him, more nimbly than I thought possible. '– Oh, shame... Oh, Dad needs to borrow the car this morning to go to hospital to see John, don't forget.'

'Get off, Guy; let me get dressed. Is he likely to pull through?'

'Who?'

'John of course.'

'Sounds like it if he can have visitors.'

'Did they say so, then?'

'Stop worrying and start living, darling. Come on. If you don't get into those clothes right now I'll take you back to bed for the rest of the morning...'

## Forty-one

I remember that morning; not because it was significant in itself, but because it was, although we didn't know it, almost the last small patch of calmness before the storm that was to demolish or uproot everything in our lives.

By mid-March several things had happened.

The epidemic – for it had now become one – had developed into a major and unprecedented disaster. Farm tracks, lanes, supermarkets and garages all had their straw-bed disinfectant baths at entrance and exit.

The government was panicking, changing their approach by the day.

MAFF was clearly out of control. The army had been drafted in to help with the slaughter and disposal of corpses; the backlog was such that some farms had hundreds of piled bodies rotting in the mud by hedges or gates, or decomposing, heaped in the barns where they'd been slaughtered. Farmers could do nothing but wait in impotent anguish for disposal, imprisoned in their own farms, their livelihood shot to pieces on the results of a piece of paper.

The daffodils were in flower.

In appalling contrast death was everywhere. It was impossible to escape from the stench; either from the carcases or from the blackish smoke-drenched winds. Across the horizon on every side, including, now, Cornwall, plumed thick smoke. A drive into Culverstock or Moorhampton revealed pairs of white-clad men cornering sheep, heifers, bullocks in field gateways or driving them into makeshift pens.

By the equinox they'd slaughtered nearly thirty thousand Devon animals, an almost unimaginable figure, even when you heard or saw the evidence. Throughout the day and night pyres burnt and burnt.

Despite much pressure on the government from farmers, vets and groups such as the Soil Association, little was being done to implement any kind of vaccination programme. MAFF dithered.

We all cut our trips away from the farm to an absolute minimum. Supplies and mail were left in a makeshift shelter at the end of the track. Despite the rain, we took to leaving the car there too and walking back and forth. I found myself learning to keep my eyes on the track at my feet rather than, as I had in morbid fascination to start with, scanning the horizon for new pyres.

Guy, a pint-a-night man, seemed to be drinking more than usual every evening.

John May had had a relapse. By the time the cattle from his and his son's farm had been disposed of he was dead, and Bob had lost a good neighbour and his chess game; and a little more of his spirit.

The rain continued.

*

The farm adjoining ours was given a contiguous cull notice, as a result of being within three kilometres of the Mays' farm. Terry Maddocks, a man not known for his docility, barricaded the gates and refused anyone entry, even the vets. With his two solid sons he paraded his shotguns and dogs belligerently throughout the day and night after being given notice. His wife Ginny, a bony nervous woman, didn't emerge from the house.

Bob rang them. ('Bit of solidarity. He must be feeling desperate.')

'Tell him I'll come and join him with my pick handle and axe if he needs back-up,' Guy told him.

Terry was nearly inarticulate with rage and frustration. 'Them – bleedin' – motherfuckers – don't know their arses from their bleedin' elbows – over my dead body are they going to bleedin' cull – over my dead body – all I ask is three more days. Give me three more days. Three bleedin' days, that's all. Time enough to get the results.'

They didn't give him his three days. The next morning early Bob had a call from Terry, breathing so hard he could barely speak. 'They're 'ere, Bob – all the crowd – '

'Who, Terry?'

'Whole bleedin' lot – arsing around with their trucks at the effing gates. Police an' all. The – whole crew. Don't stand – a bleedin' – chance now.'

'Do you want us to come over?'

'What the – bleedin' hell – what am I going to do?'

'I don't think there's much you can do, Terry. I'll come over if you want, give you a bit of moral support, but even if your tests come back negative they'll cull. You're within radius. Nothing you can do. At least you showed them that you won't just lie down.'

'Storming of the bloody Bastille. Nah, I'll show 'em. Here goes, mate. Ta for listening.'

'Give me a call, Terry. Anything I can do. I'm sorry.'

Bob put the phone down. 'Poor fellow. Brave front, but they got him in the end. All he managed to do was stall them, buy forty-eight hours' grace. Sounded like Ginny was crying, in the background.'

Trudy took her glasses off. 'I'll give her a ring in an hour or two. Might not be anything else we can do.'

'How many's he got, Dad?'

'Maybe a thousand head. Eleven hundred. Mostly sheep but a couple of hundred cows and bullocks.'

'Shit,' said Guy. 'Us next, d'you think?'

Bob didn't answer. He got up and quietly put his coat and boots on, opened the back door into the yard and stood there for several minutes, staring out at the rain, before stepping through into it and closing the door behind him. I watched his hunched shadow pass across the scullery window towards the barns.

The next day we had the vets in to check our stock. We were out of the contiguous cull area – just about – but were served a 'D' notice which meant that we couldn't move our stock off the farm for sale, or buy in. The government-designated vets would be checking on us every other day.

The bottom pastures stayed waterlogged and impassable. The higher pastures had better drainage, but were exposed to all the winter weather. By the time that lambing started not only had the rain turned to hail and sleet, but, worse, the government had forbidden all movement of animals even from field to field within a farm if that movement involved crossing a public byway. If we had been just a day earlier moving our sheep down there wouldn't have been a problem; but there hadn't been anywhere they could go that wasn't waterlogged, and the barns were taken up with the cattle. Now we couldn't move the sheep at all, as the lower pastures on the slopes of Wolf Tor were only accessible by the lane to Culverstock that skirted the tor. It was possible to apply for a licence, but that might take up to three weeks to process, we were told.

'The only option we've got, as I see it,' Bob told Guy, 'is to build some makeshift shelters up there.'

'Far too much wind up there, Dad. The walls don't break it and there's no trees for shelter. Can't see how we can expect anything to stay upright up there.'

'I can't cull, Guy. That's the only other option. Can't see any of the lambs surviving this –' he gestured towards the window – 'and it'll weaken the mothers too. That's what some people are doing – welfare grounds. Can't bring myself to think about it, personally.'

'We're not at that stage yet, Dad. There may be a break in the weather, too. Worry about it when it happens.'

'The Pencarrows hired a marquee.'

'A marquee for lambing bloody sheep? Must have cost them an arm and a leg. What did they do, remortgage their fleet of Mercedes?'

'Worth finding out. If the pegs will hold in all that mud.'

But the contractors couldn't help. Their marquees were either out or being overhauled; they weren't allowed to travel onto farms in the area at the moment anyway; and they doubted very much that they'd be able to erect one in the winds we were having; nor, they thought, would the pegs hold given the condition of the ground and the level of exposure we were talking about up there on the slopes of the tor.

Bob and Guy were utterly exhausted. They took it in turns to do the night vigil with the lambing ewes, taking the quad bike and a Thermos up through the storms to the high pastures.

I came down early one morning and they were both in the kitchen. Guy had obviously been drinking; thumping his fist belligerently on the table at the farming news on the radio. Bob was just sitting quietly, as was his wont, head propped on his hand by the Aga. Both men were saturated, wet weather gear strewn all over the backs of chairs and various surfaces.

'What's fucking Brown and his limp-wristed cronies know about farming? Shut in their warm fucking offices. Balls to them. Lost more fucking lambs than we saved last night. So far the innings is about two to one dead,' he shouted. 'What's he know about that?'

194

'Let it go, Guy,' Bob counselled. 'It's a tough job he has. I wouldn't like it.'

'But did you hear that? Mass cull in Devon? How the hell are any of us going to come out of this fucking mess alive? Load of wankers. Load of effing wankers! I'm going back up the hill.'

He threw his waterproofs on and stormed out of the house. We heard him cursing as he crossed the yard.

Bob managed a wry smile. 'Did you know you'd married a temper, Tamar? – We never thought he had one until lately.'

'No, me neither. He never used to swear, either. Stress.'

'Eliot did all the temperamental stuff when they were younger. Artistic, he is. Always thought Guy would be stable and solid and quiet.'

'Well, he is, normally, isn't he? It's hard for him to face the possibility of – losing everything. You too. You must be completely wiped out, Bob. Can I make you some breakfast?'

'Love it, Tamar. Thanks, love. Trudy out doing the hens?'

'Think so. Or lighting the fire next door. Tea and toast and eggs?'

'Grand. You're a good woman. Hope Guy knows how lucky he is.'

I smiled. 'Thanks, Bob. He's a good man, too.'

## Forty-two

The thing about trauma is that in the event you don't think about how different life might be. It wasn't only that I didn't ever have time to imagine how my life might have turned out if I'd stayed in France; or if I'd married someone other than Guy – or if I'd married, say, a photographer; or editor or explorer rather than a farmer; or if I'd not married. It's true that there wasn't time; but in trauma the events are so all-absorbing that past and present might as well not exist. I didn't think about anything other than the trouble that was exploding all around us, and how we might all survive it.

There are moments when intuition and premonition are linked, and you know without doubt that something must happen. An old part of the brain kicks in, and you simply act on your instincts.

Did I know that the net was about to close in on us? Perhaps it was just that we woke to the single late March day that offered a clear sky and a flicker of sunshine, and cabin fever had set in. Whatever, I spent fifteen minutes persuading Guy that we desperately needed a day away from the farm. Three weeks would have been more like it; but three weeks would have been out of the question. Even a weekend was inconceivable – at any time of the farming year, but especially now. And Guy would in any case be hell, kicking his heels on holiday, lost without the routine of the agricultural day.

'I can't,' was his immediate reaction. 'You know I can't, Tay. Dad needs me here.'

Days off together were practically unheard of in our married life; Guy was a conscientious man who took his responsibilities very seriously. So it took a fair amount of effort to twist his arm. In the end I pointed out that since he'd done the night lambing watch Bob would in any case expect to take the bulk of the day's responsibilities himself; that was how the two of them worked it. That didn't really carry much weight, so I rather unfairly pulled the trump card.

'I can't hack this much longer, Guy. I really need to see you, to spend some time together, to talk about things that don't involve foot and mouth or MAFF's latest blunder or the weather or the dwindling stocks of fodder.'

'What things?' Guy suddenly looked alarmed.

'Oh, nothing in particular. No need to look so anxious, darling! I just feel we've lost sight of each other lately.'

'How can you say that, Tay? I see you every day; most mealtimes too. More than most couples.'

'That's not what I mean, Guy.' Did I really have to explain? 'We hardly ever get time just to ourselves; to each other.'

'But we've had several evenings in our sitting room on our own recently.'

'Us and the TV.'

'What do you want to talk about?'

I sighed. 'I just want to talk, Guy. I have foot and mouth all day and then foot and mouth all evening on the TV too –'

'I'm a farmer, Tay. I need to know what's happening.'

'I know that. I just feel we both need a break from it, that's all.'

'And you know we shouldn't be driving more than necessary. How would we both feel if we brought it back from somewhere?'

'Maybe we need to balance the chances of that happening against our marriage, Guy.'

'That sounds like a threat, Tamar. Are you saying I'm not enough for you? Aren't you happy with what we've got? I can't do any more than I do for you, Tay.'

197

I couldn't admit that actually no, I wasn't very happy. I guessed that none of us was, right now. How could we be, with the present difficulties and the future so uncertain?

'I just want to get away for a few hours. Please, Guy. I don't often ask. We can go somewhere where foot and mouth isn't a problem.'

'Like?'

'Oh, I don't know. The coast? What about Boscastle?'

I could see him thinking. I knew we could take a route that skirted all possible foot and mouth areas. I opened my mouth to forestall his objection, but he surprised me.

'OK. If you insist. Let's go. As long as we're back before dark.' As he talked he pulled a jumper on over his jeans: his moss-green one that I'd got for his birthday rather than his usual tatty old Guernsey that he habitually put on under his overalls. I noticed, as I always did, how well that colour suited him: brought out the green in his hazel eyes. His head emerged, hair awry, and he smiled at me. 'You're right, Tay. Time out. You win. D'you still love me?'

There was a new puffiness under his eyes. I was aware of a pang as I looked at his familiar face: kind eyes, generous mouth.

'Of course,' I said. 'Of course.'


Our motives for everything are so mixed, aren't they. He was a good man: a good, kind, decent, caring man who lived in as honest a way as he could. I knew he wouldn't let me down. I knew I could trust him. He would also, had things been different, have made a fabulous father.

We had things in common: Dartmoor, a passionate interest in animals and the land, an appreciation of a way of life not founded solely on commercialism and consumerism. I already felt part of the Delaney family. In the first year or two of my time on the farm we seemed simply to gravitate towards each other. We laughed, and time together was easy.

I wasn't thinking romantically. It wasn't like that with Guy, though he was romantic in his own way. I imagine, if I'd thought about it, that I would have said that I was happy just being single. Certainly I was wary of relationship, after Mark and then Oliver. So when I realised Guy was in love with me, for a long time I shied away. I see now he employed the same tactics with me he employed with animals – a gentle, consistent, unthreatening but unrelenting forward movement. And it worked. So we might not have had a wild passion, but we did have a deep affection for each other, and we were also friends. The best basis for permanent relationship, I told myself. Mum concurred. Louise liked him. I needed stability. He needed me.

As we sprayed our boots and then the car tyres with the disinfectant bottle at the end of the track, as we did every time we entered and left the farm now, straw bed notwithstanding, I had the sense that we were making a break for freedom.

'I know we're lucky, compared to some,' I observed to Guy, 'but still there's a sense of siege in the air, isn't there? – I feel as if we're doing something wicked, escaping for the day.'

Boscastle was exactly what I needed. We walked out alongside the harbour – clear green water – and up onto the cliffs. Though the little harbour was sheltered, the ocean was torn and choppy, great gunmetal waves assaulting the rocks, seabirds keening above. The cliffs were dotted with kittiwakes and jackdaws pressed back against the rockface.

We followed the coast path in single file. The wind was too wild to talk, and I revelled in that kind of internal stillness that is only possible when you are caught up in the elemental world;

when you forget your humanness. The wind filled my head and I felt a sense of crazy freedom; I wanted to shout and dance. I hadn't realised before quite how oppressed I'd felt lately.

In Tintagel we found a small out-of-season teashop and warmed our hands on mugs of tea. The teacakes were home-made and spicy.

'God, these are good,' said Guy. 'More? I could eat that all over again. Or maybe the hot apple cake this time? Hey, Tamar, you look great with some colour in your cheeks and your hair all mussed.' He stretched across and patted my hand. 'You were right, love. We needed a day out. Ought to get moving again soon though. I wonder if they're licensed? Could do with a beer first.'

I have a photo – two – we took of each other on the pier of Boscastle Harbour. ('Holiday!' He'd said, picking up the camera as we left. 'Need to record this; just so you can't say we never do.') Guy's in his grey fleecy jacket with a scarf around his neck. He's smiling; his smile helped, I suspected, by the three pints he'd swiftly downed in the pub nearby. He also looks older – more like a man in his forties; his hair thinning slightly. I'm sitting looking out to sea and the wind's coming at me. My hair, still its dark chestnut, is quite short, curls tugged across my face in the gusts. I'm wearing jeans and wellies, and my green woollen jacket is open over a plain sweater. All I ever seemed to wear on the farm were jeans and sweaters. Gone was the starchild look, the mass of hair, the sarongs and swirly skirts and bright colours. Looking back I can see too how the intervening years had worn me a little ragged. There's a shadowed look in my face, somehow, and with my shorter hair I look altogether more sober and sensible.

'God, you're going to have to drive, Tay. Sorry. Bit pissed. Went straight to my head. Guess I'm tired after last night.'

Dark was closing in. The outlines of the tors on Bodmin

Moor shaped the southwestern horizon; soon Dartmoor would appear to the front and on our left. At our backs Venus had just lifted into visibility. I'd forgotten what stars looked like, with all the low closed skies we'd had for as long as I could remember.

I put the lights on.

'I'm a bit concerned about Mum and Dad,' Guy said suddenly.

'Mmmm?' I was careful, these days, how I responded on the rare occasions when Guy talked about feelings. Anything other than an unemotional neutrality in my voice prompted him to declare me over-reactive, and to then close down or take refuge in frivolity.

'Mum just seems, I don't know, more and more withdrawn somehow. I remember her being much more fun when I was young. Guess maybe – Eliot – she's been, you know, a bit more kind of quiet since then. And Dad seems so depressed sometimes.'

'Well, they're getting older, love. People do get quieter as they age. More introverted. And life's hardly been a bundle of fun lately.'

'I've been wondering whether' – he looked sideways at me, sheepishly – 'whether we should umm send them on holiday maybe?'

'Guy Delaney! You bloody hypocrite! You don't believe in holidays!'

He had the grace to grin rather shamefacedly. 'Yeah OK. But even I can see that they need something. I don't mean now, obviously. But maybe in the summer for a couple of days? When all this is over?'

'Where would they go? I know Bob used to travel a bit but I'm not sure I can see it, nonetheless. They're grafted onto Culver.'

'I wondered about Mum's sister Gwen. Couple of days in Oxford; Stratford maybe. Something different. Or maybe even to Ireland to stay with Dad's brother? Home from home, as he farms too. Have a chinwag. They could fly from Plymouth. Or Bristol maybe. Think it's only around a hundred quid. Less, even...'

'Oh Guy, you dreamer. Great idea. They'll never go though. But we could ask them... What about us? Would you consider leaving Culver for a few days?'

'Dunno. I'm worried about it all, truth be told. About farming and about the farm.'

'Thought you didn't take the current crisis too seriously?'

'Well, somebody's got to keep a spark of humour round here. But I don't know what would happen if – wasn't that our turning?'

'Who's driving this car?'

'Sorry. Anyway. Won't happen.'

'D'you think it might?'

'About as much chance of that as of you getting pregnant.'

'God, Guy, that hurt.' I'd heard the bitterness in his voice. I drew a breath. I knew he wasn't getting at me. 'Does that still bug you?'

'Sorry. Of course it does, Tay. How could it not? I wanted children. I wanted our children. And anyway no bloke likes to think he's firing blanks.'

I reached my hand to his knee. 'We've other things, sweetheart. We'd have even less time together if we had kids. And it doesn't make any difference to my feelings for you. And "firing blanks" is such a gross way to put it!'

'Yeah, well.' I sensed rather than saw his head turn away towards the window and the night.

I didn't know what else to say to make him feel better. The

silence drew on, mile after mile.

'Music?' I asked, eventually. I felt his shrug, but he bent to the box of tapes at his feet. The car filled with Bach. I knew that was for me. He'd have chosen rock.

'Let's go and get some chips in Launceston, shall we?'

'You still hungry?'

'Not really. Just seems like a day-out-ish thing to do.'

'Yeah, OK. If we wait till we get to Culverstock we can pick up some fish and chips to take back to Mum and Dad too. And a bottle of something.'

'OK. Lovely idea.'

## Forty-three

'Guy,' said Bob after supper. 'Something we need to do. A word?'
He stood up and he and Guy went through to Bob and Trudy's
sitting room.

Trudy and I looked at each other. We also stood up,
simultaneously, and started to clear the plates and wine glasses.
'Nice to have a drink,' said Trudy. 'We don't seem to drink much,
Bob and I.'

I wondered if the comment was loaded, but decided not.
God, I'm getting paranoid.

'Though it's a blessing, sometimes,' she continued
conversationally, sweeping crumbs into her hand and dropping
them into the dog bowl. 'Stops me from picking all that blessed
interference up in the airwaves.' She smiled at herself and looked
up at me. 'So to speak. My head doesn't half feel cluttered much
of the time. They call it a "gift" but it's often a curse.'

I looked at her enquiringly.

'You know what I'm talking about, Tay, don't you? I
sometimes wonder if you don't have a touch of it yourself. I knew
you were going to persuade Guy to have a day off today; and you
knew why you needed to, don't you?'

'Oh, I was feeling really shut in. He looks so strained, too.
And Bob. So tired.'

'Well, might have been your last chance, today. I've a feeling
things are going to change fast now.'

I looked at her with some alarm. Her face didn't look any
different, and she carried on stacking dishes on the counter top,
emptying teabags from the pot into the compost bucket, filling
the washing up bowl.

'What do you mean, Trudy?'

She shrugged. 'Our turn's coming, I think, Tamar. I'm glad

you managed to get Guy out. Do him good. Glad that the wine loosened Bob's tongue, too, a little.'

'He even cracked a joke!'

'He's a good man in a storm, Bob. I was lucky when I met him. I need him, you know.' She sniffed and put the radio on, thus signalling the end of the unaccustomed moment of confidences.

'Guy and I were wondering whether we might persuade you both to take a little break sometime? Maybe in the summer? We couldn't remember when you last went away. Isn't it your wedding anniversary soon?'

'Thirty-nine years.' She smiled wistfully. 'Gone in a tick. But a holiday? We'll see, Tamar. Hard to get Bob away.'

I nearly said that it was harder still to get her away, but thought better of it. I didn't remember any occasion in my time at Culver when she'd spent even so much as a night away.

Thirty-nine years. I tried, and failed, to imagine how it would be to be married to Guy for that long. I couldn't quite give a shape to the future in my imagination; probably because of the current uncertainty.

My mind registered continuing uneasiness. I returned to what Trudy had just hinted at, before we spoke of holidays. I opened my mouth to pick up on it: what did she mean, things were about to change? – but when I glanced at her face I saw that the conversation was closed.

We worked side-by-side in what was, for us, a reasonably comfortable companionable silence. Easy domestic stuff. Trudy was boiling dishcloths and teatowels, labelling a couple of tubs of leek and potato and apple and parsnip soup to be frozen, and sorting through the freezer to make room. I was mixing a batch of dough, ready to rise above the Aga and be kneaded last thing to leave to rise again overnight. I hadn't ever grown out of the pleasure of preparing bread ready to be baked first thing the next day.

'I don't know why you don't use the Mouli,' said Trudy. 'I shouldn't have thought that your feminist ideas would allow it, hand-kneading. We have the technology to free women these days, you know! Here, do you want some rosemary?'

It seemed to be a day for confidences. 'The first time I met you, Trudy, you told me about rosemary – how you used the ointment as a universal panacea. That must be thirteen or fourteen years ago, now. Yes, please. Is there one of the little red onions in that basket still? – Thanks. I just really like making bread by hand. Guy offered to get me a breadmaker, but it's just not the same.

'I remember the day. It was the first time I came to Culver; Bob was telling me about apple trees. It all seemed so idyllic. God, Guy was still at college, and I was already grown up. I could never have imagined I'd end up living here. You brought out warm scones and gooseberry and elderflower jam.'

'Fancy you remembering that,' Trudy's voice was soft. 'If it was fourteen years ago Eliot must still have been here...'

'I think he was away on the day I came. I didn't meet him, anyway.' I felt almost shocked, hearing her speak of him, and so soon after Guy had mentioned him too. As if they'd both broken a taboo. No-one normally ever said his name. Strange, the things that crisis brings to the surface.

That niggling sense again. Something disturbing.

'Trudy –' I said, then stopped. I couldn't ask her.

Trudy glanced swiftly at me then looked down at the vegetable basket in her hands. I thought for an instant that she was about to say more; but then the phone rang and the moment passed.

'The men are late,' I said what seemed like hours afterwards. 'I didn't hear them leave the house, but I guess they must have done, ages ago.' I looked up from the photos and papers I was going through. My current piece had grown out of the water-garden piece I did on Trescarrow – the same editor wanted a series on working waterwheels in Devon and Cornwall. 'Did they go up to the sheep?'

Trudy looked up at me over her glasses. She was working on slender needles and soft fine wool, turning the collar on a little jumper she was knitting for Johnny and Rosie's new baby. 'Oh no,' she said. 'They'll have gone up to Betty Woodman's.'

'Betty's? What do you mean? How can they have done? She's been culled. They wouldn't do that.'

'I think they have, dear,' she said enigmatically, and carried on counting stitches.

I knew better than to push Trudy for an answer. I felt a momentary flash of something approaching anger. We'd had what was for us quite an intimate conversation; and then once again the blinds were pulled down. Moments like this I felt like the outsider I was; and, in some ways, always would be. I fought an adolescent urge to slam back my chair and storm upstairs. I made myself bend my head again to my research, while my mind somersaulted. What on earth had they gone to Betty's for? And why the secrecy?

I was in bed when, hours later, I heard the loo flush and the shower running.

Guy groped his way towards the bed.

'I'm awake.'

'It's late. You should be asleep. Did you set the alarm?'

'For the night watch, you mean? No. I didn't know where you were, did I?'

207

'You know I set it for three on my nights on.'

'For all I knew you were already up with the sheep. Where did you go?'

'Betty Woodman's.'

'That's what Trudy said. But why? That was a stupid risk, Guy. You're crazy. Why on earth?'

'Tell you in the morning.'

'No. Tell me now.'

'I need some sleep, Tay. Get off my back.'

'How do you expect me to sleep now?'

'OK OK. We went up to put a tarp on her hayrick, OK?'

'A tarp on her hayrick?'

'Barn roof blew off last night in those gales. She's on her own, Tay. That would have been all her fodder wrecked else.'

'What? But she's been culled! There's nothing to feed the hay to! For God's sake Guy! What's the matter with you Delaney men? It's illegal, apart from pointless, apart from stupidly dangerous – entering a recently-culled farm! It's the highest risk category! Have they burnt them yet?' Trudy's words replayed in my head: Our turn's coming. I felt afraid.

Guy was silent. I felt him turn over, bury his head in the pillow. I lay there, my mind spinning. I couldn't believe what he'd done.

'Guy?'

At length he spoke. 'What d'you expect me to do? I can't kick someone when they're already down. No-one else would help.'

'But why?'

'Because her hay's the only chance of a bit of income she has left!' He was nearly shouting.

'But you're prepared to put Culver at risk for that? Everything we've got?'

208

'Yep. Hope some bugger'd do the same for me if I needed it.'
I could have sworn his voice had a break in it. Simultaneously
with my sense of fear and outrage was a sense of huge and
disconcerting tenderness. I told you he was a good man. I loved
these two men for what they'd just done, even though my mind
could scarcely encompass the level of risk they'd just taken.

'Is that why you went after dark?'

'What?'

'Because if you were reported the authorities'd have you ten
times over.'

'Dad's idea. Couldn't say no.'

'Have they disposed of the carcases, then?'

'Nope.'

'What do you mean, "nope"? They're not still there?'

Silence.

'GUY? Where are the carcases?'

Silence.

'Guy!'

Now I was sure he was sobbing. I couldn't remember having
ever heard Guy cry. I was shocked into numbness.

Then anger surged up again. 'Answer me, for God's sake! It's
my business, too!'

'Outside in the yard. Piled against the kitchen wall.'

'Christ almighty –'

I could barely hear him. 'Hold me, Tay. Please.' He was
shaking. 'The stench. I can't tell you. She's in her seventies, Tay.
It's her life's work. The stench. She's on her own –' He tailed off.

I held him.

'They've been there two weeks waiting disposal. She can't go
out. Tay, there's blood –' a great gulping sob – 'there's blood
from the carcases running under her kitchen door. We couldn't
not go.'

# Forty-four

I don't remember any details of the next three interminable weeks. I do remember, however, the feeling of doom.

'Did you know, Trudy, what they were going to do?' I asked the next morning.

'Depends what you mean by "know", dear. They didn't discuss it with me, no.'

'You mean Bob didn't even mention it?'

'That's right.' She stared at me levelly.

'Would you have let them go up there if you'd known?'

'I did know.'

I ignored that. 'I mean if they'd told you in any normal way.' I couldn't stop the edge to my voice.

She ignored my words, in her turn. 'I can't stop them, any more than you can.'

'But at what price! The risk!'

'Yes.' Lips tight. Conversation closed.

The phone. I took it.

'That was the vets'. They'll be up a bit later.'

'Remind Guy they need to tell them to take a look at the shearlings. He's on today. Bob'll be out there too, though, no doubt. He's worried sick. They're up to their bellies in mud and there's nowhere else to put them. They'll starve; or drown. If we don't get permission to move them soon it may mean a welfare cull on the RSPCA.'

I looked at her. Trudy wasn't given to melodramatics. The reality of the situation, even without our contracting the disease, began to hit home for me. I went cold. 'OK,' I said, simply.

It must have been a couple of days later that Guy came in looking haggard. 'Two of the heifers are limping.' He threw himself into a chair. His eyes were wild. 'That's not all. The vet thinks he's found a lesion in one of the yearling ram lambs.'

Trudy and I stared at him in horror, digesting this information.

'And two of the shearlings down in the home meadow are dead and the rest look terrible.'

'Dead? Dear God. Has it happened, then?'

'It can't have happened overnight –' Trudy and I spoke together.

'No grass; too much rain; too cold. Just a mudbath. No sodding chance. The shearlings, I mean.'

Guy stood up again and paced to the window, shoving his hands in his pockets. 'For the rest, God knows. Dad's up there now. They're testing again. He's talking about slaughter. On suspicion. The vet.' He swung round to face us both. 'Before the results. He says. This is it. Yep. Our turn. I need a beer.' He reached up to lift a pint glass from the hook on the beam, then strode into the larder. I heard him yank the lid off the homebrew bin and plunge the glass in.

'But it can't have been that quick –' I said, as he returned, wiping the glass with his hand and licking the froth off his fingers. 'It was only a couple of nights ago –'

'Not from Betty's. No. 'Course not.'

'How does he know the lesion's not orf?'

'He doesn't. Says he can't take risks.' He turned back to the window abruptly. 'Out of control in the county now. Over a quarter of a million carcases to be burnt still and thousands to slaughter.'

'But surely –' Trudy whispered. She was white. 'But surely we get twenty-one days?'

'What for?'

'From suspicion. I mean if no animal develops foot and

mouth from the initial suspicion? Aren't they spared?'

'Depends. We're too close to infected farms.'

'But they're your father's whole life –'

'And mine, Mum. And mine.' He tipped his glass to his mouth.

I couldn't speak. I could feel panic rising, a white acid heat. All those animals. MyGodMyGodMyGod.

Guy finished the beer and strode out to the scullery to pull his boots on. 'Going to find Dad,' he said gruffly, and slammed the door.

Bob moved like an old man. He bent to pull his boots off, one by one. His face was grey and gaunt, and he wouldn't catch our eyes. He slumped into the chair by the Aga.

'Guy told us,' I said. 'I'm – so desperately sorry, Bob.' Pitifully inadequate words.

He nodded, eyes fixed on Fly at his feet.

'What will happen?'

'Don't know, lass. Where's Guy?'

'Upstairs. D'you want something to eat?'

'Not much of an appetite. Thanks.'

I wanted to ask him what the vet had said, when we'd know, what the chances were, but his silence was dreadful. Forbidding. I glanced at Trudy. She was watching him, her lips moving slightly. It felt very private.

'I'll get some vegetables,' I said. I couldn't think what else to do.

## Forty-five

I don't think I'll use the words 'agony', 'despair' and 'turmoil' in the casual way I used to ever again. I realised during that period how privileged my life had been, and that only once in my thirty-seven years had I ever really suffered agony, and that was on hearing of Mark's death. And to a lesser extent in the wake of Oliver's disappearance – for disappear he did, silently and untraceably.

In both cases it was my suffering that was paramount.

It's quite a different thing watching people you love slide inexorably further and further into desolation.

You could be forgiven for thinking that the government was playing a cat and mouse game with us. It was impossible to think clearly in the next few weeks; in fact it was impossible to think at all.

We were under siege: imprisoned and hopeless. To start with, we simply didn't know from day-to-day what was going to happen – were we due for slaughter, or not? We lived on our nerves and litres of tea.

Later, we all seemed to fall into that kind of apathy that I gather happens to caged laboratory dogs: electric shocks are sent through the floor bars on one side, so the dog moves. Then the charge is switched to the other side, so the dog moves back. The next stage, though, is random charges. Eventually, in despair, the dog gives up trying to avoid the electric shocks and simply lies down and takes it.

Early April now. The slaughtermen were due to arrive on Tuesday morning at nine o'clock. Nine o'clock came and went. Ten o'clock. No-one and nothing. Then a call at noon to say it would be two-ish. No-one that day, or the next.

Bob and Guy took it in turns to call the vet, MAFF, the county council helpline, the Farm Crisis Network line. Then all of them over again.

No-one could answer with any certainty.

- There was a backlog.

- They were going to wait for results.

- They weren't going to wait for results.

- They'd get to us as soon as they could.

- We weren't a priority as we weren't confirmed.

- Yes, they knew we weren't allowed any movement on or off.

- Yes, they were in any case looking into a welfare cull on the shearlings if they could find a haulier.

- No, they couldn't after all transport the lambs for cull as the abbatoir was waiting for clearance.

- Yes, they slaughtered cattle on site but currently sheep were taken away if it was a welfare cull.

- No, no-one could visit the premises except to slaughter.

- No, we weren't after all a priority as the farm was isolated and no longer adjoining anyone with any stock, diseased or otherwise.

- The virus spread up to three kilometres.

- The virus only spread for a kilometre.

- Dead animals were safe animals.

- The virus wasn't destroyed by burning.

- Yes, it could be carried by humans, birds, animals, dead or alive, the wind.

- No, it couldn't.


In other words, no-one had any idea what they were doing.

Various farmers we knew faced bankruptcy. Various were at

the limit of their borrowing: the banks on their backs as well as MAFF.

The rain continued.

On a towel in an apple box by the Aga were today's three tiny lambs, more dead than alive.

So far we'd continued to lose more lambs than we'd saved. Bob and Guy had dragged these three out of mud in the top pastures at dawn, sodden rags. The mother of the twins was dead; the other mother simply too weak to feed hers. The dead one had to stay where she'd fallen, for foxes to find her; another one of this season's many casualties. As it was the men technically shouldn't have brought these lambs back – wrapped in Guy's coat – as it involved the lane; but you'd have to be a monster to leave new young life to simply die. They were probably the only glimmer of hope any of us had.

'It's a bastard,' said Guy. 'Dear Jesus. You save them, knowing full well that they might be shot in a day or two anyway. But what can you do?'

Trudy sat and looked at the milk powder, jug, bottles and teats piled at the back of the Aga. 'This time of year I pray for it to end, normally, this feeding every couple of hours. Right now I'd give anything for these three little ones to stay alive, I'd feed them round the clock if I had to, sleep or no sleep.'

Bob said very little; hunched and grey in his chair by the Aga, he drank mug after mug of tea and stared at nothing.

## Forty-six

I was beginning to feel concerned about Guy. He seemed to me to be coming loose; unravelling. Every time he came into the house he'd plunge his glass in the homebrew, often not even taking his oilskins off; then standing steaming by the Aga in his socks he'd down it in one or two, and go back out into the weather. He alternated between frenetic action outside, and total lethargy in front of daytime TV, looking at first for the foot and mouth bulletins, but very soon watching anything – sport, chat shows, game shows, schools' programmes, children's TV. The even-tempered placid man, the epitome of stability, someone who barely watched television at all, seemed to have become a morose non-communicative manic depressive.

And I? Well, obviously I was part of it all, and deeply depressed. Like the rest of us I was captive. I couldn't even walk the dogs, let alone ride.

I could still work – I had a fax machine and email. I had no heart for it, though, despite deadlines.

From the yard we smelt the pyres – round the clock, day after day, then week after week, and despite the rain. All I could think of was the obscene, and probably pointless, massacre: the reality of death piled on death, incomprehensible numbers of animals and associated livelihoods, while in Whitehall they debated whether or not to vaccinate. Devon was, as far as the rest of the world was concerned, closed for business.

We had only the supplies we already had in, though friends would drop a box of groceries at the end of the lane, by the disinfectant bath, where the guardian of officialdom sat vigil in his car watching the rain, next to our taped-off entrance and FOOT AND MOUTH – DO NOT ENTER signs.

The phone was our lifeline: our only connection with the

outside world, with friends and family, with other farmers, with the Farm Crisis Network.

But still the call we were waiting for, the one to say whether or not we would be culled, didn't arrive. You know how it is: the uncertainty in a life and death situation is often worse than the actuality. And we still didn't know if we had foot and mouth.

Guy brought now an urgency, a desperation, to our lovemaking. Whereas before he'd turn to me gently, maybe once or twice a week, now he seemed to need to make love to me every night, sometimes twice; reaching for me, breathing hard, with an impersonal blind look in his eyes. Often, he couldn't make it; then he'd roll off me, groaning. I'd smell the alcohol on his breath; and long after he was sleeping, I'd still be awake.

Then one night he started to question me about my past. He'd not previously shown anything other than a mild, affectionate interest in my life before him; and, while not disinterested exactly, had had no curiosity about previous lovers. He knew I'd been in love with someone in France; I'd told him about Mark when we first got together, in relation to whom he'd shown towards me a depth of care and sympathy.

That night he questioned me sharply: how much did we make love? Did I love them? And before them, how many others, where, when, who were they? At first I felt puzzled, then distressed; at the point where I was starting to feel angry he suddenly broke off mid-sentence; two minutes later he was snoring.

Once again I stayed awake, long into the early hours, trying to make sense of it all: of the horrors happening around us, of the future of the farm, of the family despair, and especially of my marriage and what Guy needed from me. And what I personally needed to keep going. That one I couldn't answer; or at least, if I had an intuition about it, the implications were too big at the moment to conscience.

The next morning brought a slender finger of watery sun flickering over the wall into the yard. Guy and I went outside together: Guy to go and investigate the night's casualties – if any; we were now so used to anticipating another lamb dead, another shearling too weak to stand – me to bring in some wood.

The yard was thick with mud, and a thin layer of slurry from the cows' barn. I turned to say goodbye to Guy as he headed off up towards the meadows – mudfields – and I don't know what happened but a second later I was on my back in the mud. I guess hysteria must have been close to the surface, because I couldn't stop laughing. Guy was back with me instantly, bent to hold his hands out to me, and suddenly he was laughing too, shoulders shaking with it. I grabbed his hands, but we were both so weak with the sudden emotional release that he couldn't pull me up, and he too ended up in the mud, straddling me. We must have been immobile there for two entire minutes, our laughter redoubled, both of us thickly coated by now.

I could hear the cows rustling in the barn.

'God, Tay,' he said, wiping his eyes with the back of his hand, and then pulling out a handful of T-shirt hem from under his jumper and jacket to wipe off the fresh swipe of mud he'd just applied, 'God. How I needed that! I'd kiss you, only –' a fresh hoot of laughter – 'I can't tell which way's up! Where's your mouth?'

That struck me as inordinately funny; and I was off again. By the time I'd recovered, Guy was looking at me seriously. His fingers were fumbling with the zip of my jacket. 'God, woman,' he said, in a low voice. 'You look so sexy all wet and muddy.' Now his hands were tugging my T-shirt out of my jeans. 'Tay,' he whispered, 'will you? Right here? Please?' There was a look in his eyes – fixed, fierce, distant – that I'd never seen before. The hairs stood up on my neck.

I couldn't help my reaction. I sobered up immediately. 'For God's sake, Guy, what's the matter with you? Get off! Right now!' I was trembling now, with outrage and fear. 'Your mum or dad could appear any second. For God's sake GET OFF!' I was pushing at him, trying to struggle free.

He resisted, holding me down by my shoulders. His face was very serious. For a minute I thought he was going to fight me. Rape me, even.

He must have felt my shaking.

Abruptly then he twisted off me and stood up, tucking his T-shirt back in. Our moment of play and frivolity had disappeared, as remote now as the few minutes' sun, already gone.

Guy stared at me for a long minute, then turned and stumbled off towards the hill.

## Forty-seven

For years, at my instigation, supper was generally an affair involving all four of us, with candles and conversation. It seemed an important ritual, even if (though) we didn't discuss anything of particular import.

Since the beginning of these hard times, though, television had increasingly replaced conversation. I didn't really see the takeover happen; but I was aware of its loud presence in the kitchen, squatting where we could see it.

It was on as normal one evening. The usual foot and mouth shots. We couldn't not look, of course; even though a bit of me wanted to scream for God's sake let's think about something else for once! Then I glanced at Guy – can't remember why – to see he'd stopped chewing and was staring at the TV. I looked too. A heap of smoking cattle bodies; maybe eighty or a hundred. Blackened, bloated, gross, grotesque. I looked back at Guy to protest. It's not that I'm squeamish, just that sometimes you need a break. He nodded fiercely at the screen.

'Oh!' Trudy's hands covered her mouth.

I looked. Out of the charred mass a grey-ish shape was moving.

'Oh my God!' I said. 'It's alive!'

'You bet it is!' Guy was grinning.

'It's a calf!'

'Phoenix the Charolais calf, found alive after being trapped for five days under the body of his slaughtered mother near Honiton, walks free...' the presenter's voice rose as the camera zoomed in on a very young grubby white body.

'But how could he have survived burning?' I could hear distress in my voice.

'Reconstruction, darling. You don't think the cameras were

there as he was discovered, do you? Superimposition. The cattle were burnt separately.'

'You mean –'

'Shhh, listen!'

'The owners of the herd are preparing to battle for his reprieve...'

Suddenly we were all cheering, clapping, laughing. Hope!

And of course Phoenix became a kind of mascot. Over the days that passed as his case was taken up by the media I noticed an increasing vigour in the farmers' resistance to the culling policies and an increasing anger, too, amongst the public. The slaughter total was almost inconceivable; much of it the results of misdiagnosis or contiguous culling. We in the Westcountry had had enough and we were going to fight back. Whole communities were fighting together against the absurd plans for disposal of bodies: resisting the giant burial pits – too close to habitation or water supplies – by banding together and physically preventing access, or keeping vigil, being vocal.

Suddenly it seemed as if a tide had turned and we might yet win. Spirits rose.

We heard about the Green Wellie fund, launched by the Western Morning News to help farmers with aborted incomes, which rose swiftly by thousands. There was in the countryside, it seemed – we were still 'gated' – an air of near-jubilation, or maybe hysteria; I imagine rather as it must have felt during the war, with a resurgence of determination as people pulled together in a common cause under siege in a way they don't, usually.

That is, out there where they weren't under notice of suspected foot and mouth. At Culver things weren't so brilliant, however. Friends and neighbours rang every day; but we were incarcerated still.

221

Guy and I had, by tacit agreement, not talked about our encounter in the yard since. Though I still felt uneasy about it, Guy was having such a tough time at the moment that I put it down to momentary imbalance; and I didn't want to make things worse by shaming him.

As the days went on and we still didn't know when – or even for certain if – we were going to be culled, the strain became almost insurmountable. Secretly I guess we all knew it was inevitable; the days piled up purposelessly, and it was not possible to take any joy in seeing the surviving lambs grow; the bigger and the more playful, the more painful it was. To watch them chasing each other up banks and leaping on and off fallen logs was excruciatingly poignant for me, and I think for the others too. We all had trouble sleeping; I also think we each, in our own way, were praying now that they would simply cull our stock and leave us alone to get over it as best we could as soon as possible.

So when the slaughtermen arrived one dry bright April morning – the cuckoo in the valley amongst the new gold-greens of the oak leaves making itself heard, and the first few swallows swooping around the buildings – our reaction was numbness tinged with something almost akin to relief. The irony in the human heart – suffering with a real and profound reason is much more manageable than the kind of imposed inertia and fear that accompanies the stasis of the unknown.

After the slaughter we could none of us bear to go outside for several days. The cows we'd had to leave where they'd fallen, in the barn; and the sheep in the mud-sodden meadows at the mercy of crows and magpies. We kept the windows closed and didn't even walk the dogs, simply letting them out into the walled garden, until one day, to our horror, Fly escaped and came back later with blood on his nose and paws.

Then the hauliers came and Culver was empty of animals; and there was no income. We couldn't restock for six months – supposing we wanted to anyway, and could find the money.

We didn't talk about any of it, really; simply carried on; though there was, of course, far less to do.

Bob took it all, of course, with his habitual quiet dignity. He arrived in the kitchen early each morning and automatically started moving towards the scullery to pull his boots on; then stopped himself and hovered aimlessly for a few minutes. I tried not to show I noticed, but it nearly broke my heart. This ritual continued for weeks, until eventually I broke the silence and teased him, made him smile a little at himself.

I knew he wasn't sleeping; I could hear him moving about most nights, up and down stairs. 'Not enough to do,' said Guy. 'He's always had a purpose and a focus. Can't bear being idle. I'll get him to come and help me fix things about the place.'

The farm needed to be scrubbed twice a day with disinfectant for several weeks, and the straw bed remained at the entrance. We were still, for a while anyway, confined.

Guy and Bob took it in turns to scrub out.

The sheepdogs grew plump; eventually their pacing stopped and they became lazy, too.

The barn stayed empty, the concrete flooring clean and echoey.

Guy resourcefully used the time, with remarkable equanimity, to mend the fences and repair machinery and equipment, fell the limbs of damaged or diseased trees, rebuild stone walls. Sometimes Bob worked with him; sometimes he'd sit in his office, ostensibly doing paperwork, but I suspect largely simply staring into space. I caught him at it several times, when I'd drop in to say hello or take him a mug of tea.

Guy had taken to whistling through his teeth, endlessly and tunelessly. When I pointed it out to him, he grinned. 'I find it stops me thinking,' he said; and carried on.

A couple of months later, to everyone's astonishment, Trudy and Bob scratched together enough money for the cheap flight to Eire and went to Cork for a month to see Bob's relatives.

I was working as hard as I could; none of the promised compensation had yet been forthcoming, which meant mine was virtually the only income.

The bank started to threaten foreclosure. Guy and I agreed to say nothing, for the moment, to his parents – and hoped Bob wouldn't go through the formal correspondence when he got back.

New evidence came in to show that contiguous culls had been unnecessary. Then MAFF changed its name to DEFRA, and its head, Margaret Beckett, was holding off announcing an enquiry. 'Changing their name means they can keep their records from being looked at for thirty years at least,' said Guy sourly. 'Can't trust the Government an inch.'

Spring turned to summer, and summer towards autumn, with none of the usual farming rituals to mark the passing of the seasons. The following winter was as wet as the previous one.

It was a dull, miserable, relentless time; and nothing seemed to shift or change except that there was less and less to live on and less and less to say to each other.

## Forty-eight

Then one soft autumn day the following year a mineshaft opened up beneath my feet.

We'd had a couple of weeks of sun, and Culver was beginning to dry out. I was finding every excuse I could to be outside. Already the leaves were falling, small brown drifts piling in corners. The southwesterly winds had been fierce on the moor, racing up from Plymouth Sound and across the tors of Bodmin and ripping across our fields even in the low sheltered parts around the farmstead, taking with them a lot of foliage, before it had time to really turn in the frosts. Many of the oaks had been mildewed, and most of the trees showed signs of waterlogging.

Still, nearly eighteen months later, I put off going out towards the empty, silent fields; the coming of autumn, usually my favourite season, was drenching me this year with that heading-into-the-dark melancholia. Too much rain, the last two years. And I knew I was fighting a depression. All we had done, each of us, was survive; and that seemed achievement enough at times.

Crossing the yard with a basket of washing to peg in the orchard I heard a motorbike draw up in the lane the other side of the house. I didn't pay that much attention; I was thinking about asking Guy if, when we restocked, as we were talking of doing – 'Well, what else can I do, Tay? Sign on? – I'm a farmer,' – we could get a dozen bantams. Their quiet crooning as they raked over the leaf-fall would be soothing.

I heard the bolt clang on the yard gate and the dogs erupt in the house, and Guy straightened up from where he was fixing a gate in the adjoining meadow.

'Who's that, Tay?'

'Dunno,' I yelled back, stretching to string the washing. Guy put down his tools and walked towards the yard.

My mind fell to mulling over a piece of writing that was giving me trouble, and which was due the next day.

As I walked back across the orchard I could see a leatherclad figure, and assumed motorcycle courier. Then I noticed Guy talking to him: even from my distance I could read defensiveness in his stance – pelvis and chin jutting, arms folded. Curious, I thought. Then Bob appeared, moving faster than I'd ever seen him, hurrying stiffly towards the stranger. As I approached the orchard gate I saw, to my incredulity, Bob gather the tall young man in his arms.

Who on earth would Bob embrace? I couldn't think of anyone, unless one of his nephews had arrived from Eire.

That it might be Eliot didn't even occur to me.

I couldn't see much, except that the newcomer was taller than Bob, and dark and bearded. I hesitated a moment, then decided to detour to put the basket back into the kitchen and allow the two men what was clearly a man's moment. As I put my hand to the door latch Trudy opened it from the inside. We nearly hit heads.

There was an expression of bewildered joy on Trudy's face such as I had never seen. She almost pushed past me, dogs dancing at her heels.

'Eliot? – It IS you! My God!'

I dropped the basket and paused on the threshold, then followed.

The man lifted his eyes from Trudy's face as I approached.

I froze. I heard myself gasp, unsure for a moment. Could it be? This man, after all, had facial hair, some lines and a few silver streaks at his temples.

His grey eyes took me in; he didn't say a word. I felt pinioned. Oh yes, it was him. I nearly shouted his name out loud.

I felt myself spin. I can vouch for the fact that it is not just soft-witted heroines from tacky Victorian romances whose knees buckle. I nearly fell.

There followed one of those momentous instants of silence when no-one moved; then everyone began talking at once.

'Where've you –' 'What on earth –' ' I can't believe my –' 'Eliot, this is Guy's –' Then over us all cut in Guy's voice, cool, steel-edged. 'Eliot, this is my wife, Tamar.' Guy moved to stand beside me.

There was a pause.

I felt myself grow hot. I knew instinctively that words from either of us would set an avalanche tumbling.

Neither Oliver nor I moved. Guy looked from Oliver to me. I was dimly aware that everyone else was watching Oliver, though Guy, I knew, had clocked his effect on me.

I couldn't take my eyes away from Oliver's face, nor act. I felt shocked. I still hadn't completely registered; my mind was spinning in confusion. What was Oliver doing here? Why were they calling him Eliot?

Oliver stared back. There was some emotion in his eyes I couldn't identify. For seconds we remained motionless, Trudy's hand on Oliver's arm, Bob's arm around Trudy. I made myself look away, back up at Guy. What was happening? I couldn't read his face, either.

Suddenly fear took me and I wanted to run.

Bob broke the tableau. 'Come on inside, son,' he said, his voice breaking. I saw there were tears on his cheeks.

I swallowed.

Oliver pushed his hands into his pockets and walked alongside his mother and father towards the house.

I started to move too, not knowing what else to do. I could barely function: I felt myself flush hot and cold alternately, and

227

knew I was incapable of coherent thought or speech, though my mind was bolting hare-like for some distant refuge, far away from Culver.

Guy tightened his hand on my shoulder to restrain me, then put his hand to my chin to turn my face to his. I read fear in his eyes, and anger, and something approaching what I can only describe as agony. Or desolation, perhaps.

'What was that about? You looked as if you knew him.'

I looked away, shook my head – more in confusion and panic than in denial.

'Well, call me paranoid, but something's going on, Tay. Look at me! – Do you know him?'

I knew I couldn't bluff my way out. I've always been a terrible liar.

'I – met him in France. In Brittany.'

More silence. Guy let his hand drop.

'Was it him?' he asked. 'The one –'

I couldn't look at him.

He answered his own question. 'I think it was.'

His hand, back on my neck, was firm. We approached – or perhaps I should say Guy marched me towards – the house.

'Let me go, Guy,' I said with some force. Thank God I'd recovered a reaction. 'You're hurting.' I prised his hand away from my neck, and he dropped it.


In the kitchen there was a chaos of emotions jangling in the air.

Bob hovered by his customary seat by the Aga, then offered it to Oliver – Eliot, I guess I needed to learn to call him.

Bob looked both vulnerable and old as he smiled up into the face of his elder son. 'Well!' he said. 'I don't know what to say... you've made my day, son. And your mother's... I... More than my day...' He beamed round at all of us.

Trudy fluttered around Eliot like a sparrow. 'I can't believe it! Can't believe it!' she said over and over. Finally she caught herself. Caressing his shoulder, she said 'I'll make tea,' then busied herself with kettles, cups and cakes; the best china, I noticed. Her eyes shone as she flung glances at Eliot. I didn't think I'd ever seen her so animated. 'Can you stay?'

Eliot opened his mouth to respond. He looked overwhelmed himself; I'd never seen him off-guard before.

'Please?' Trudy had a plea in her voice.

Then Guy went to lean against the rail of the Aga, his expression what I can only describe as surly. Eliot's face closed down as he looked over at Guy, though for an instant, to my now total confusion, I thought I saw a flicker of softness.

Eliot looked at me, where I was still hovering at the door, in turmoil. He said something. His voice sounded strange: forced nonchalance. His eyes were unreadable again.

I couldn't speak. The world as I had known it was about to explode. A thousand questions were thrashing around in my head like fish in a net, and I couldn't voice any of them. I was hot to the verge of fainting.

Eliot was still staring at me. I tried to make sense of his question. He repeated it: 'So how did you two meet?'

I couldn't think. Bob, however, perhaps sensing my discomfort, stepped in. 'We're all in a state of shock, old son! It's been so long. Don't know where to start...'

Then there was a babble as we all talked over each other, and stopped almost simultaneously.

'Well, brother, tell us what brought you back here, then?' I could tell Guy was making an effort. Nonetheless his voice sounded strained and challenging.

I lasted just long enough to hear part of the exchange. I couldn't bear it. I felt I'd already experienced my avalanche, and

229

was still falling. I could make no sense of anything. I couldn't gain any kind of foothold, or purchase, and what was more was starting to feel sick.

'Saw the foot and mouth footage on French TV. Last year.'

'And?'

'They showed the Mays' farm. Reckoned you might need a hand.'

'What?! Need a hand?? – Yeah, every hand in the world, back in the spring of last year – except yours!' He raised his voice, and waved a hand wildly towards the yard. Bob tried to interject, but Guy continued loudly. 'Can you see any animals out there? What's the use in coming back now, all this time later, with them all gone? Well, cheers.' He stared at Eliot. I saw sweat on his forehead. 'Well, let me tell you. This is my farm. And Dad's. When we needed you was last year. Now, you're not welcome. End of story.'

'GUY!' Trudy's voice was shocked. 'Leave him alone! He's only just got here.'

'He can stand up for himself. You're out of luck, mate. Lost your right to be here a very long time ago. And your claim on the place. Now piss off.'

Eliot hadn't said anything, merely watched Guy, legs stretched out and relaxed back into the chair. Only his clenched knuckles on the arms of the chair showed his tension.

'Well?' Guy demanded belligerently.

'Not a lot of point in coming earlier. Heard the farms were closed. Looked it all up on the internet: *Western Morning News* site. They listed Culver.'

I was impressed at his restraint.

'So why the hell are you back now then? We've done very well without you all these years.'

Bob stretched out an arm towards Guy, who flung it away.

Bob's face turned troubled. I wanted to put out my own hand to him, but felt incapable of movement.

'Well?'

'Reckoned you might need some moral support.'

'You can stuff your patronising fucking moral support.' Guy was shouting now, his eyes wild and his face red.

That seemed to get to Eliot. 'Learnt to swear then, baby brother, at last?'

Trudy looked close to tears. Bob stood up.

I left as silently as I could, shugging my boots on in the scullery. The more timid dog, Jess, slunk after me. I stumbled across the yard towards the meadows. I needed to get out, fast, and think. Or maybe just throw up.

When I came back, what seemed like ages later, Guy was slouching in the doorway.

'Where the hell did you go, then?'

'Out.'

'I could see that. What about loyalty? Standing by your man? Don't the vows mean anything to you?'

'What are you talking about? You didn't need me.'

'Are you my woman, or not?'

Six months ago it would have been inconceivable that Guy would have spoken to me like that. My panic, which had receded a little up on the shoulders of Wolf Tor, had come back with a vengeance as I crossed the home meadow. Now, under Guy's aggression, I could feel acid rising in my throat.

'Have you been drinking, Guy?'

'What if I have? What's it to you?'

I hadn't learnt how to handle this new Guy. I didn't know how far he would be capable of going.

'Has Ol – Eliot – gone?'

'Oh yes. I told him where to get off. This is my farm.'

'But it's not, Guy. It's Bob's –'

'Whose side are you on? Mine, or lover-boy's?' He pushed his face close to mine. 'This is my farm. You're my wife.'

'You disturb me when you're like this. You're like a stranger. I can't stand it. Now let me past, please, Guy.'

For a moment I thought he wouldn't; then he shifted his body a few inches to one side of the threshold. Jess darted in with me. Guy stayed, staring out at the empty fields.

I felt dislocated, disembodied, alien. My worlds had spun round and collided. Who were these people? What was I doing here? What right did Oliver have, to walk in on us and shatter what little stillness we had struggled so hard to re-establish? Who was he, anyway? What did he mean to me now?

I walked forward into the room like a puppet. One foot, the other. One foot... Part of my mind was replaying. How did I look through his eyes? Older, not so slender, the ubiquitous jeans, hair cut short... my hand strayed to my head. I caught myself. What was I doing? What did I care how he saw me? – But all my quietness had gone. I didn't know where I belonged.

I registered Culver kitchen. Brought myself back. They mustn't know. I guessed they'd be too involved in their own feelings to notice mine, though.

Trudy's stiffness as she washed up cups and plates at the sink suggested that she was only just holding on. Spontaneously I put my arms around her, and suddenly a huge sob escaped her. She dropped the washing-up brush and bent her head and wept. I found myself crying, too. Behind us Guy slammed the kitchen door. I heard the door of our sitting room bang shut.

'Where's Bob?' I asked when I could speak.

'In the office.' She sniffed and rubbed her eyes with her wrist. The drop on the end of her nose wrenched my heart. 'He's gone again. My son… I've missed him so much. What am I going to do, Tamar? I don't know what's happened to Guy these days.'

'No, I don't know, either, Trudy.' My voice, I knew, sounded hopeless, pathetic.

'He was so angry. And – I hope I'm not interfering, dear, I'd never want to be a prying mother-in-law – but he seemed very angry with you, too…?'

My stomach churned suddenly. What did she know? 'What has Guy said to you?'

There was a silence. Trudy looked at me through her reddened eyes. Her face was more open than I'd ever seen it. There was compassion in her gaze; no judgement, no intrusiveness.

I swallowed. I tried again. 'About… ummm….'

'You already knew him, didn't you,' she said quietly, not taking her eyes from my face. 'Eliot. I saw it.'

I tried to process this, my mind circling frantically. 'Was it that obvious?'

'No. I mean I saw it. No-one else would guess, no.'

I stared at her. She stared back. She opened her mouth to say something, then closed it again. Then: 'It's hard, isn't it, being a woman sometimes. Being married to someone. Even if they're the best husband in the world… Even if it's my son.' She smiled gently at me. I saw with distress that her eyes were filling again; and mine, too. I wanted to ask her what she meant; and I couldn't.

I moved towards her. We held each other a moment, then, in a rare intimacy, woman to woman, in silence; then let go, each into our own solitude.

## Forty-nine

The market was packed; electric. This was the first cattle market since the Westcountry had been declared 'open' again, and every farmer who still had any will to farm must have been there.

It was hard not to feel bombarded by the noise level within the auctioneers' building: men yelling, shouting, roaring with laughter; the knock of sticks on metal, the bewildered bellowing of frightened cattle. The shed was warm with bodies, the air thick with human perspiration and the slightly sweet, slightly sour smell of bovine sweat, straw and dung. The cattle were penned into the galvanised hurdles, rolling terrified eyes and licking wet nostrils with rough tongues. I hated the way the stock handlers thumped and prodded the captive bony rumps.

I could feel Guy beside me, tense and focused. A fortnight's wrangling with Bob had seen him victorious: Culver was going to restock, with the help of the remainder of Bob's already-meagre savings. Compensation, we were promised, would be forthcoming. Sometime. Guy was counting on its arrival to back his argument. Meantime there was still no real income and Bob's savings had been all that had kept us afloat, apart from my erratic freelance earnings.

I was worried about Bob's state of mind. I couldn't shake off the memory of him when eventually he'd agreed – or rather, he'd bowed to Guy's persuasion – to come up with the necessary cash. The final decisive transaction had taken place in Bob's office, so neither Trudy nor I had witnessed the process, though both of us had heard the raised voices. Then they emerged: Guy, a healthy sturdy man in his prime, a young stag bursting through the door in vigour; Bob, bent, a bony old buck, trailing him. He looked broken. Guy strode over to put the kettle on; Bob had moved towards the scullery without a word, bending to put his boots on, then calling Fly and Jess. I guessed he was going up the hill.

And yes, of course, it wasn't just that memory that dogged me. Eliot's face, those grey eyes, still burned somewhere behind my retina, try as I might to forget that whole appalling scene and what it had stirred up.

Now, I was aware, Guy's whole attention was focused on the cattle going under the auctioneer's hammer.

Culver had sat out the post-cull fallow period, and Guy was wanting to restock with South Devons again. There were several individual heifers here, and one or two very small herds, and Guy was hoping to find a bull at next week's auctions in Bristol. But I'd seen him taken aside by a small huddle of farmers, and seen the way he'd come back: alert, tense, slightly agitated – I knew him well enough to know he was on the trail of something.

'What is it, Guy?'

He shrugged me off. 'Nothing; just a lot I'm interested in.'

'Tell me more?'

'A whole herd – the Smallacote herd.'

'Will Maddocks is selling up?'

'Will Maddocks is dead. Topped himself.'

'Oh my God! – When? – But he was clear, wasn't he?'

'A few months ago now. Yep. But remember the ones who never had f and m were sometimes worse off than most of those who did: no hope of compensation, no movement of animals, sales of British beef rock bottom, imported meat on the supermarket shelves, milk prices too low – you know the story as well as I do... Come on, this way, they'll be the next lot... Hi Jim, Dennis –' We were weaving in and out of the crush of farmers. Guy shouted back to me over his shoulder: 'No income, cattle still to feed, going nowhere fast with no hope of recovery within the foreseeable future. Some poor buggers couldn't hack it; simply couldn't see any way out.'

We were there. 'Family farm being sold to pay the mounting debt. He saw it coming. His wife's had to deal with it; now she wants to forget all about farming and go and live with their daughter in Stroud. D'you wonder we all wanted to go on the march?'

That was something he continuously brought up. He and I had had one of the bitterest conflicts of our married life about the Countryside Alliance march; certainly one that had left me feeling lonely and not understood. Not for the first time, I questioned my decision to marry Guy: we seemed to share increasingly little in terms of ideology, values and inner lives. Of course I saw the ruralists' point – I too felt strongly about it – but I couldn't support what was clearly, to me, a pro-foxhunting initiative hijacking the other agendas. Needless to say, I didn't go – sparking quite a lot of what Guy would call tongue-wagging within the immediate community.

He shouldered through to the front of the men surrounding the Smallacote herd. I followed him, aware of eyes looking me up and down – very few women here, as usual. I'd come really as a gesture of solidarity to Guy and the farm – despite all the time we'd had the last year we seemed to spend very little of it together; and Guy had specifically asked me. I'd have come anyway, though. Each of us was, I think, trying our best to hold the marriage together through what had been a very testing time.

'Yes, there they are. Maddocks in his younger days was a South Devon judge, so his cattle should be A1.'

'It's – it doesn't seem right. Buying his herd. Talking about it so coolly, so matter-of-factly.'

'Somebody's got to buy it. It'll continue his work too. And it's money for his wife – hold on, there it is coming up now.'

'But Guy just beef cattle? Why? No milkers at all? And do we have the money? – Guy? – Answer me, dammit! It's my life too, and Bob and Trudy's –'

'Shut up, Tay. Leave this to me, OK?'

And so it happened that an hour later we were the new possessors of thirty-seven South Devon cows, sleek chestnut creatures, plump after a summer of good grass.

'Somebody's smiling on us still, Tay.' Guy flung his arms around me in the car park. 'Up and running again! I hope Dad's pleased. And no more being tied to the milking routine. I knew we wouldn't go under! Delaneys don't.'

I smiled back at him. This was the old Guy – laughing, upbeat, optimistic.

He continued. 'Sheep next. Shall we get Wiltshires again? Or Blackfaces?'

'Whatever you like. You're the sheep man. And hens? Bantams.'

'Mmm, OK. D'you still love me, sweetheart? I know I've been a pig sometimes. It's been tough for us all.' He swung me round to face him, his hazel eyes smiling into mine, kissed my lips. 'Mmm? – And –' he put his mouth to my ear – 'you're even sexier than you were when I married you...'

'Of course I love you,' I said.

When we got back there was a handful of letters for me on the side, along with my copy of Dartmoor magazine, which Bob must have picked up for me in Culverstock. I swept the letters into my bag after a quick glance – bills mostly, and a hand-addressed one in a script I didn't recognise.

Guy had bought a couple of bottles of cheap champagne. They sat incongruously with the warmed-up chestnut, celery and

237

stilton bake I'd made up the night before. Trudy and Bob as usual shared our supper; Bob was, not unusually, quiet; but both parents seemed pleased for us.

'You're fun tonight,' I said to Guy. He was laughing, teasing, engaged; relating anecdotes, exaggerating wildly, resting his arm on my chair back, stroking my hair. For the first time in months I started to relax.

Guy was getting ready for bed, singing in the bathroom. When he was pleased with himself he'd sing rock or country music solos in his warm tenor; when he was brimming with it and horny as well it'd be the sax lines from jazz pieces. Tonight it was jazz, which made me smile. I felt a rush of affection for him. Maybe we'd pull through after all.

I took my bag into my study and emptied it out, which I'd got into the habit of doing at the end of each day. I'd forgotten the handwritten envelope. I ripped it open absentmindedly, half-listening to Guy and mulling over the day, our new Culver herd.

A single small sheet of paper, torn from a diary by the looks of it. I unfolded it. Black ink. Spiky artistic script.

*Tamar*
*Got to see you. Six o'clock Wednesday, back of Wolf Tor (west side)?*
*Oliver*
*PS It's important.*

My heart started banging hard, and suddenly I couldn't breathe. I caught myself looking wildly round the study for somewhere to hide the letter. I flung it in the bin, then immediately retrieved it. I thought about tearing it into pieces. I stood paralysed with it in my hands.

Guy flushed the loo, and without even thinking I switched the study light out. In the dark I felt myself blushing at the deception. Pull yourself together. I knew I only had seconds before he'd come looking for me. I stuffed the sheet into the pocket in the lining of my bag, then went to open the window – swiftly and surreptitiously – and took great gulps of the cool star-ridden night. I willed my heart to stop thumping, and took some very slow breaths.

Of course I wouldn't go. I also knew I wouldn't tell Guy. I was protecting him, I told myself, and this resurgence of fragile hope that today had waved at us. Also, I didn't want any more conflict. Best for everyone if I say nothing, I told myself.

The bathroom door opened. I willed myself to think of something else – anything. Picture the Culver fields full again; lambs, calves and brown bantams. Picture spring, and the drifts of snowdrops on the grassed tops of the bleak stone walls of the lane. Was that an owl, its white blur as soft on the darkness as its call was shrill? Picture Guy, strolling naked towards our bedroom, unlatching the door, lighting the lamps, opening the window. Whatever, don't think of him...

'Tamar!'

'Coming –'

I said nothing. We made love.

Guy held me afterwards; put his lips to my hair and murmured. 'Tamar, I'm so sorry for all the times I've been a shit to you.' Then he turned, pressed his warm buttocks and thighs against me, and slipped swiftly into open-mouthed sleep, innocent to the deception which I hadn't even committed, I told myself, but which drifted nonetheless in the air like puffball spores ready to root themselves and send out lightning-swift networks of underground mycelia, take hold of our lives.

Two owls called to each other. Where had I read that owls

239

represent the soul?

Why Wolf Tor? He couldn't know that it was somewhere I went for refuge, for restoration. I almost considered it mine.

There was a gibbous moon the other side of the barns. I lay staring into the darkness, wide awake, gazing at the bare silhouetted shoulders of the tor, my heart stamping for attention, my breathing shallow.

## Fifty

I was quite clear that I wasn't going to meet Oliver. Eliot. What would it serve, except to fuel a restlessness in me?

And the truth is I did love Guy. He'd taken a lot of care, too, to be attentive and gentle with me recently.

And yes, of course I was lonely. That deep insidious soul loneliness that pervades you when you are not with your kind.

That made me vulnerable.

Or maybe that's an excuse.

I was upstairs in my study, working; which meant, not unusually recently, that I was sitting behind my word processor staring out towards the tor, watching cloud shadow pattern its shoulders.

Somewhere I could hear a robin's song. I drifted into it. It seemed, lately, that I only felt any sense of peace and stillness when I was on my own shut away here, or out on the moor.

Snatched moments. Downstairs I heard a door, then Guy's voice bellowed up the stairs:

'Tay! You there?'

No! I wanted to call back. 'What d'you want, darling?' I said instead.

'Father Christmas has come early!' His voice was irritatingly sing-song. 'Come and see!'

I closed the file I had been (not) working on and pushed my chair back, trying not to resent the intrusion. The patterns on the hillside had faded, now; what the weather forecast would call 'bands of rain' were massing in the far west, over Bodmin Moor, bent, presumably, on marauding incursions into our moor.

Guy was waiting, still in his coat, at the bottom of the stairs, a grin on his face. He didn't move, merely looked at me expectantly. Obviously I was meant to say something, or notice

241

something.

I looked at him: his head, his face. 'No, not my hair, sweetheart. Yes, I'm always clean-shaven. OK – mostly. No, haven't bought a new shirt, either... and my hands are empty... ah! Did you hear a squeak? A clue...'

Bulges in his waxed jacket pockets. Ears! Each side... two kittens!

'Who needs kids!' He said. 'Kittens don't need schooling and aren't lifelong limpets...' He lifted them out gently in his big farmers' hands. A black and a tabby. Mewing, and still blue-eyed. 'Stan was going to drown them. Only little fellas... Here. Yours!'

I took them carefully from him, felt their scrabbling, bent my face to their fur. Inhaled. Allowed myself to be moved. Composed my face. He really needed me to be delighted. I didn't have the heart to remind him that I am a dog person, by nature; can't stand the nasty predatory ways of cats, and I love the wild birds and mice too much, if I'm truthful; although I liked the farm cats well enough. But who can resist kittens? – and of course I too would have rescued them from drowning. They were symbolic, somehow. Were they supposed to be a focus for my (no longer terribly dominant) maternal urge? Well. They were beautiful, and I loved Guy for saving them. I lifted my face.

'You old softie. And I'm so pleased you saved them. Aren't they sweet? What shall we call them?'

'They're two toms. Mum thinks they ought to be Laurel and Hardy or Morecambe and Wise or something.'

'Too pretentious. Could go with Eric and Ernie, though...'

'OK, E and E then. Let's go and have lunch. Guess they need feeding, too. They're only little. Should it be four times a day?'

'S'pose so. Haven't had kittens for years!'

'And,' he said, 'I haven't finished. And –'

I looked at him expectantly.

He chuckled, savouring my impatience. 'I've found you some bantams.'

'Guy! You star! Where are they?'

'Back of the Land Rover in a couple of boxes. A trio – cock and two hens – and five more young hens. C'mon... Give the kittens to Trudy a minute.'

I ought to feel happy, I wrote in my journal that night. We've come through slaughter. Maybe we can start over? We've restocked. Guy isn't drunk tonight. There are two new kittens warm in a box by the Aga. And bantams installed in the orchard. I know these are his gestures of atonement after all his anger and withdrawnness since Oliver's appearance. Why then this sense that I was living in an earthquake zone? – But my dreams seem to be full of death and destruction. I wake feeling exhausted. I'm not interested in making love. I don't laugh much. I feel as if I'm on the edge of a cliff all the time, or walking between fault-lines, trying to step over gaps.

Tomorrow's Wednesday. Of course I shan't go to meet Oliver (Eliot). Is this what my anxiety's about?

Or am I just processing the awful stuff that's happened now, after the event, when it's safe to do so?

I guess you'll have seen through my self-deception.

It was Wednesday. All day I'd tried to force my mind into a straitjacket – a totalitarian regime of one. And of course – because that kind of brutality never works – my mind returned constantly to the one thing I'd forbidden it. All day I'd been twitchy; jumping at anything and anyone, until Guy had become irritated almost, I feared, to the point of suspicion. I've never been any good at lying, even by default – and to me dishonesty is as much about not saying what is true as saying what's not. I'd felt that I must be broadcasting my treacherous thoughts every time I looked at anyone, so I avoided their eyes.

Still I told myself that I was going nowhere; and the day ticked past menacingly, and I achieved nothing – no work, no peace, no focus. The kittens' feeds were tricky, and their third feed at the end of the afternoon was a disaster: too young to lap properly yet, they couldn't cope easily with even the smallest of the lamb-feeding teats. I nearly choked Eric, who promptly vomited, and most of Ernie's milk went over his shoulders, back and chest, and my thighs.

'Why aren't you using a syringe or dropper?' Guy's tone was one of incredulity.

Because I hadn't even thought of that, that's why. It was obvious, of course; I'd reared numerous birds and small animals over the years and had a range of pipettes, droppers and syringes.

Big Ben struck six on the kitchen radio. I tried to look unconcerned, but after I'd succeeded in spilling my tea on Guy's stretched-out legs, he snapped.

'For God's sake, Tay! What the hell's the matter with you? – Take the dogs out, or something, for Christ's sake!'

'Don't talk to me like that!' I snapped back. But hardly even aware I was doing it, I marched to the scullery and lifted my jacket off its peg. Jess and Fly were there immediately. I pushed my feet into boots and yanked the door open. Cold air swirled round me. If I'd thought I suppose I would have justified myself on the grounds that Guy's words had given me permission.

But I wasn't thinking. I set off up the lane, in the opposite direction from Wolf Tor. Already the track was littered with russet beech leaves, stippled with occasional scarlets and lemons from the single bird cherry and the scrubby hazels.

I could avoid all responsibility and say 'my feet of their own volition carried me back off to the left across the fields, and

244

before I knew it...' etcetera. But I'll resist. Of course I turned off and headed back up the hill. Ten past six. He probably wouldn't have waited. Certainly the old Oliver wouldn't. It'd be OK then, wouldn't it, just doing my usual walk?

He was there. I saw him before he saw me, and I hesitated. My heart was thudding and I felt sick. I could still walk in the other direction – maybe. Then the dogs raced towards him and he turned his head my way. He leaped off the rock on which he'd been perched, and took a couple of strides downhill towards me.

We stopped a few yards apart. I suppose if I'm honest I have to say that my thoughts had strained towards this – if we did meet alone what would we say? – I hadn't been able to imagine. 'How've you been?' 'What do you want?' – All a bit pitiful and totally inadequate.

For several minutes we didn't move or speak; simply watched each other. Jess did that collie thing of pushing her muzzle into his hand and gazing at him. He stroked her head with his other hand. I tightened my lips. No. I wouldn't succumb to that. Jess! What about loyalty?

Then we spoke simultaneously.

'I don't know how to apologise –'

'Why did you leave like that? In France –'

We both laughed at the concurrence, me a little nervously. He was still watching me. Did I imagine it, or did he look almost shy? He spread his hands. I looked away.

'Tamar.'

I gathered myself. This felt dangerous. I didn't know what on earth I was doing there. What good would it do any of us? My anger rose. Did he know what he was playing with?

I should have turned back immediately. Instead I spoke.

'Why did you want to see me, Oliver? Or Eliot, I suppose I should call you now.'

'How could I not?' He answered simply. I was expecting him to be guarded, too; and his directness threw me. I swallowed and focused on the lichen-covered boulder at my feet. If I looked at him I knew I'd be lost. The wind was icy. I started to shiver.

'I'm married now, Oliver. Things are different.'

'Then why did you come?'

'Just tell me what you wanted to say; then I suggest we go, and leave it there.'

'Why did you come? No, don't avoid it, Tamar. Just tell me. Why did you come?'

My mouth was dry. I glanced at him then away again. I was afraid he'd see the terror I was feeling.

'Where are you staying?'

'Don't avoid me.'

'I don't know why I came. I hadn't intended to.'

'But you did. You're here.'

'You never used to be this direct.' Fatal, referring to the past. Alluding to a time shared.

'Things have changed for me, too. I've grown up. Going grey, even.' He hadn't taken his eyes from my face. I could feel them. 'Even though I haven't married.'

Why tell me that? Did I imagine the inflection on the 'I'? And was he referring to the growing up or the going grey in relation to marriage? 'That's none of my business, Oliver.'

'Actually, it is. I wanted to tell you that – that – '

'Why should I want to know?'

'Let me finish. You're being defensive.'

'What do you expect?' I was nearly shouting. The dogs looked up at me. 'Look, I have to go. I was stupid to come.'

'Stop. You can go in a moment. I need to tell you. Something. That there's scarcely been a day since – that I haven't thought about it. About you. I mean.'

246

In a rush my eyes filled with unexpected tears. It released me. I swung round and stumbled towards Culver, whistling for the dogs. Oliver didn't speak, or move to stop me.

At the bottom of the slope I glanced back. I could just see his silhouette against the darkening sky, the slightest softening of angles amongst the jagged rocks of the tor.

\*

On the Richter scale, about five; lower than when Oliver arrived in the yard, and lower than the foot and mouth stress and all those deaths. But cataclysmic enough in terms of what it did to my equanimity.

Another handful of pomegranate seeds.

I love Guy. I told myself over and over. He's the kindest most thoughtful man I know. I love him.

## Fifty-one

I've long known that we manifest what we focus on. What we think is what we get, in other words: our daily lives mirror back to us our inner processes, the effects of our thoughts and beliefs. That's one meaning of karma.

So no surprise that, unable to wrench my mind away, it was only a matter of days before Oliver and I coincided again.

This time it was at the opening of a new alternative energy centre attached to a wind farm in the north of Cornwall. I was there to write it up for *Wessex Today*; Oliver, it turned out, was there as press photographer for a syndication agency.

I was waiting in the restaurant for the opportunity to have a few words with the new director, currently talking to the TV crew, when I felt, rather than saw, Oliver approach me. He stopped to my left, a couple of yards away. I caught my breath, then slowly turned my head towards him. He was in his biking leathers, helmet over his arm and camera round his neck. My heart started pounding hard. Whoa, Tamar, you're here to work. Focus on the director... I turned my head back; a moment late, as it happened: someone else, microphone at the ready, pushed in front of me. This was an aspect of journalism that I hated.

I glanced back at Oliver. The faintest crinkle – sardonic, sympathetic – at his eyes.

'Can't afford even a moment's lapse, hey. In this business. It's a bugger.'

'What are you doing here?'

'Same as you, I imagine. Life as a freelance.'

'But haven't you only been in England a week or two?'

'Nope. Came back in the summer.'

'Oh! Where are you living?'

'What's it to you?'

The old Oliver. But did I imagine, this time, a glimmer of amusement? Nonetheless I didn't feel inclined to give him any slack. Instead of replying I concentrated on stilling my heart and slowing my breath, focusing on the subject of my forthcoming interview, who was laughing with a woman colleague. Against my will, I found my eyes flicking over her: lipsticked mouth, the same cerise as her plunging T-shirt. Short black skirt; nice legs. As usual I was in my jeans and walking boots, with a clean but ancient white shirt under my jacket. I was glad I'd washed my hair. I risked a surreptitious glance at Oliver. He was watching the pair. To my annoyance I felt jealousy rise in me. I'm not a jealous person. Oliver stirred stuff in me that no one else did.

I moved away slightly, closer to my interviewee. Oliver moved too.

'Who's sent you?'

'*Wessex Today.* And you?'

'Oh, I work with an agency. Have been for years. International. If I'm lucky it'll end up as an infill in the middle pages of a broadsheet or two. Only in England though.'

I didn't pick up the thread. I'm getting better at just allowing silence. To be truthful I had no idea what to say, and my heart was still thumping hard enough for me to fear that my voice would shake and betray me to Oliver. Just then the director turned my way and I seized my chance.

When I next looked Oliver had disappeared. I'm not sure which was stronger in me: disappointment or relief.

I queued for coffee and took my tray outside into the thin sun, installing myself on a bench. It was important to get some notes down while my impressions of the place were fresh. I fished out the leaflets I'd picked up at reception. Thankfully I was interested enough as to be able to think clearly, and I'd filled a couple of pages of my notebook and finished my carrot cake before I next looked up. Still no Oliver. Well, that was OK. Much better not to see him. I flexed my fingers and put my gloves back on. Cold. Time to go.

A chaffinch appeared on the picnic table and I brushed the crumbs off my plate for him, then finished my coffee and stood up.

Oliver was lounging by the entrance to the car park, back propped against the new earth bank, one leg crossed over the other. His pose was so familiar it hurt, even after all the intervening years. I kept walking. He looks older, I thought, face more creased. He inhabits it now. I pushed away tenderness. Not helpful. He spoke as I drew level.

'When did you go to Trescarrow?'

'What?'

He repeated his question. I stared at him. I couldn't think what he meant. 'I saw your piece on the watermill.'

'What? Oh! Did you know I was at Culver, then?'

His eyes looked shadowed. 'Course not. It didn't say, did it? Fucking thunderbolt, seeing you there. Married to my brother.' He looked away, out towards the distant sea. I saw his Adam's apple jump.

I'd intended to keep walking to my car. Somehow I couldn't move.

'It's close by.'

'What? What is?'

'Trescarrow of course. D'you have to keep saying "what"?'

'Sorry.' Why 'sorry'?

'Will you come with me?'

I opened my mouth to say 'what do you mean', but thought better of it. 'When?'

'Well, now.'

'Where?'

'To Trescarrow!'

'To Trescarrow?'

He sounded exasperated. 'Tamar. Fuck.'

I looked at him, ready to be angry, then saw he was almost smiling.

'Yes. Will. You. Come. With. Me. To. Trescarrow. Now?'

I couldn't think how to reply. My mind circled in confusion. What about Guy? What about my work? What about your bike? Or my car? I don't want to see you again. I can't. I can't not see you again. I don't want to go home... I must go home...

'I need to go home.'

'Why?'

'You know why.'

'No. Tell me.'

'Oliver, this is a crap conversation. Whatever was between us was a long time ago. You behaved like a shit. I'm married to Guy and my life is at Culver. I need to go home.'

'Did you know you had a crumb on your lip?'

I felt myself blushing. He wrongfooted me so easily, still. Now I did feel angry. I started walking towards my car. He followed.

'Tamar. I'm sorry.' (Oliver, apologising? Twice now, if you include his confession on Wolf Tor.) 'Just that there's so much unsaid. Give me a chance. Please.'

'Just leave it. Leave it, Oliver. Let it go.' I put the key in the lock.

'Is that really what you want? Look at me, Tamar.'

I paused. He put a finger to my chin and raised my face; I heard my intake of breath.

'Come on. Please. Half an hour. That's all. We can drive separately. If you prefer. And it's on your way back, anyway.'

I was just about to drive out when he leapt off his bike and raced towards me again. He was urgently searching his pockets. 'You got a mobile, Tay?'

'Yes, though it'll be switched off; I barely use it.'

'I've dropped mine somewhere. Can you ring it?'

I fished around in my bag, found it, switched it on. He gave me the number. I rang. Another phone answered, with a little burst of something Afro-Cuban, from under his bike.

The paths wound through green darkness. Tree rhododendrons tunnelled above us. Everywhere was the sound of water.

I suddenly felt hugely, safely, peaceful.

We walked side-by-side; single file in the narrow bits. Oliver didn't touch me.

There was a sudden burst of blinding light as we emerged by the carp pool. I loved that moment; I'd experienced it before. We looked at each other; I knew he too had been aware of it.

The sky was caught in the massive lily pads. A single late butter-icing-coloured flower raised its face. Fat carp swayed lazily in and out of the stems.

No sound but water. No time.

I squatted at the edge. He too squatted down, further away. He'd got his phone out, fiddled with it, then swapped it for his camera and started adjusting the lens.

BeeBEEP. Text. 'this is how it is / the path gives out here / at the lily pond'

I noticed I was shaking. He strolled back round and grinned at me.

For minutes we didn't talk. Then: 'I didn't know you knew about haiku.'

'Been practising Zen for years. Didn't I tell you?'

'Of course not. I haven't seen you! Does that practice include

252

haiku?'

'Well, I include haiku. Part of my contemplative streak. Goes with the photos. As I see it. Capturing the moment. I'm a crap poet though. Matter of fact, not all of that's mine anyway. Basho's idea. Or Buson. One of those old haiku masters, anyway.'

He moved along the stone edge of the carp pond.

He was leaning out over the water, focusing his lens close to the surface of the pool.

Him and me and water. I didn't mean to say it, I swear. But there it was, out: 'You're not going to fall in this time, are you?'

He looked up at me and grinned broadly.

'Or should I say: at the lily pond / Oliver's barely balanced / will he, won't he, fall?' I extemporised, feeling pleased with myself.

Oliver laughed; a deep warm laugh that made me want to laugh with him. I realised that I hadn't really heard him laugh before, in France. I looked at him, unable to suppress my own smile.

'I felt so stupid. Trying to impress you. Thought I was going to drown.'

Then his smile vanished and we both fell silent. Perhaps he too was remembering what I was remembering, hot with embarrassment as well as the memory of desire: what had happened afterwards. Oh God. When would I learn to think before speaking? Suddenly the laughter had evaporated and my peace had gone. I stood up and stretched, and wandered on down the path, away from the pool.

When he caught up with me I was standing beneath the gunnera, watching the cascade of water over the mill wheel.

'Are you happy?'

His question took me by surprise.

I didn't want to answer. It would also be disloyal – though I

253

recognised that I was hardly standing on moral terra firma as it was.

'I need to go now, Oliver.'

'We've only just arrived! What have I said?'

'It's not you,' I said. 'It's me.'

I could see him register my admission. Worse and worse. I turned away again.

'Tamar,' he said, softly. 'Tamar.' I couldn't bear the sadness in his voice. I couldn't bear any more pain at all, anywhere.

'Don't you smoke any more?' I heard my voice, cool and brittle. The question was irrelevant, trivial, distancing. Ironic, too, because it was Oliver's distance that had been so hard before.

Oliver looked at me. I raised my face and looked back. Once again his grey eyes were unreadable. He shook his head. 'So?'

I fled.

BeeBEEP. '???'

I let it go.


An envelope arrived, addressed to Tamar Delaney, a couple of weeks later. A private view invitation: Oliver McDermott at the Foreshore Gallery, St Ives: Recent Photographs.

Still using a pseudonym, then.

It occurred to me, with a cold shock of fear, that of course Guy's brother – my ex-lover – was a criminal, a wanted man. Someone who'd caused death by dangerous driving. He'd never been caught after jumping bail. Somehow, up until now, I'd resisted allowing the implications of it all to penetrate. How the mind tricks us.

The thought sobered me. I put the card away in the pocket in my bag, and did my best to forget Eliot Delaney.

## Fifty-two

I turned into a liar. I've wondered since: at what point does deception start? Starting points. I said at the beginning that they interest me. When did I cross the threshold beyond which I could not turn back? It fascinates me, this notion of time as a linear unfolding; the fact that things – actions, words – cannot be undone. A torrent of leavings disappearing in one's wake, like islands.

Atonement is maybe the best one can hope for; and even that is not always possible. Atonement, then; or remorse. That's the choice. Remorse is a soiling and sordid state of being. It tars your wings. That's why Catholics have confession. It's something to do with revisiting, taking responsibility for and thereby lifting the weight of the past: a cleansing. Not exoneration but some kind of liberation. The possibility of redemption.

But that's a digression.

Did the deception start with Oliver's note, which I chose not to mention to Guy? Or our next two meetings, the second by 'chance' (if such a thing exists), the first by calculated self-delusion?

Or maybe that afternoon of slant light – a photographer's dream, apparently: late October, milk-smooth sea, and nothing but ocean between us and America.

It was certainly the first time that I knowingly made an arrangement that would ensure that I saw Oliver, without telling Guy.

How the universe conspires. I remembered that *Gardens* had, months previously, shown an interest in my doing a short series on Devon and Cornish Gardens. I'd not followed it up before because I'd been more interested in placing environmental research I'd been doing: BSE, organophosphates, water purity, mercury in fillings, sweeteners in food. And of course foot and mouth. Well, now I remembered, and called them up with a view to kicking off with the tip of the peninsula, working my way northwards, or northeast, up through Cornwall and into Devon over the next few issues.

I suggested the Barbara Hepworth sculpture garden, which of course is in St Ives.

They bit.

I went.

It's shocking how easy it is to fall into deception, isn't it? Just a handful of words, an impulse, an unpremeditated step.

The Foreshore private view was at lunchtime. I was up early, agonising about what to wear. It was still soft and sunny. Jeans and jumper seemed somehow more honest – more habitual, less of a 'message' that our meeting mattered. Less likely, too – I hate to admit that I thought this – to arouse suspicion. On the other hand, it was a private view. But at lunchtime. OK, I am a writer – everyone knows that writers simply wear black and dress to please themselves.

I hate the transition from bare feet or sandals to socks and boots. But it was borderline for warmth, and my sandals were too chunky and scuffed to look smart. In the end I wore long boots and a simple black skirt and top, with some solid but not too ostentatious silver and turquoise Nepalese jewellery. My hair was growing a bit, and I felt more feminine than I had for ages.

'No jeans, Tay! Where are you going today?'

'St Ives. Barbara Hepworth garden for a mag and I'll probably call in at the Tate. There's a private view I might drop in to...' I made a show of searching through my handbag. 'Seen my keys?' I prayed he wouldn't ask more; I knew I'd probably be flushed with the almost-lies.

'You passing Trago? Will you go that way?'

'I could,' I answered, relieved. 'What do you need?'

'Sheep nuts.'

'Does Trago do animal feed?'

'As far as I know. Don't they? Otherwise one of the ag merchants, could you?'

'OK. Do I need to look for a special supplement or anything? I mean the ewes're pregnant by now, aren't they?'

'If that young fellow knows how to do his stuff. I knew where I was with the old ram... Nope. They're fine. Good shape, considering. Better take the farm cheque book.'

At the wheel of the car I felt alternately elation, guilt and nervousness. Even with a detour to an agricultural merchant I drove far too fast and arrived early enough as to be able to spend a good chunk of time in the sculpture garden before going to the Foreshore.

The town was still busy, prior to entering the winter quiet after half-term. I snaked through the narrow streets looking for a central parking spot, but everywhere was full. Never mind – I'd park at the top of Barnoon and allow myself a few minutes' wallowing in the view: the 'island' chapel, the tumble of lichened roofs leading down to the harbour, a fishing smack or two with their streamers of white water and gulls, and in front of me and off to the left too, towards the coast path and Rosewall Hill, sea. Sea, sea, sea. Azure, jade, indigo. A scattering of surfers, like punctuation. Everywhere the call of seabirds and soft salt air.

An extraordinary sensation suddenly made itself felt: as if every cell in my body was fizzing. Gradually I became aware that I felt hugely, intensely, alive. On an instant I felt freer than I'd felt for months. Years, even. I wanted to dance down the steep path, skip down the steps, run down The Digey, singing out loud.

The gallery was full of light.

I was breathless.

He was standing slightly apart from the hubbub. He too was dressed in black. In his alert stillness he looked like an exclamation mark in the white room. When he saw me enter he reached for a glass of red wine – what I would have chosen for myself – and brought it over to me. He had a slight smile at his eyes. He handed me the glass and lightly touched his fingers to my hair. I coloured.

'You look lovely,' he said, simply. 'Glad your hair has grown.'

This new Oliver was confounding me. From our history, I couldn't help but be braced for, if not warfare, then at least some fencing – the need to be permanently *en garde*. The fact of not having to be defended was leaving me feeling somewhat naked.

'Thank you,' I said, once I was fairly confident my voice wouldn't shake.

I lifted my eyes to the photographs. All black and white; an impression of space, of vastness. I could breathe.

'Must be years since you saw my photos,' he said musingly. 'Galerie Chateaubriand, I guess.'

'Mmmm, probably was,' I replied. Then a thought occurred to me: 'How do you know that? You weren't there!'

'I was. I saw you come in.'

My heart started beating erratically. 'You hid from me?'

He looked out of the window at the shore; nodded for me to look, too. The light had glossed a pathway: a wide swathe of sand and sea was illuminated, as if cut and collaged from a different day altogether. I felt him drift away for a few moments. When he came back, his eyes had a new expression in them. 'Did you ever read Henry Williamson's book *The Pathway*, set in North Devon? There's a story within a story: *The Starborn*, I think it was.'

'Yes,' I said. 'It was a favourite when I was growing up.' I knew exactly what he was talking about. This was the interior Oliver: a privileged brief glimpse. I looked down into my glass. We were silent. Then someone came up to him, took his arm, led him over to speak to an older smart-looking woman, and the three of them moved towards a triptych at the far end of the gallery.

I took the chance to look at his pictures.

Yes, spaciousness. The pictures had the feel of Zen gardens to them; a harmonious meeting of shapes and patterns and forms without the distraction of colour.

He clearly had something. The composition was very simple – a gamble – but what had happened was that he used the subject not to fill the frame but to frame something else: maybe something akin to a question. What I mean is that the composition was intended, I think, to be transparent: to gesture to something beyond itself, even while being fully itself.

One sequence, for instance, was composed entirely of fluid forms – ripples – photographed at close range and printed large. In a way the actual subject was unimportant; what mattered was the juxtaposition of several versions of the same movement in different textures or elements, from soft to hard. As far as I could tell in close-up he'd used ripples in water, in sand, in a ploughed field, in the whorls of a human thumbprint, on bark, on what I thought must be a huge ammonite, and finally on stone.

I suddenly realised with a shock that the shapes on the stone were manmade; and were in fact from one of the chambered stones we'd seen on our day near Carnac, all those years ago.

Beside the sequence the information board enigmatically read:

nothing but this

waves

then

no waves

I was mesmerised by the sequence. I moved from each to each of the seven prints several times, entranced. Then I walked back the other way: from hard and ancient and durable to soft, transient and recurring. I was fascinated. And there was something profoundly right about the sequence, like when you see something that is constructed according to the golden section, or the Fibonacci sequence; or hear a perfect scale. It soothes something in us.

I was still staring when Oliver came back. He just stood beside me quietly until I turned to him.

'These are extraordinary, Oliver.'

'Thank you. It – matters that you like them.'

'Do I recognise the stone carvings?'

He looked pleased. 'You remembered!'

'Oh yes.'

Someone else was approaching him. 'Have you sold any?' I asked.

'One or two. That woman wanted the triptych for her café. Do you know the Porth Ia?'

'Yes. Look – someone wants to talk to you. I'll leave you to it.'

'Meet me later? Coffee, maybe?

I hardly hesitated. 'OK. Porth Ia?'

'An hour?' His eyes held mine, smiled; then he turned his attention to the man waiting politely just out of earshot.

I wandered round the gallery, stopping by each photograph. Yes, I could live with any of them.


Paradise.

Cafés are important to writers. Or at least writing's a good excuse... This is my favourite anywhere. Afternoon sun drenched the terrace of the café in soft light, bounced off the chrome chair legs, lounged on the wooden decking. A young speckled herring gull stood on the railing and fixed me with its yellow eyes.

The clear sea, glass green in the shallows, was close enough for the murmur and shush to take over the air. The sea in West Cornwall is exceptional: it really is the colours of those exaggerated postcards.

I'd caught the café just in time for some lunch: antipasti – a bowl of spicy olives, slippery with herby oil; a plate of red bean and cashew paté, cold roast pepper and aubergine, and orange roast butternut squash with chopped coriander. Warm home-made bread; rocket salad. Sparkling Cornish spring water. A feast for all the senses. I had my notebook beside me, and scribbled more notes about the sculpture garden in between mouthfuls.

Despite my deception, despite my guilt and trepidation, I felt totally serene.

'I wasn't hiding,' said a voice behind me. 'I was just having a difficult day. Wasn't sure you'd come in to see me, anyway.'

I smiled and held out the bowl of olives. 'Why else?'

He took one. 'Not my style to come bounding down the stairs. Making assumptions.' His grin was wry. 'Heard Jean-Yves doing his lines. Hoped you'd noticed his very naff shoes. Can I get you a coffee?'

I couldn't suppress my smile now if I wanted to. 'Please. Was the photo in the gallery the one from the time I knocked your tripod in the market? The first time we – I – umm met you?'

He was there immediately. 'The lobster. Yes. You did see the poor bugger on the fish stall then. Knew you'd hate it, too...'

'Claws bound with twine. Yes. – Have you eaten?'

'Not hungry. Big breakfast.' He pulled out the chair next to mine, and dropped his camera – perpetual accessory – onto the table, lifted his hand for the waitress. Stared at the sea for a moment. Then he turned his grey eyes to my face. They were serious, searching. Just as he opened his mouth the waitress appeared. I carried on eating.

He waited till she'd gone. 'There's something, isn't there? Still. It never went. Fuck knows what to do about it though.'

There was a pause. I stopped eating.

'You're different,' I said eventually, feeling terribly shy. Self-conscious.

'I told you. I've grown up. Got tired of running. Hiding. But you. You didn't answer my question?'

'Was it a question?' I knew I was playing for time. 'I liked your little poem, by the way.'

The waitress arrived with our coffee; I was glad to have something to do with my hands. I glanced out at the sea. The tide was coming in. It was then that I saw them: two seals in the near shallows, close enough to see their markings. I'd never seen them that close. 'Look!'

We watched them for six or seven minutes, until they were out of sight over towards the rocks where, earlier, I'd seen two young gulls glutting themselves on a flickering mass of little silver fish, trapped by the tide in a rockpool.

I could feel, or maybe sense, Oliver's breath on my neck.

It was then, inexorably, that something turned. Coincidence; synchronicity; call it what you like. We inhabit a symbolic and multi-tracked universe. Some places the veils are thin.

For the briefest moment, this was the man I'd been with forever. I turned my head and our eyes collided.

At the risk of labouring my metaphor, I swallowed the final seeds. No turning back from here on.

Then we fell back into our separate places.

For a moment Oliver had looked as if he were about to take my hand. He didn't, though.

I'd sobered instantly on landing back in my separate body. What was I doing here with my husband's brother? Illicitly? I pushed the thought away; and as if sensitive to all the nuances Oliver shifted levels. 'Tell me about your writing, Tamar. What are you doing with it?'

'Well, right now of course there's all the foot and mouth business... and I've been doing some investigative stuff to do with environmental toxins,' I began, in relief. 'Mercury and fluoride and aspartame and organophosphates. But I'm down here to do a piece on the Barbara Hepworth sculpture garden for a magazine; I arrived early enough to visit; it fitted in nicely,' I gabbled. 'Next week –'

He'd listened patiently. Now he interrupted: 'No, I mean why you write.'

'Well, because I'm interested in my subjects; and we need –'

'I mean your creativity. Why do you write?'

'Creativity. No time for it, really. Umm –'

'If someone gave you six months. If someone said you only had six months. What would you do? That's different?'

'Uh, I – God, Oliver. What is this?'

'Just wondering what your vision is these days. Had you down as a dreamer; cooking up poetry while you gardened.'

'Gosh. OK. Six months. Well, I'd spend more time walking and riding. I'd spend a lot more time reading. Gardening, of course. Friends.'

'And your soul, Tamar? That's what I'm talking about –' He smiled wryly, self-deprecatingly. 'Yeah yeah I know. No other way of asking. What does it need?'

'I'd withdraw from the world a bit, I guess. Out in the wild. And write more – I suppose – "from the heart". Yes, poetry. I'd write and write and write. Journals, letters, philosophical essays, stories, explorations with no goal – oh, everything! There are so many things I want to explore and imagine but circumstances don't – well, don't really allow. Time, and the times...'

His eyes creased at the corners at my enthusiasm. 'On your own? Do you share those things with – anyone?'

'I don't think you should be asking me that.'

'I just did. So?'

'What about you?'

'Oh, I know I need to photograph. What I see. That's my path. And a certain dose of solitude. But I've lacked a travelling companion.' He glanced away, after the seals. '"You have to do it alone but you don't have to be alone to do it." I've always been alone.' He pushed back his chair suddenly. 'Going to see if I can spot the seals again.' He indicated his camera. 'Coming?'

'Yes, to that question.' I took a breath. I could still taste pomegranate. 'And no, to the other. In response to your honesty.'

Oliver picked up the bill. 'Thought so. You're solo, deep down, aren't you? Still?'

I gasped. 'That's outrageous, Oliver. I'm – married. Out of order! And hey! – that's my bill!'

He shrugged, and strode into the café.


A seal-less hour later we strolled back across the beach. A tide had left crescents of mussel shells necklacing the sand – indigo, amethyst, French navy. The sea, with dusk approaching, was milky, opalescent. Motionless. We walked side-by-side, not quite touching. The sand was cool and slightly moist. Our bare feet sank fractionally.

With the old friction between us gone, silence was comfortable. We spoke, or didn't. It didn't matter. We were new lovers; or we'd been together forever. Either; both. Of course there was electricity between us; always would be. But it was different now. The tension felt creative rather than antagonistic. Strange, when there was still so much to say, and considering how it had been left, all those years before. Our afternoon was easy, warm; a gentle flow of spoken and unspoken conversation both ways, continuously.

The irony wasn't lost on me. This was the man beside whom I wanted to walk. And wake. And I was married to his brother, a good man whom I had no wish to hurt. There are times when you wonder what joker in the universe, or in the psyche, is dealing the cards.

At the end of the beach he turned to me and simply opened his arms. We were standing at the edge of the water; now and then a wavelet swayed up and licked our ankles. Clutching my boots awkwardly I tentatively stepped towards him. He threw his boots clear of the tide then reached for mine and chucked them after.

I barely came up to his shoulder. I'd forgotten. He rested his chin on the top of my head, and we just gently held each other. For a long time.

'I can feel your heart beating,' I said in that rather banal way that people have in such circumstances. Then: 'I must go in a minute.'

Silence again. The light was falling slantwise. The lichened roofs were lit; somewhere in the distance a window had caught the setting sun. The fields sloping down to the water on the headland were meshed with rays. The air was soft.

'What're we go to do, Tamar?'

'I don't know what we can do.'

'Will you let me stay in touch?'

'I don't know where you live, even.'

He put his hands on my shoulders and leant back to look into my face. His expression was serious. 'Best for everyone if you don't know. OK? Don't ask me.'

He let go of me and squatted down, picked something up. He opened his fist: a whole mussel, both halves attached. He gently separated it at the cartilage, handed me one half of the bivalve, grinning.

We drifted back to the town, went our separate ways.

Five minutes up the hill going home: beeBEEP. 'tomorrow, remember today. x'

## Fifty-three

Night had long fallen when I got back. I felt terrible. And I felt filled with joy. How can two such conflicting emotions co-exist in the human heart?

As I opened the door Guy's raised voice was coming from Bob's office: haranguing, rising and falling. I knew immediately he'd been drinking. I dropped the bags of shopping I'd picked up at on the way back and paused in toeing off my boots in the front hallway to listen. From time to time there was a deeper quiet but firm interjection from Bob.

I have to admit to a rush of guilty relief. If Guy was both pissed and angry he might not notice the highly-charged aura which I was sure I would be radiating. Nonetheless I stopped a moment and leaned against the hall wall to try and compose myself before encountering Trudy, who was unlikely to miss it.

I picked up the bags again and breezed into the kitchen. The kittens came tumbling and mewing towards me. I dropped the bags and scooped them both up. 'Cup of tea, Trudy?' I said, dumping the kittens in the chair by the Rayburn.

'Hello, dear. Good day? Love one.' Trudy lifted her head from the newspaper and looked at me. She paused, and her grey eyes looked extraordinarily dark and inscrutable for a moment; or maybe I, with my conscience, imagined that. My pang of unease was accompanied by a different and poignant sensation as I suddenly recognised Oliver's farseeing look in hers.

Then her face cleared. 'Have you had anything to eat?'

I went to sort through the bags. 'Not yet. Picked up some groceries, though, including the things on your list.'

'There's a couple of baked potatoes in the oven. I fed the men – didn't know when you'd be back.'

'No. Great. Thanks. Think I've got some salad bits in here –

267

oh, did you cut any lettuces this morning?'

'A couple. And some of your rocket.'

'Oh good. What're those two arguing about?'

'Heaven knows. They were at it this morning, too.'

Just then the office door opened and Guy strode out.

'That's my last word, son –' Bob's voice followed him.

Guy looked black. 'Hi,' he said to me, and walked towards the larder. I held my breath. Yes, the homebrew. Trudy and I glanced at each other. He re-emerged. 'Good day? – Good,' he said, before I could respond, and took his glass out into the yard.

I made the tea. Several minutes later I took my mug and strolled out after him. In the dark I could just make out Guy's shape, leaning on the gate through from the yard into the lane. My heart was pounding – guilt, no doubt, as well as anxiety about what had happened in Bob's office. There was a sprinkling of stars through a light haze, and a thin moon. Frost before dawn, maybe. I went back for a jacket.

'Got your sheep nuts,' I said casually, by way of a preamble.

He grunted.

I carried on. 'What was all that about?'

'What?'

'You and Bob.'

'A bloody great fuss about nothing. The old man's so effing stubborn sometimes.'

I sipped my tea. He didn't seem inclined to continue. To deflect any possible attention away from me, I asked baldly: 'What were you shouting about?'

'The farm business is mine, Tay.'

His words stung. I looked at him.

He must have felt my stare in the darkness. He added without turning his head: 'Sorry. Difficult day.' He stretched out his arm and touched me briefly on the back.

We leaned on the gate side-by-side. Now I felt annoyed as well as guilty. I didn't know what to say, but was afraid he would ask me about my day and then I'd have to lie, at least by default. The darkness would cover a rising blush, however. God, I was becoming a scheming bitch.

As it happened, he was too absorbed in whatever was going on for him to do more than barely register my presence. If he had been the type, I'd have said he was sulking. Certainly he was emanating a grouchy surliness.

Guy and I were a couple of feet apart; to an onlooker, we would, no doubt, have seemed quietly companionable. The hypocrisy was palpable. What was I pretending? I felt squeezed in the present by both the past and the future. As long as I could stand here, the loyal farmer's wife, and focus on nothing other than what we had: a (mostly) affectionate and (mostly) bearable marriage, a beautiful home, and a newly-restocked farm, I could be almost content; and, more importantly, not have to risk rocking any boats. And, after all, those things should be enough. More than enough. Shouldn't they?

But as soon as my thoughts strayed, as they did constantly, to Oliver and the day, then a wild and unstable joy rose in me, coupled inextricably with a choking sense of deception and despair.

I shook myself mentally. Think of something else.

'Did Trudy feed the bantams today, Guy, d'you know?'

'Yep. Fox got one last night apparently. Feathers everywhere. Sorry, Tay.'

'Oh God. D'you know which one?'

'No. One of the younger hens, I think. Why don't you get another coop and shut them up?'

'I don't want to. They're safer up in the trees. Remember I lost the last lot because we shut them up at night and something

269

got through the planks.'

'Something got one in the trees, too.'

'I know. But only one. The young ones aren't always as quick. Sad, though. I love those little birds. I'm just going to go and check them. And see Saracen. If it's dry tomorrow morning I might try for an early ride. Feels like weeks since I took the horse out.'

'Rain coming,' said Trudy next morning.

'But we had a light frost this morning.'

'It'll change before evening. Wet. And chilly.' She's always been a reliable forecaster. 'The wind's rising and backing. Can you give me a hand with the rest of the eating apples, Tamar? We need to get them in, really. Cider ones are going on Monday. What have you got on today?'

'I was going to ride, but I'm up a bit late for that. I do have to write up some notes from yesterday, though. If you could do the animals while I make a start I can give you a hand after that for a couple of hours. Is that OK? What about Bob and Guy?'

'I think they're still fencing, and rebuilding that stone wall in the top pasture. Lambs'll be over that in a tick. Guy wanted to run the harrow over some of the pasture and spread some calcified seaweed over the next few days, too.'

'Did you hear that they're wanting to ban the use of that?'

'What, calcified seaweed? We've always used it.'

'I know; but apparently it all comes from the entrance to Falmouth harbour, and it's a kind of coral, I think. Anyway, it's ancient and nearly exhausted, they say.'

'Hmm. We'd have to go and pull in fresh seaweed instead, then. Can you imagine how much we'd need? Anyhow, you go off to your computer and I'll see you later.'

## Fifty-four

The trailer was already parked out in the orchard, ready-loaded with a stack of big empty baskets. The air, noon-warm, was fragrant with fruit: ripe and heady. A few drowsy wasps made half-hearted assaults on the windfalls, half-buried in lush grass and dandelions. A robin flitted over to sit on an apple twig and watch us.

'God, it's so good to have had a break from all that rain. This sunny spell has been good for late grass, too, hasn't it?'

'Mmm. Smells good, too.'

'November next week. Here, have this bag.'

Trudy and I slung the canvas bags across our bodies and helped each other prop and stabilise the ladders. Trudy started on a russet, I a pippin. Both of them had taken the wet badly; there was quite a lot of scab on the fruit. Nonetheless, it had been a wonderful harvest season, and the hedges and banks around were still crimson with hips and haws and bryony berries, and the track flushed pink with spindle. Most of the rowans had gone now, but on the larder windowsill we had jar after jar of crab apple and rowan jelly, deep amber in the glass, alongside the gooseberry and elderflower, and plum jams.

We picked in comfortable silence. The sun was weak, but I was still aware of it on my neck, exposed because I'd piled my hair on top of my head out of the way.

There's something very soothing, meditative, about picking fruit. It's partly the rhythm, and partly the primal satisfaction that comes from gathering harvest. It's also a deeply nourishing act; and as talk of possible war had started and the whole world, not just my personal one, was feeling rather destabilised it was good to lose myself in the mindlessness – mindfulness – of gentle physical movement. And to daydream.

From time-to-time one of us would chuck a bad one to the ground, or descend the ladder to empty our bag.

We had both arrived at the trailer at the same moment. I went to empty my bag first, while Trudy stretched her back. I'd noticed she was stiffer climbing the ladder than she had been last year. 'Your back OK?' I called over my shoulder, lifting rather than tipping the apples out so as not to bruise them.

'Yes. Bit stiff, that's all.'

I finished and Trudy stepped forward.

'Trudy, do you know what they were arguing about last night?'

'I've a fair idea.'

Silence.

'Will you tell me?'

She sighed. 'Men are so stubborn sometimes. Intractable. They just can't see the bigger picture.'

'Mmm?' I tried to sound encouraging.

Trudy leaned against the trailer. 'Guy wants to sell a couple of the fields.'

'My God, Trudy! What on earth for? And why am I always the last to hear? Sometimes I feel so – so –'

'I know. He means well, does Guy; just he likes to do things his way.' She smiled sheepishly. 'Can't think where he gets it from. Don't take it personally, dear. He always talks when he's ready.'

I swallowed the urge to say don't tell me how to manage my husband. My irritation seemed to be close to the surface. Instead I said: 'But why on earth?'

'Says he wants a new tractor.'

'What? What's wrong with the old one?'

'Well, nothing. Still serviceable, as far as I can tell. But it is

272

ancient. We had it when we took over Culver when the children were little. But he wants one of those new Japanese ones.'

'But Bob would never agree to selling off Culver land!'

'I know. Can't think why Guy thought he might.'

I brooded on this back up in the next tree. How marginalised I sometimes felt; patronised, too. And angry. Once Guy and I would have talked about everything. And sad, too – where was the happy-go-lucky easygoing man I'd married? But come to that, where was his open and honest bride?

Pandora's box. Next time we coincided by the trailer what Trudy had to say was of far greater import.

'D'you want some water, Trudy?' I poured us both some from the jug and glasses I'd brought out and left beneath the trailer and took hers to her.

'Thanks.' We leaned our backs against the trailer and sipped.

'Trudy – I – feel a bit anxious about Guy sometimes. You must have noticed how different he is from the old Guy.'

'Of course. But it's been such a tough time. He's grown up a bit, that's all. He'll come through.'

'But he bullies Bob. I hate that.'

A worried look came into Trudy's eyes. 'I know, dear. That makes me sad. Bob's frailer than he used to be.' She swallowed and looked down into her glass.

Neither of us said anything for several minutes. I moved to pick up my bag again.

'Tamar – how are you? Is everything OK?' Trudy didn't look around at me, just put the glass down and started emptying her apples.

'Y – yes, yes; I'm fine. Just on a short fuse at the moment, that's all. Annoyed that Guy didn't tell me. Bothered about his attitude to Bob. Otherwise I'm fine, yes.'

'I don't mean about Guy and Bob or what we were talking about.'

'Huh?'

'I meant are you OK?'

'In what way?'

Trudy never normally asked personal questions, except in the broadest way – apart from the time when Eliot had appeared in the yard and she'd revealed what she knew. We'd not spoken since of any of it; and although I often railed about this family trait of reticence, the last few months I'd been grateful. I couldn't talk to anyone about it, and anyway I'm not sure I could have borne it; my feelings were so confused and it was already costing me all I had of willpower simply to function. And I'm hopeless at dissembling, brazening things out.

'I just wondered.' Still she didn't look at me. 'I wondered if perhaps you'd seen Eliot?'

I dropped my glass. Splinters flew across the trailer. I froze. Trudy turned and looked at me then, her grey eyes searching, but with no judgement in them, only a kind of fierce longing. She smiled a little smile. 'How's my boy?' Her voice was low, vulnerable.

We stood facing each other. I couldn't meet her gaze and I couldn't start to speak.

Silence stretched between us. My mind was whirling. How did she feel about it, knowing I was married to one of her sons but in touch illicitly with the other?

Trudy broke the silence. 'Tamar, there's something I want to tell you. I wanted to tell you in the kitchen that time after – Eliot. I've never told anyone. I need your word that you'll never mention it to anyone else.'

Did I want that responsibility?

She looked at her hands a minute, ran a thumbnail around the margins of her fingernails. When she looked up, her face was grave, and sad. 'Will you give me that?'

I hesitated, then nodded.

'I don't know why I'm telling you this. It's no-one else's business, and even the boys don't know. Maybe that's wrong of me.' She glanced down again. 'I'm a private woman. Perhaps that's partly because I never had a daughter. I wanted one. Sons are different, no matter how much you love them. You're the nearest I've got, Tay, and I'm lucky. I trust you. I think of you as my daughter.' She looked up into the branches of the apple tree, then turned her head and smiled at me, a luminous smile that I practically felt on my skin.

It crossed my mind that we were all unravelling.

Trudy continued. 'Times like this... Somehow it seems important to tell you. I don't know –' she smiled at herself. Her face looked very vulnerable; I saw how beautiful she must have been in her grey-eyed enigmatic way. 'I don't know why. It might help you to know. And I guess you'll understand. ' She looked away a minute. 'And perhaps I need to get it off my chest. Here goes.' She drew a long breath and looked away from me, out over the moors. 'Guy – Guy isn't Bob's child. I was very stupid. We were going through a hard time; Bob was away working a lot, lecturing. I had a small child – Eliot – and was lonely. I knew I loved Bob. I knew it; but I still did it. Stupid, ridiculous. Selfish. Bob – forgave me. Loved me still. He's a bigger man than – anyone.' As she spoke she gazed off over my head into the distance, towards the moors. A pair of collared doves was crooning on the telephone wire.

'But –' I began. He even looked a bit like Bob. 'But –' I couldn't finish. Once again, I had nothing I could say. I was past shock. After the past year – not to mention the recent past –

275

there was little room left for intense emotional response. I simply stared at her.

'So it was hard enough for me to hear Guy throwing Bob's son out, throwing his weight around about "his" farm. I can't begin to think how it was for Bob. He'd never say anything, though. As far as he's concerned, Guy's his son too. And after all, he's been the loyal one.'

When Trudy had refocused her eyes on me, I saw they were full.

'There,' she said. 'There, Tamar. My confession. Bob has been the best husband I could ever have had; and the best father to both – both of – my – our – sons. There. Now you know my secret. Maybe it will explain things. Maybe not.'

She blotted her eyes and sniffed, then picked up the apple bag. 'There. Enough. And – I don't want to know –' she paused. 'Anything else. I'm just longing to know how Eliot is. That's all.'

# Fifty-five

That winter was gentle.

Looking back, I realise that it was the first winter for a long time when I didn't feel constantly embattled by the Dartmoor micro-climate; when I wasn't forever climbing in and out of wet clothes. Taking hay up to Saracen in the mornings – the weather was kind enough for him to overwinter entirely outdoors – with the dogs was the pure pleasure that it ought to be, and I got in quite a lot of time riding up amongst the tors and down the ancient trackways, too.

The moor in winter has a dark and commanding grandeur that is entirely missed by the summer trippers; winter suits it. It feels bigger, somehow, and more feral. I'm always amazed, too, how when you look, even though the amethyst of the autumn heathers has gone, its apparent sere uniformity is in fact a subtly dramatic palette of ochres, fox-reds and rusts, acid greens and peat blacks, linked by the white rush of one of the leats or brooks. Sometimes, in winter, coming out early into weak sun, a whole hillside will be winking – sheets or ragged patches of ice where bogs sit, or where rills have left gloops of themselves as pendula, ice chandeliers, at their margins.

Winter is a time for the buzzards and kestrels and sparrowhawks; sometimes a peregrine or merlin speeds across your vision. Single ravens cronk from the tops of tors, and the foxes come down lower to hunt or scavenge, appearing frequently in daylight in our fields or on the lane.

Things looked set for an upturn – very welcome, long due.

Culver's new animals were thriving. Healthy sheep inhabited the home meadows, and the new South Devons wintered well in the big barn and its two adjacent fields. The kittens became bolder, and Ernie in particular – the black – took to strolling off down our track to investigate the banks and their inhabitants. Even the bantam numbers remained stable.

By January, though we'd had some snow and quite a few frosts, my leeks – the only things I'd managed to plant – were showing abundant greenery and thick white stems in the vegetable garden. And first snowdrops, then celandines and dandelions, followed by primroses, violets and stitchwort lit the banks.

I'd landed a small 'Dartmoor Diary' column in a national weekly broadsheet: 300 words on our continuing recovery from foot and mouth, and a record of the changing seasons. Undemanding, and it helped me pay attention to the small details of natural life: something I love. It gave me good reason to spend time wandering, musing, observing without feeling guilty at all the domestic and farm things that also needed doing. Plus it paid. Maybe it would buy me the time to start a larger writing project.

Money was very tight, still, but the promise was there: we had received some compensation, and there would be, we'd been assured, more coming. We'd lost a good year's income from stock, and it would be a while before we had more to sell. Nonetheless, on the home front, things seemed to have eased. There was, admittedly, a dip in collective spirits when the bank statements arrived, but we seemed to be getting by. Maybe we'd simply got used to all the uncertainty. We were good at 'making do'.

There was no sign of any new tractor, but Bob and Guy seemed not to be arguing about it.

There was a quietness about us all. Sometimes I worried that it was a deadening: that we'd all been dulled by what we'd gone through. But there was also relief.

Guy was altogether calmer. He was drinking less, though it seemed to me he was more withdrawn. A strange phenomenon, which I suspect is not uncommon in such circumstances: since I had been seeing Oliver, ironically, Guy and I, as far as our daily lives were concerned, were getting along better, although there was a distance between us. I can't say our recent communication really had much depth – in truth, I suppose, it never had; but we had a shared past and there was still warmth between us. We'd been through a lot. And survived it. There were, and always would be, differences between us: exemplified in such things as my vegetarian diet and his carnivorous one; and now, in our relative positions on the possibility of war in the Gulf, which was looking increasingly like a probability. Sometimes we argued about the latter; often, recently, we had chosen to keep our views to ourselves.

Though Guy was noticeably angry for a time, we had never spoken again of my connection with Oliver, though we were, I think, both aware that the knowledge squatted between us: a quagmire which we skirted.

But now we were somehow more gentle with each other.

It all sounds perfectly reasonably contented on paper. It was, I suppose, on one level. What was really hard though was the continuing undercurrent of deception. I knew I was living a lie and I didn't know how to start to address it. It coloured and clouded everything – everything felt mottled, muddied, equivocal.

For yes, of course – you will have guessed – Oliver and I continued to meet. Is it an abdication of responsibility to say that there was an inexorability in our coming together? – I did, for a very long time, resist it. I cannot condone or defend my behaviour. I have a depth of remorse and guilt that will remain.

But regret? – I came alive; and in so doing realised how close I had been to losing my spirit. Soul loss comes about when you have to lop off bits of yourself in order to remain in a situation; in order to survive, to exist. In some parts of the world, this is imposed on people. Here, in the West, we choose to do it – and frighteningly, it seems to me, we often call it love.

Compromise is necessary in order to live with others, you might say. Well, I would answer, it depends what you compromise. And why. If it's your soul, in order to not have to live out your own truth – in other words, out of fear of the consequences of living out your truth – regardless of whether it's anyone else's – then I cannot agree. And if living your truth means hurting another? What is your personal responsibility? What does it mean to be responsible to and for yourself? To be selfish? To be selfless? Well. Philosophers and theologians over centuries have debated these things.

There comes a time when we each have to choose, maybe. It is never black and white. It is rarely clear exactly where the greater good lies. And truth is not always where we expect to find it.

Of course I trip myself up, over and over. The middle of the night is worst: knowing what I do now, would I still do what I did then? – I asked that early on in this story. You could justifiably ask me now.

I have no answer.

This is not to disparage what Guy and I shared in our marriage. After all, I chose not to leave him. It is also not to exonerate myself from what happened later. I take full responsibility for my actions and their consequences. But Oliver is, was and will be my beyond-all-other lover; my only full and wholehearted lover. Once we had voiced this, to ourselves and each other, words and justifications became irrelevant.

And the first time, this time around, that Oliver and I made love – in the white light of a late December afternoon, by the fire in Louise's candlelit cottage where I was staying to caretake her animals while they were away for a few days between Christmas and New Year – I knew that my marriage to Guy could not come alive again.

And of course we were left with the 'how'. Oliver had thought about coming back to Culver to confront Guy, but I persuaded him not to, after we started to meet. In the scheme of things a deceit is still a deceit, but it would have compounded my feelings of guilt terribly and I could barely imagine what it would do to Guy. So we met wherever we could – either in Cornwall or somewhere in Devon, depending on our work and other circumstances. It took a long time before I visited his flat; but there came a point where I was so deep in that to keep demurring was both pointless and even more false and cowardly than I was already being.

I had no idea what to do about anything. It would be many more months before anything at all was – for the sake of any other word – resolved; before anything came clear.

## Fifty-six

On the news that morning they were talking, as every morning lately, about the war in Iraq. I remember it clearly; it was the first time that the news scarcely touched me at all. How could it, after what I'd discovered first thing that morning after a sleepless night, peeing on the little coated stick that came with the Boots testing kit? And then making an excuse after breakfast to drive back in to Culverstock, and buying another kit... and another, just to be sure...

It seemed to me crazy that anyone ever thought war could be decisive, and could be over in days. I'd been very involved with anti-war work – letters, emails, marches and demos. I also found myself so upset by the news bulletins that I rationed my intake to once a day. Nonetheless I continued to show up at the daily peace vigils in Culverstock, where new faces joined us each evening.

Just the previous week I'd been blind with rage at it all – the hypocrisy and deceptions, the cover-ups and forgeries, the stupidity of nations who think that violence can ever solve anything. And after the rage, once the war had started, came a deep sense of despair.

But now suddenly, in the light of everything, I found I didn't have any feelings left to respond to the war. I'm ashamed to say that events here overtook my social and political conscience.

Outside spring kept coming, despite war, personal conflict and tragedy. Spring, after all, is inevitable, although it's hard to believe sometimes. From time to time, in the midst of all the whirling pain and chaos that followed, I could still feel a clear note sound somewhere inside me: green and fat and simple, like spring; like the first spikes of bluebell shoots – now long over – in amongst the dog's mercury. I hung on to those moments with all

I had.

I hadn't been able to bring myself to face Guy, be honest and direct. I found myself waiting until supper to find a way to tell him, lying on the couch in my workroom in the late afternoon wrapped in a throw and staring out at the bleak March moors. That wasn't the plan; but it was how it happened.

I watched until the grey light had faded, and the shapes outside the window – bare ash tree, uneven barn roof, gate, stony bank and hedge – had been swallowed by dusk. One by one the features of my room dissolved: the computer, the little bronze horse on the shelf near the window, the photos and paintings on the walls, then the Chinese silk shawl with its dragon, draped over the back of the couch. In the far distance, above Wolf Tor, a thin moon climbed slowly into the darkening sky, its horns diamond-sharp. Already a hazy aura proclaimed frost again, though above and behind the house thick clouds still hung.

I was shivering; just as likely to be extreme anxiety as the chill, though as I stared out of the window a stray flake or two of snow drifted past. Out of nowhere came a faint memory of Communion wafers from my convent schooldays – the certainties, the safety, the promises of childhood. I latched onto that thought, desperate to dispel other more disquieting mental intrusions. Not now; there would be plenty of time to deal with all that later. For the moment, the task ahead of me took all the emotional energy and courage I could rally.

The faint murmur of the TV from downstairs heralded newstime. I was feeling far too vulnerable to face the prospect of images of bombs and devastation; nonetheless it was time to face them all.

I could hear Trudy clattering in the kitchen. I didn't need the smells thickening outside the room to know that there would be Yorkshire pudding with onion gravy again. It was Trudy's night for cooking. She always took Sunday nights; she believed in a serious roast 'for the men', which I should now be used to but which irritated me intensely for a number of reasons, including my vegetarianism (though to be fair she often prepared something small for me to replace the meat), and also because her assumption of the matriarchal role for this night made me feel undermined.

Trudy and I had always co-existed quite comfortably in the kitchen, accommodating each other. Just now and then, though, and tonight was one of those times, I found myself angered and alienated by having to fit around her way of doing things. And annoyed that we shared a kitchen, as well as the cooking. I guess it was a mother-in-law moment, and shouldn't surprise me – every woman needs, even when she has established her place 'out there' in the world, to feel she owns her own place at the hearth. It's a primal, rather than rational, requirement for a sense of personal power, I suspect.

I pushed such ungenerous thoughts away, welcome though the distraction was on some level; and remembered that Trudy and Bob had raised the topic of building a smaller 'retirement' cottage, maybe a wooden cabin, down in the valley near the copse where there were the remains of an early mediaeval farmstead. Planning permission in the National Park was, and is, very difficult to obtain, though, so I didn't hold out too much hope; but separate dwellings would be blissful – I needed the sense of having my own, or our own, self-contained dwelling. I still hadn't ever really had that, unless you count my tiny rented place in Bath. I hadn't realised until that moment how strong the urge was. I couldn't truthfully ever really imagine Bob retiring, however; and even the memory of the way I felt Guy sometimes sidelined him on his own farm set up an acute almost physical pain in me.

I swung my feet off the couch and pulled on an old jumper. I'd knitted up one for each of us the first winter I'd been here, from our own fleece which Trudy and I between us had handspun, and which I'd then coloured with plant dyes; mine was in shades of lemon, gold and orange from onionskins and gorse blossom. I needed the emotional comfort it gave me that evening, quite apart from its warmth.

I took a deep breath and headed for the stairs.

At the door I paused. In the kitchen the kettle rocked and spat on its damp bottom on the Rayburn. I could smell, mingled with boiled spring greens, the usual faint odour of stockinged feet, recently released from wellies, sheep, and dogs. Tonight they made me feel nostalgic, full of a strange yearning. Premonitory, maybe; the anticipation of loss. Or just guilt and apprehension. Actually, I was terrified of facing them all.

Trudy's grey-clad cardiganed back was bent over the stove, where she was stirring something. My eyes scanned the men: Bob, khaki and brown, balding head bent over *Farming News*. Guy's feet were propped on a chair; I noticed with a twinge of tenderness Eric the tabby on his lap, and with a pang of guilt the holed socks. No doubt Trudy had noticed, too; she'd say nothing, and probably darn them herself, to my faint resentment and exasperation. But the truth is I simply wouldn't – wouldn't want to – make time to darn them myself; though I hate the idea of waste and throwing things out unnecessarily, life is simply too short to mend socks.

I knew as clearly as if he had spoken them Guy's thoughts behind his closed eyes: mentally he'd be checking off the ewes who had bagged up, ready to lamb. After that, he'd be running through the list of feed needed on Friday when he went in to Culverstock for the market, and picturing that in relation to the bank statement that had arrived this morning.

Suddenly something snapped in me, rebelled against the predictableness, the ordinariness, the careful colourlessness underneath the tension of it all. The fictions we had built, the things that remained forever unsaid. All the secrets.

I took a step into the kitchen. And it was out before I could stop myself.

'I think I'm pregnant.'

Oh my God. The worst possible way to tell them. Guy would hate it. And my own shame and anxiety flooding up to my face in red waves. Words that could never be unsaid – ahhh! The hypocrisy of raging against the unsaid only a moment before! – And a sudden searing certainty that I had changed our lives with those four words irrevocably, irreparably.

In that moment I hated myself.

For an instant there was a surge of near-joy in the kitchen that was tangible. Six eyes turned my way. Trudy and Bob's eyes were momentarily lit. But Guy, ominously still, commanded all our attention; and the look in his eyes as we all turned to him was terrible: ice-fire. Wild hope flared in his eyes; followed by a volcanic fury, and horror. As he held my gaze something passed between us and then beyond us, out into the cold night, and died, leaving me dizzied and swaying.

Silence swooped over the kitchen like a lava flow. We were frozen in a ghastly tableau. Then three things happened in swift succession. Trudy dropped the gravy boat. The cats scattered. In the passageway the phone started to ring; Bob, without looking at any of us, without a word, rose to answer it.

And Guy was staring at me still: a long, shocked anguished look that I felt at my breastbone. Slowly he levered himself from his chair, and, without taking his eyes from my face, reached behind him for his jacket. He looked like a sleepwalker. Skirting his mother and the oozing brown china-strewn puddle on the flagstones he moved towards me in that same slow mechanical way. A muscle was working in his cheek. I felt fear fist itself into my stomach.

He stretched a hand towards me, then withdrew it. He tilted his chin towards the yard. Without a word we both moved into the scullery and he stood aside to let me go before him. I lifted my old red woollen jacket off the hook and bent to push my feet into cold wellingtons; beside me Guy did the same.

No sign of the moon; swallowed into thin low cloud. The yard was still and dark, a light shroud of feathery snow and the faint glimmering from the tiny dewpond across the lane offering the only relief from blackness.

I could hear Guy breathing heavily beside me. My stomach churned. Our breath hung in little pockets in the chill air. I felt alien with dishonesty; separated from myself. This is what limbo is, perhaps – being divided from your true nature and incapable of inhabiting your own skin. Wandering outside yourself. Watching yourself: this deceiving adulterous woman, bringing anguish into the lives of people who didn't deserve more pain.

In the home meadow a sheep bleated. We'd still exchanged no word.

Side by side, almost as if in companionable accord, we crunched across to the gate into the orchard, and stopped there.

I felt Guy turn towards me. We didn't touch.

There was a faint but discernible catch in his breath as he opened his mouth. I felt him bring his voice back under control. For a pragmatic man Guy's accurate intuition winded me. 'It's his,' he stated in his slow careful farmer's voice; the one he'd used to tell us that a calf had died back in the 'old' days; or, more recently, that he'd had a letter from the bank. 'It's his, isn't it?'

## Fifty-seven

### Dartmoor
### OLIVER

Why did I come back? You expect me to know the answer to that? Yeah, yeah. I know. Who else?

OK. I'll try.

Comes a time, I suppose. Travelling's great. Liked the work. Liked the variety. Liked not being tied to anyone or anything. Thought that was how it would always be – then suddenly. Found it was only up to a point.

Was thinking a lot.

Was thinking about home. In the abstract, I mean. What is home? A tent? A bike? A bar? My camera? Other people's dreams and dramas? Other people's galleries/magazines/businesses? Rooms rented here for two weeks, there for six. B&B. A night in the arms of this woman, a year in the home of that one. Don't mean to sound pejorative. Just – not enough.

Then found I was thinking about HOME. Dartmoor, I mean. Wanted to be there.

I'm a granite person. It's different from limestone or sandstone or clay or slate. Granite's hard. Ancient. Durable. Fire-made. A conductor. Piezoelectric. Glittering where the light strikes. Crystal and mica. Radioactive in the fissures. Light and dark. We survive, we granite people.

Granite. I needed it, its electricity, for creativity. Needed to be there. That landscape.

At first just a question. What would it be like. Didn't take it seriously. Wondered what it would be like on a different

288

continent, too: Africa, Canada, Australia. Latin America. Interested in them all.

Then I dreamed about Culver. Two nights on the trot. Everything going down the pan.

Next I dreamed about HER. That shook me.

Next time, I dreamed about her at Culver. Yep. She's granite, too.

I meditated on that the next few mornings. Tried to let it go. But something had me by the throat by then.

The next few assignments screwed up. I mean I screwed them up. Told me something.

Still ignored it.

I was down in southwest France. Heard about the foot and mouth a week or two after those dreams. It gave me the 'flu for a fortnight. Mum used to say that – one of those 'coincidences' would knock her out for days. Unless she took notice. And sometimes then, too.

Well, I turned away. Too big a risk going back. Couldn't see it. And didn't know where SHE was anyway. So no point from that direction. And Culver? Well, I'd given it up, hadn't I? Had no right. No right at all. And besides, there was the little matter of a court case. If they got me. Hard to prove the truth of that one. Didn't want to have to. For reasons. Easier not to try. And best not to think about that event. Pain, still. Too much.

So for a year nearly I did other things. Fell in with some people who organised groups for the Camino – you know, pilgrimages to Santiago de Compostella. That was fantastic. Walked with them, took photos, watched them arriving. Lifetime's dream, some of them. Some of them badly ill, but hanging on, hanging on. Courage. Faith. Walked with a guy whose daughter died doing the route the year before. So he was finishing it for her. Walked with a guy in a wheelchair struggling and bumping and the chair tipping and catching. With an old woman who struggled the last mile on her knees. A young girl with leukaemia. Photographed their faces as they entered the cathedral at the end.

Blew me away. I mean it. Blew me away. Yep. Late twentieth century and pilgrimage is still here.

It humbled me. Humble. I like the feel of that in my mouth. Its sound. Not a word I've given you cause to suspect of me, is it? But there.

So that's why I didn't go back. And one of the reasons why I did...

Why I did: well, HER. Didn't know where she was but she wasn't here. Bit of a chronic ache these days. Can you get arthritis of the heart?

And what happened for me on the Camino.

And Culver. Mum and Dad getting older. I needed to know, badly, about foot and mouth. How they were doing. It was my home.

And I was thirty-something-pushing-forty. Not so cool, a guy of my age still running. Time to face the truth and the future.

OK. Another reason: another paternity suit. Here. France. Yes. Shit. Till they found I'd been done. Could have told them. Did

290

try. Bastards had to go through my medical records; held it all up, of course.

Finished me off though. The woman was OK. I thought. Pretty. Generous. Bright. Sexy. And a devious bitch who was hot only for marriage. And jealous of my work. Not to mention duplicitous. Not her fault I couldn't love her, though.

Sad, isn't it? Bloke of my age. You know, that bastard J-Y put his finger on something: 'Alors, Oliver, un homme has to choose his future by the time he's thirty-five. And your choosing? You wish to keep being only on your own? I am envying of you; but more, I am pitying of you.' Bastard.

## Fifty-eight

Could've hit me with a sledgehammer and I'd not've noticed. At Culver, I mean. My brother. My fucking little brother. Married. To her. My woman.

Can't tell you what a kick in the balls that was. And Jesus, did it hurt. After everything.

What it cost me to go back. And to have him good as sling me off the farm.

After I got back into Britain – same way I got out – it took me two months to screw up the courage to go back. Home. Can't tell you how difficult it was to turn off the lane and ride down the track, open that gate. After all these years.

The silence. Jesus. The silence. Not an animal anywhere except the dogs. Bad enough.

Then Guy. Not over the moon.

Then

HER.

Thought I recovered pretty quickly. Afraid for her when I left though. How she'd be. What he'd say. My little brother. No fool, Guy.

Took me another month just to draw breath. Didn't know anything could get to me like that. First, I thought I'd just forget it. Forget the lot of them. But Mum and Dad... I don't know. So pleased to see me I nearly wept, too. Cracking up in my old age.

Wasn't sure I could ever face seeing her again, though. Or – him.

Got a flat in Penzance when I came back from abroad. Nothing special: bit crowded there, too many people. But an attic with a dormer window, and I could see the sea. Kept me going. Got the exhibition together – was in process when I went to Dartmoor. But then I crashed. Haven't ever been that low in my life. Had no idea.

Didn't want to see Culver again. It was OK the first couple of days. Shock. And anger. And then – got worse and worse till I couldn't sleep. Eat. Couldn't think of anything else for more than five minutes – even the show. Then – I had to see her.

Gave J-Y a call. Don't know why.

'Fuckin' 'ell, Oliver! What are you playing for?'
'At,' I said automatically.
'Merde! Waiting at! They don't have children, yes?'
'Not as far as I know. But they're married, J-Y. My brother.'
'They are happy?'
'How the hell should I know?'
'Was she looking as if happy?'
I thought. 'Not really,' I said. 'But it was a strange situation.'
There was a silence. I could hear J-Y breathing.
'How long are you wanting to play this, Oliver? Not telling this woman your feelings?'
'Are you saying their marriage doesn't matter?'
'I'm not saying anything. I am asking you if you let your

293

feelings, ever. Talk with her, Oliver. Talk with yourself.'

'Cheers, J-Y, you bastard,' I said. Hung up.

It didn't get better. Got worse.

So I told her. Felt like shit about Guy. But she was mine – I'd always known it. And yeah, yeah, we don't own anyone. Especially not someone like her. But we – Christ – I can't say it, even now. But she said it once. 'Belonged.'

Course it was tough. Couldn't work out for months what she really felt. Everything gets muddled up with responsibility and guilt and duty and habit, doesn't it? That's why I stayed alone.

Asked her if she'd leave him. She said no. What I expected. Asked her if she loved him. She looked away. No answer. What does that mean? Told her I loved her. Saw her eyes. How can I forget?

So. We met when we could.

And I didn't go back to Culver. Didn't trust myself around my brother.

## Fifty-nine

Don't know what it was that made me go. That second time. Woke up one morning and had to drive to Culver. No question. Get it from my mother – you don't stop to analyse these things. Just do it.

Took the bike and headed up there fast.

Hadn't been back since the shock. Out of anger: my brother, married to my woman. (Not that he saw that, of course. But there. Laid down in the stars, or something; nothing to do with legal rights or bits of paper.) For her sake. She didn't need external conflict as well as internal. And cowardice? Probably.

Can't pretend I was comfortable with it, but took what joy I could, when I could, with Her. Ironic. Now that I was sure, now that I'd admitted she was the one for me. Knew she felt the same. But somehow I managed to live with how it was – respected that in some way she loved Guy, and wouldn't promise me she'd leave him. But. All I wanted was her. The smell of her. Her skin against mine. The speaking without words. Couldn't believe how much I'd wanted to get away from her all those years ago. Different person, I was then.

Anyway.

Remembered on the way up they'd probably be lambing. Or maybe I was too late. Culver used to lamb early. But Tamar had said they'd only restocked a month or two before Christmas. Maybe they'd be late this year.

Might be a way back to Guy. If they were. Gesture of reconciliation. If he'd take it. Offer a hand with lambing. Something was up – had to be there, find a way in.

Bumped up the track. Sunny. Primroses everywhere. I loved Culver. I admit it.

Heart pounding. Long time since I needed something so badly. If ever.

Guy was bent over something in the yard. Bit of machinery. Straightened up when he heard my bike. Stopped at the gate. Don't think I'd ever seen him so angry. Last time paled into nowhere. He'd put on weight; his eyes seemed smaller in his now-flushed face. He was glaring.

'What the sodding hell do you want?'

'Is the lambing over?'

'What the fuck's it matter to you?'

I couldn't afford to blow it. Not before finding out what was up. I swallowed my reaction. Tried a different tack. 'Thought Bob looked – frail. Last time. Thought I'd see if you needed a hand? Give him a break.'

He held my eyes. 'No thanks.' He bent back down to what he'd been doing. Chain harrow coupling mechanism broken, by the looks of it.

I swallowed. Looked around. No sign of lambs, but ewes in the home meadow.

He glanced up at me. I took a step forward. 'What's wrong with that harrow?'

No answer.

'Trudy about?'

He flung the hammer he'd been using in the direction of the toolbox. The clang echoed off the buildings. He took a stride towards me; kicked the toolbox; spanners and screwdrivers rattled everywhere. 'Look, mate.' Teeth gritted. Hands balled at his sides. 'GET – OFF – MY – FUCKING – LAND. GET IT?'

Never imagined Guy was capable of such rage.

Opened my mouth to answer. As I did so I saw Mum and Tamar in the porch just yards away. I vaguely registered the postvan arriving, and the postman getting out and hesitating.

Threw me off track. Guy's fist landed on my cheek.

Enraged me. Lost it. I raised my hand to smack him to the ground. Thought better of it. Dropped it but found myself bringing on the serious guns.

'Fifteen years ago, Guy Delaney, I saved your pissing little arse! Do you remember?' I was shouting. From the corner of my eye I noticed the postman start to move our way. 'I protected you. You killed that poor sod. Who was actually driving? WELL? Have you forgotten? Have you any IDEA what my life's been like, covering up for you, LYING for you, all these years? You – cowardly – little – piece of – shit? – Don't you fucking threaten me!'

I heard the women gasp. The thought that Mum would so hate the postman to be witnessing all this flashed through and out of my mind.

Guy's face was up close. I could see the receding hairline, the pores on his cheeks, nostril hairs. This was my little brother.

'Do you call screwing my wife, impregnating her, protecting me?' Guy's roar banged against my eardrums.

I took a step back. Took me a minute to take in what he'd said. 'What? What did you say?'

'Well it's not my fucking baby.'

No words. I couldn't open my mouth. Nor move. Just stood there like a bloody moron. Tried to make sense.

'Who – whose baby?' Of course. No need to ask. She was there. Yards away. Looking terrified. Wanted to go to her. Touch her. Pull her into my arms. Couldn't move. Everyone was staring.

'Well. You've wrecked my life now. Had your revenge. Now get – out. Just GET OUT.' Tears in his eyes. God. What a fucking mess. He turned his face towards me, slowly, lumbering, like a goaded bull. There was pain, under the anger. Something broke in me. I opened my mouth but he got there first, teeth gritted, forcing the words out. 'It's my farm, Eliot. Just – fuck – off. Now. Last time.' His mouth collapsed.

Suddenly Mum was there. Her hair was coming unclipped; she looked wild. 'THAT – IS – ENOUGH. GUY. Let me tell you something. Maybe you should know. It's about time. No, Eliot, you stay right there. Now.' Her voice was commanding. Strident. Her eyes fiery. She looked mad. I'd never seen her like that. Wondered if she was beginning to lose it. Alzheimer's or something.

'Not now, Ma. For Christ's sake!'

'Yes, right now, Guy. Come here.' She was twisting a teatowel in her hands. She shot a glance back towards the house. Steadied her voice. Guy thrust his hands in his pockets. Didn't move. 'Guy. This is NOT just your farm. You might have farmed it, but Eliot has at least as much claim. There's something you need to know.' She drew a shaking breath. 'Bob is not – not – your father.' She sniffed. 'Not your father. There. Enough.' Her voice rose. 'And you, Eliot –'

I couldn't make sense of what she was saying. Of anything. Babies. Fatherhood. Everything was swimming away from me.

There was a moment's silence; ominous. Like between lightning and thunder. Before you know how close.

Guy made a low moan. Glanced at him. He raised his hands to his face. Swayed. Thought he was going to fall. He veered away across the yard, his voice rising to a wild wailing bellow, like an animal's.

Couldn't breathe suddenly.

We were all transfixed. Fixed, anyway.

'Eliot.' Mum again. Her voice was low, slow, quiet; her eyes almost black. Spooky. Her small frame somehow looked huge, forbidding. I was goosebumps. Pinioned. This whole scene – surreal, appalling. 'I've had enough. We've all had enough. This

298

has got to be sorted out. What d'you think you're messing around at? Don't think I don't know. Face up to your responsibilities. Come clean, Eliot. Be honest with yourself. And your brother. Now. Before it's too late.'

Looked away from her. Looked around for Guy. Couldn't see him.

Felt completely crazy.

Tamar was coming towards me. She was wrapping her jacket tight around herself and crying.

Then the roar of a bike being revved too hard from beyond the gate. My bike. My God! He was in no state. And the helmet still in the mud where I'd dropped it when Guy took a swing at me. I swallowed. 'Can – errr – can he ride a bike, Mum?'

She was staring at me. Through me. She shook her head.

Broke the spell. Ran for the Land Rover, wrenched the door open. Keys in it. Thank God. 'Open the gate!'

Tamar and Mum arrived at the gate at the same moment. I tore through in second gear. Bumped and rattled and roared up the track. He needed to know. Not my child. Couldn't be. He needed to know. My mind swung between anger and confusion and Mum's words. Guy not Bob's son. Tamar pregnant. His, not mine. Can't be. Couldn't be. Thought she'd said infertile. Him. But me – I knew for certain I was. What??? Was she still making love with him then? Yes, of course. Or – couldn't be, surely? But Christmas, OK, for certain – she'd told me about Christmas. How long? Jesus Christ – which way'd he gone? – Got to the end of the track and knew suddenly. Whipped the Land Rover to its top speed. Turned right. Christ, please let it be in time. Sweet Jesus. Not that way. Not that way to die...


Because I knew I'd be too late. Already I was too late. Mum's words. The shock. A curse. This 'gift'.

He had to know it was his child. Nothing else mattered. I had to get to him in time.

The old Land Rover rattled and coughed. Last time I'd driven it was that terrible night fifteen years ago. Travelling again down the same road. The irony didn't escape me. I felt heavy with fear. Sound of someone panting filled the cab. Me, I realised.

No hope of catching up. Accelator flat to the floor already.

The bend. Picture came in to my head. Small river bridge less than a mile ahead; right hand bend starting practically on the bridge. Call me fanciful but the dead it had claimed hovered there still. Felt them, thickening by the year. Known that since I was a kid. Black dread. Narrow lane, possibility of ice or frost in the shadows from last night, or damp from icemelt.

I was shaking. Calling his name. Over and over.

For a moment I thought it'd be OK.

Heard the impact over the engine. Thought I did. Then silence. So loud I thought it would wipe me away.

I was too late. He must have hit the curving wall of the bridge head-on. Could see the skid on the tarmac. Twisted. Bike off to the side. A smear along the road. Picked up his glasses' case from where it had fallen out of his pocket. Didn't know he wore glasses. Don't know why I picked it up. Seemed respectful. Don't know why the glasses made me cry. Wiped it on my jacket. Blood.

No movement. No breath or pulse. Still warm – awfully appallingly warm. Couldn't stop looking at his face.

Don't know how long I sat there. His head gently placed on my thighs. Was stroking it. His blood all over my fingers. My clothes. Told him. Told him everything. Over and over. Until someone came. Then the ambulance. Then the fading light.

300

## Sixty

### Dartmoor
### TAMAR

I'm hesitating here, my pen hovering like a kestrel waiting to stoop and commit myself. So many endings. Do I still want to declare to you – to myself – that I believe in redemption, in miracles, in happy endings?

Since I last sat down at my desk overlooking Wolf Tor there's been another death. The funeral was yesterday, after the inquest ('took his own life while the balance of his mind was disturbed').

I'm not sure I'll be able to write this. Perhaps I'll keep it very brief and spare all of us the details.

It was Eliot who found him, early one morning. I can't imagine how you live with finding both your brother and your father dead. Of course it's marked him. How could it not?

Fly had been scraping at the barn door and whining. The door had been wedged shut from the inside, so he had to break it down.

I loved Bob. I can't tell you how much I know I'll miss him, though at the moment I'm numb.

It seems he had cancer. None of us knew, except Trudy. Throat cancer's one of the worst, and apparently the prognosis was not hopeful.

And I wonder whether, after surviving foot and mouth, Guy's different way of approaching Culver's future, the shock of Eliot's return and what followed (and I'd always had a sense that Eliot had been, covertly, Bob's favourite), and then Guy's death, the war was the final straw for him. A lifelong pacifist, he had been devastated by what was happening.

Apparently he was propped against the bags of feed. He had wedged the shotgun between his knees. By one of his hands was a photograph: he and a smiling Trudy and the two teenage boys in the front garden. No note.

Looking back, I realise that he'd found his own way to tell each of us that he loved us, some weeks before. Despite everything.

Right now, I don't know how to hope for the future, except maybe by remembering the lessons of the past: how well our fragile/robust spirits continue keeping on.

I've had the title from that Michael Ondaatje book in my mind for months now: *Coming Through Slaughter*.

It's not an event, but a process, over and over mending our lives.

Some time in the future, I know, it won't all be open wounds, ours, or our species'. It will be their memory that aches, now and then, reminding us what it is to be alive: these new spring flowers, these old scars.

What births and deaths ultimately teach us is how to live in the present, with what is. Eliot insists that I take time to meditate with him, in the mornings. It helps.

In an hour or two I have to go in for an antenatal routine and a scan. Astonishing, this pregnancy; and with it, at times, a surreal calm.

After the clinic I shall go and pick up my parents from the station. I need Mum here at the moment; and Dad'll know what to do with my shell-shocked family.

Through the open window outside I hear Eliot's boots crossing the yard, and in the home meadow the increasingly-strident bleatings of this spring's lambs mingled with the crooning of the bantams. Trudy's tame orphaned lamb, far too big to need any maternal care now, still insists on following us into the yard, and slips in to bed down by the Rayburn with Eric and Ernie, or the dogs, if we leave the door open.

We carried on sharing the spring lambing through the nights, the three of us. No matter what else is going on, that can't stop: new life happens when it happens. It was one of the hardest things I've done – carrying on 'as normal' after the tragedies, and doing what Guy or Bob did for so many years, without them; and also maybe the one thing that pulled us all through.

Of course our pasts catch up with us. I've lost a husband and now a father-in-law; Trudy's lost a husband and son. Those kinds of memories steal a part of you. I will pay, probably for the rest of my life, in remorse, guilt. Trudy, as always, will deal with life as it is, and her feelings, in her own largely private way. She and Bob shared a rare, private, silent intimacy. I see, too, in retrospect, how had I known to look for the signs I would have seen that she had known Bob's – what? Destiny? Fate? Karma? – for a long time.

She has regained Eliot, as have I (and I'm learning to call him Eliot).

And we are all about to gain a new and unanticipated member of the next generation.

I don't know what will happen when Eliot's past, as it must, closes the distance. I have to assume he'll be cleared; though I guess there'll be a re-trial. I have to assume we'll handle it. Whatever 'it' is.


But this moment is what we have, and love is deepened at the most implausible times.

I finger the mussel shells – paired, once again – sitting before me. Over the tor a buzzard rises on the thermals, and then a second joins it, and they flip and roll for a moment in play.

I rise from my desk. In a minute I shall go and make tea for Trudy and raspberry leaf tea for myself, and take a mug of coffee out to Eliot where I guess he'll be sitting, under the little old oak tree in the home meadow with the dogs beside him, watching the lambs. His fingers will be itching for a roll-up, and he will probably, instead, be whittling something – a whistle, or a spoon, or a small mammal from a piece of ash or holly or lime. Or maybe he'll be digging-in compost and manure into Bob and Trudy's old vegetable plot that he turned over last week. We talked yesterday about extending it. Maybe one day we'll manage the veg box scheme; who knows?

But more fittingly, we're going to be planting a big new orchard, for Bob and Guy. The old cider varieties, and a row of beehives to pollinate them. Eliot's signing up for cider-making and beekeeping courses. We're talking of selling the sheep and cattle. Even Trudy feels that's right. That part of our life has gone.

Call it a sop, a propitiation to the old lost gods of the underworld, if you like, the dark ones; but we're going to be planting mulberry and walnut among the sunny apples and bright cherries. And when pomegranates come back into the shops, then I shall germinate some of their seeds in our new greenhouse, too.

Eliot gets a lot of nightmares. He blames himself, of course. He's finding it impossible to do nothing for more than a few minutes at the moment, but can't concentrate, either, and his cameras are in hibernation on top of the wardrobe in our temporary bedroom, the old downstairs sitting room. (It's hard to know where to sleep at the moment, with the house so full of the recent past.)

I'm sleeping heavily, though I frequently find myself waking up weeping. In the daytime I seem to be mindless. When I think about the baby, I slide into something more positive; something approaching a cautious optimism.

We don't, of course, know what will happen in the future. After all, Eliot's still a fugitive as far as the authorities are concerned, regardless of what did or didn't happen in truth; and the only witness to the first fatal accident is – try to write the word – dead.

But then several of us witnessed the final truthtelling.

And he's here now, with me. This time is what we have.

And this child belongs to the three of us, he says: me and him and his brother. My late husband.

I'm still light on my feet, though there's not too long to go now. Perhaps I'll manage another ride or two out onto the summer moor on Saracen, Dancer's now middle-aged son, before I have to stop for a while.

A shaft of sunlight slips across the yard and enters the room.

I close these pages.

ALSO FROM ROSELLE ANGWIN

# *IMAGO*

What if the veils between time, people and places are thinner than we think? And if the past and the present are continuously interwoven, even overlapping?

When Annie, just beginning to heal from a near-fatal crash, sets off for a conference in France, she has no idea that this will be the catalyst for a dramatic journey.

It starts out innocently enough: a late summer party on a Devon riverbank, a full moon. But two things happen as a result of that night: Annie's husband is killed, and the 'accident' jolts her into a 700-year-old 'memory' that will take her to the Pyrenees and the inferno at the heart of the Cathar inquisition, into a turbulent love affair, and towards another encounter with death.

*"If you enjoy a book that is vivid and gripping, complex and rich in metaphor and meaning, a book that makes you carry on thinking long after the last page, then this is most definitely for you."*
Amazon

INDIGO DREAMS PUBLISHING

ISBN 9781907401381

286 pages £7.99   Kindle £4.62

Indigo Dreams Publishing
24 Forest Houses
Halwill
Beaworthy
Devon
EX21 5UU
UK

www.indigodreams.co.uk